THE PRIME SUSPECTS

"Okay, yes, Pamela wasn't a very nice person," Jinx conceded. "But there has to be a better reason than that to turn someone into a killer. And since the murderer is more than likely still among us, the clues must be here too."

"So who does that leave?" Helen asked.

"Cathy, Patrick, and Max," Jinx said.

"Don't forget Stephanie and Charlie," Alberta added.

"It has to be one of them. I mean, it's highly doubtable that it's someone we haven't met yet since the roads have kind of secluded us here since last night, making it impossible to escape," Freddy surmised.

"So to sum things up, we have five main suspects," Alberta said. "I think it's time we started investigating . . ."

Books by J.D. Griffo

MURDER ON MEMORY LAKE

MURDER IN TRANQUILITY PARK

MURDER AT ICICLE LODGE

Published by Kensington Publishing Corporation

Murder at
Icicle Lodge

J.D. Griffo

KENSINGTON PUBLISHING CORP.
www.kensingtonbooks.com

KENSINGTON BOOKS are published by

Kensington Publishing Corp.
119 West 40th Street
New York, NY 10018

All Kensington titles, imprints, and distributed lines are avail-
able at special quantity discounts for bulk purchases for sales
promotion, premiums, fund-raising, educational, or institu-
tional use.

Special book excerpts or customized printings can also be created to fit specific needs. For details, write or phone the office
of the Kensington Sales Manager: Attn.: Sales Department.
Kensington Publishing Corp., 119 West 40th Street, New York,
NY 10018. Phone: 1-800-221-2647.

Kensington and the K logo Reg. U.S. Pat. & TM Off.

First Printing: December 2019
ISBN-13: 978-1-4967-1398-8
ISBN-10: 1-4967-1398-2

ISBN-13: 978-1-4967-1399-5 (ebook)
ISBN-10: 1-4967-1399-0 (ebook)

10 9 8 7 6 5 4 3 2 1

Printed in the United States of America

This book is dedicated to all the figure skaters I've loved and admired for decades. From Dick Button to Rosalynn Sumners to Michelle Kwan to Nathan Chen. A never-ending line of amazing athletes and dazzling artists to which I now add the one and only Pamela Gregory.

ACKNOWLEDGMENTS

I want to thank the cozy mystery readers and my fellow writers for welcoming me into this wonderful, crazy, cozy community. And a special thanks to Larissa Ackerman, Kensington publicity whiz, for spreading the word that J.D. Griffo and the Ferraras are here to stay.

CHAPTER 1

Chi non è meco, è contro a meco.

Looking out her kitchen window Alberta no longer felt as if she was living in a dream. She touched the gold crucifix that never left her neck and was filled with gratitude. Finally, Alberta accepted that this was her reality.

It had taken a while, but at last she had gotten used to the fact that the huge expanse of crystal blue water known as Memory Lake was her permanent view. She no longer felt she was trespassing in someone else's home every time she looked out her window. Her life had indeed changed.

Sighing, she remembered what the view was like from the kitchen window of the first apartment that she and Sammy rented in Hoboken, New Jersey, when they were first married—the soiled, decrepit brick wall of the tenement next door. A building, so close, that if Alberta climbed into the kitchen sink, opened the window, and stretched her arm, she could touch its rough façade.

Her memories fast-forwarded several years to when she and Sammy had moved to the suburbs and the view from the kitchen window was obstructed by her neighbor's tall privacy fence, made out of sturdy white plastic, so all she could see while washing the dishes was her own backyard patio and a few feet of grass. She gazed out that window so often that the lightning-bolt-shaped cracks in the cement and the unattractive mixture of green and yellow patches of dried grass were etched into her memory. She often joked that those images were like mental cockroaches and would survive the inevitable dementia that would grip us all in old age. Alberta had always been a "glass half empty" kind of gal at heart, but that—much to her surprise—was slowly changing.

Ever since she moved to Tranquility, a part of New Jersey far different than the urban landscape of Hoboken or even the cluttered and overpopulated suburban towns that dotted the state, it was as if Alberta had absorbed the slower pace of the town and the peaceful nature of its idyllic and panoramic vistas allowing them to rewire her, shift her mind-set, so she could see life differently. Alberta embraced this new energy and felt revitalized. But, just when she had gotten used to her new surroundings everything around her was about to change yet again.

"Look, Lola," Alberta said. "It's snowing."

Miss Gina Lollobrigida, Alberta's cat, who was almost always referred to as Lola unless she broke some cardinal house rule like flipping over her food bowl or deciding she needed to gussy herself up by wearing Alberta's lipstick, which as unbelievable as it sounds had happened on more than one occasion, lounged on the linoleum floor in a speckle of sunlight that streamed through the window and purred. Her black fur glistened in the sunshine and the white mark over her left eye stood out even more vibrantly than usual.

Lola was wearing her usual expression—eyes half closed so it appeared that she either knew all the mysteries of the universe or she didn't care to acknowledge there was information beyond her grasp. She was content staying right where she was, but Alberta would have none of it. Even though Alberta was rather certain Lola didn't care to know what was happening outside, she was, after all, a doting cat mother and wasn't going to let Lola miss the first snow of the season. Or, Alberta thought with an acknowledged hint of sentimentality, the first snow of their new lives.

Alberta placed the last breakfast plate in the plastic draining rack to dry, quick-washed her hands on the dish towel, and scooped up Lola into her arms. Lola might not care about the view, but she would most certainly care about being grabbed by two wet hands.

"Isn't that *bellissima*, Lola?" Alberta cooed.

Lola let out a long, sultry purr that Alberta chose to believe meant that her cat agreed with her wholeheartedly. And how could she not? The world right outside her window could pass for a scene from a holiday movie like *White Christmas, Holiday Inn,* or Alberta's favorite, *Meet Me in St. Louis.*

She parted the red and white plaid curtains that had recently replaced the more summery yellow and white gingham window dressing and smiled. Sure, she might be sixty-five years old, but Alberta Ferrara Scaglione felt like a kid again. Although Alberta had lived her entire life as a skeptic, not imagining life could get much better, she was forced to admit that there was magic in the ordinary.

"*La prima nevicata,*" Alberta gushed. "The first snowfall." She nuzzled Lola closer to her cheek and the cat squirmed delightedly. "*Our* first snowfall."

Even though Alberta had only moved to Tranquility

in the past year, she had visited the town when she was a young girl. However, those trips were always during the summer months so this was the first time she'd be spending winter here. That meant she was about to celebrate another first—her first winter season in her new home.

No, the landscape had not yet turned into a winter wonderland, but a transformation had begun. The oak trees in the backyard had lost all of their leaves, the spindly ends of their bare branches reaching up to the sky like greedy oversized children eager to be replenished. The bushes were still green and full, but they'd lost their luster and were littered with brown spots. The biggest change, of course, had to do with the lake.

Memory Lake was huge, flat, and blue, deceivingly simple adjectives that didn't quite describe its majesty. Now as a light smattering of snow fell in perfect vertical lines, too numerous to count, and disappeared onto the surface of the water it was as if the heavens were feeding the lake and offering it nourishment for the harsh weather that was surely to come.

The snow that fell wasn't sticking, but evaporated the moment it touched lake water like an emotion that couldn't be maintained once it was acknowledged. But like all strong emotions, the snow would return, and the next time it would probably stay a little bit longer.

Alberta didn't know how long she remained in front of the kitchen window, swaying side to side and softly humming "Micio Miagolio," an old Italian children's song about a hungry kitty cat who doesn't share her meal, and one of Lola's favorite lullabies, when she heard the phone ring.

Holding Lola expertly in one arm like a sleeping

newborn baby, Alberta picked up the phone out of its cradle. "Hello."

"Hi, Gram, it's me, Jinx."

"Lovey!" Alberta squealed. She was always excited to hear her granddaughter's voice. But whenever she heard her granddaughter's voice unexpectedly on the other end of the telephone she grew concerned. "What's wrong?"

"Oh my God!" Jinx shouted. "You have got to stop assuming something is wrong when I call!"

"Ah, *Madon*! I'm an old lady, we always assume the worst."

"First of all, you're not old. And second of all, knock it off!"

Alberta smiled and loved that she and Jinx had grown so close in the past year that they could yell at each other good-naturedly. There was an easy back and forth to their conversations filled with mutual respect, nothing like the conversations Alberta once had with her own daughter, Jinx's mother Lisa Marie, which were knock-down, drag-out fights overflowing with hatred and words that were carefully chosen to wound and degrade. Alberta shuddered, not only at the memory, but at her role in shaping it. Whether those arguments were the result of conscious or subconscious thought didn't matter, Alberta had a starring role in them and there was no way she could take back any of the words that had spewed out of her mouth or wash away the shame she'd felt ever since. All she could do was look back in regret and look forward with hope. If she couldn't reconcile with her daughter, she could at least make amends by creating a life with her granddaughter.

"Alright, *basta,* let me start over," Alberta said. "To what do I owe this surprise phone call?"

Ignoring her grandmother's attempt at sarcasm, Jinx replied, "I want to meet for dinner tonight."

That's all? Alberta thought. "Of course, I'll defrost a lasagna. And I have some leftover stuffed peppers. And you like shrimp scampi, don't you? I made too much last weekend."

"That all sounds delicious, Gram," Jinx said. "And can you invite Aunt Helen and Aunt Joyce to join us?"

"Of course," Alberta replied.

Ever since moving to Tranquility, Alberta hardly ate a dinner without her sister Helen or her sister-in-law Joyce so at first she didn't think the comment strange, but then she realized it was odd for Jinx to make a special request to invite the entire family to dinner. Something had to be wrong.

"Jinx, what's going on? Why do you want us all to have dinner together?"

"Because I have super fabulous news to share!" Jinx cried. "I'll see you at seven."

Jinx hung up before Alberta could question her further to find out exactly what her super fabulous news was. Not to worry, instead of asking Jinx she would ask the other members of her family.

"What could be so important that Jinx needs to gather us all together at a formal dinner so she can make an announcement?" Alberta queried the room.

Helen and Joyce were sitting around the kitchen table munching on Entenmann's raspberry-filled Danishes and sipping raspberry-flavored vodka, a sort of appetizer to the evening's meal. They had been discussing what Jinx could possibly want to tell them, but thus far hadn't come up with any realistic answers. They did, however, have many questions.

"Did she say she was bringing anyone with her?" Joyce asked.

"No," Alberta replied shaking her head. "She only said she'd meet us here for dinner at seven."

Munching on a piece of Danish, Helen said, "It has to do with a man."

"Why do you say that, Helen?" Joyce queried.

"Because whenever a woman wants to have a pow-wow with other women it always has to do with a man."

"That's a little old-fashioned, don't you think?" Joyce retorted. "Jinx is a young, independent woman starting her career as a reporter, she doesn't base her self-worth on another man."

"I'm not sure that's entirely true," Alberta declared. "She has grown very fond of Freddy."

For the past few months Jinx had been dating Freddy Frangelico, the local snorkeling instructor, and the two of them had grown extremely close. Alberta wholeheartedly approved of Freddy and considered him an ideal boyfriend—he was courteous, respectful, handsome, and, most important, he made Jinx happy. But there was a lot about him that Alberta didn't know so the fact that Jinx's announcement could involve Freddy made Alberta anxious.

"You don't think they've gotten engaged, do you?" Without waiting for a reply, Alberta chugged her glass of raspberry vodka for emotional support.

Joyce placed a well-manicured hand to her mouth and her eyes widened so even if she wanted to hide her surprise at Alberta's comment, her body language gave her away. "Berta, I never thought of that. He's a nice kid and all, but also too, they just met."

Helen broke off another piece of Danish and said, "Maybe they *have* to get married."

"Of course they *have* to get married," Alberta replied. "They're in love."

Joyce patted Alberta's hand gently and clarified the statement. "I think what Helen means is that they may *have* to have to get married."

Confused, Alberta looked from Joyce to Helen for more explanation. When Helen spoke, Alberta got more than she ever expected.

"Jinx might be in the family way!"

Typically, if anyone brought a conversation to a screeching halt, it would be Helen. However, this comment and its not-at-all-subtle implications not only brought the conversation to an abrupt stop, it caused Joyce to refill all their jelly glasses with more raspberry vodka. When their glasses were once again empty, Alberta was the first to find the courage to speak.

"Jinx would never . . . she's a good girl."

"Oh, Berta," Helen chided. "This has nothing to do with being good or bad. Unmarried women get pregnant all the time even if they take precautions. Remember Cousin Louise?"

"The one who married that mechanic," Alberta replied.

"The one who *had* to marry that mechanic," Helen corrected.

Shock took over Alberta's expression, like a grenade exploding in the middle of a field of daisies. "Louise got married because she was pregnant?" Alberta asked, flabbergasted.

"They would've gotten married anyway and they stayed married until death did them part," Joyce explained. "So it didn't make any difference, but yes, the reason they got married was because Louise was pregnant with little Jeannie."

"And Gumpa Marco's daughter, Angela?" Helen continued. "She wasn't putting on weight, she was pregnant, which is why Gumpa Marco shipped her off to Sicily to marry her third cousin, Giuseppe, before she started to show."

"That marriage didn't end as well," Joyce added. "Let's just say Angela was never cut out to be a fisherman's wife."

"Who among us is, Joyce?" Helen asked, knowingly. "Who among us is?"

"Ah, *Madon*!" Alberta shouted. "How many other girls got pregnant when we were younger and had to get married?"

"Tons!" Helen replied.

"How come I never knew about any of this?" Alberta asked.

Cutting off yet another slice of Danish, Helen explained, "You never wanted to see the world for what it really was when we were kids. That's why it hit you so hard when you were an adult, you didn't prepare yourself like I did."

Alberta didn't want to contradict her sister and open up a can of worms, but Helen was wrong. From a young age Alberta realized life was far from the proverbial bowl of cherries, and it took her until she moved to Tranquility to understand that it was filled with hope and promise. However, Helen was right about Alberta being naïve when it came to controversial subjects like unwed pregnancies and girls not behaving like the good little girl Alberta was taught to be. She wasn't ignorant that such things occurred, but she didn't dwell on them so the thought that Jinx could be pregnant and planning a quickie wedding was the furthest thing from her mind.

When Jinx burst into the kitchen it was the first question out of her lips.

"Jinx, are you pregnant?" Alberta asked.

"What?"

Greatly relieved, Helen and Joyce let out a collective sigh.

"I guess that settles that," Helen declared.

Not convinced, Alberta pushed Jinx for a real answer. "Well, are you, lovey? It doesn't matter if you are or if you aren't, we will support you either way, but please just say it, are you or are you not pregnant?"

Throwing her coat on the hook of the hutch next to the front door, Jinx shook her head—simultaneously bemused and annoyed by her grandmother—and bent down to greet Lola. "I am definitely not pregnant."

"Thank God!" Alberta exclaimed as she kissed her gold crucifix, looked up to the heavens beyond the ceiling, and made the sign of the cross.

Standing up, Jinx buried her face into Lola's stomach making the cat purr in sheer delight. Replacing her fingers with her face to continue playing with Lola's tummy, Jinx said, "I thought you said it would be okay if I were pregnant?"

The three women answered in unison: "We lied."

Laughing hysterically, Jinx sat down in the empty seat at the kitchen table. "Well, that's good to know so I can plan accordingly if I should ever find myself in that situation, but why in the world would you think I'm pregnant?"

"Because you called us here for a very important meeting," Alberta replied.

"And you said you had fabulous news to share," Joyce added.

"So Berta assumed you got yourself into trouble," Helen lied.

"That is not true!" Alberta shrieked.

Jinx and Joyce smiled at each other as Alberta and Helen continued to argue over who was the first one to bring up the idea that Jinx could be with child until Lola meowed so loudly it made them all stop and remember that they still hadn't learned the truth as to why Jinx called this impromptu dinner.

"If you aren't pregnant, what's your news?" Alberta asked. "Are you engaged?"

"No!" Jinx cried. "Why does your mind automatically go to marriage and pregnancy—and not necessarily in that order—when I say I have some good news?"

Shrugging her shoulders, Alberta replied, "Because I'm Italian. The best news is always about weddings and babies."

"Well, my news has nothing to do with a man," Jinx asserted. "It has everything to do with me."

"Good for you, Jinx," Joyce said, raising a glass of vodka.

Alberta felt ashamed that she had assumed her granddaughter's good news could only be tied to a man. But after spending decades playing second fiddle to all the men in her life, whether she was coerced into the role or entered into it willingly, it was a hard habit to break.

"Good for you, lovey, and I'm sorry for jumping to the wrong conclusion," Alberta offered.

"Thanks, Gram," Jinx said. "Technically my news isn't only about me, but all four of us."

The women exchanged looks that ranged from surprised to concerned to exasperated.

"*Basta!*" Helen shouted. "I am no longer a woman

of the cloth and do not need to adhere to a vow of nonviolence. Tell us your news before I clobber you! The suspense is killing us."

"Okay, but before I tell you I need to know one thing," Jinx declared.

"What?" Alberta asked.

"Chi non è meco, è contro a meco," Jinx said very slowly, overenunciating her words.

Again, the three older women looked at each other with expressions that now ranged from bemusement to alarm to utter amusement because Jinx sounded like she was channeling Woody Allen channeling Marlon Brando.

"Do you mean to say, are you with me or against me?" Helen translated.

"Yes!" Jinx squealed. "That's exactly what I said."

"Well, not *exactly*," Joyce corrected.

Alberta leaned back in her chair and spread out her arms to her sides, "What kind of *pazzo* question is that? We're always with you."

"Even if you were having a baby out of wedlock," Helen said. "We might not be with you from the get-go . . ."

"But we'd get there very quickly," Joyce added.

"So tell us, lovey," Alberta pleaded. "Whatever it is, we're with you one hundred percent."

"Good!" Jinx beamed. "Because I might not be having a baby, but start packing your bags because the Ferrara ladies are going on a vacation!"

CHAPTER 2

Molta brigata vita beata.

"A *vacation?*"

Alberta didn't mean to, but she said the word as if it were blasphemous, like one of the dozen or so words her father had forbidden his daughters to say out loud regardless if they were in public or at home, and warned them that if they even thought of any of the words even for *uno momento,* it would turn them into the type of woman no man would ever want to marry. She quickly backtracked to soften her statement.

"A vacation sounds delightful, lovey," Alberta added. "But this announcement of yours is all so sudden, you've taken us by surprise."

"A better surprise than making us carpool to the maternity section of David's Bridal," Helen quipped. "But a surprise nonetheless."

Grabbing an empty jelly glass and filling it to the rim with raspberry vodka, Jinx replied, "Oh come on, Aunt Helen, would it really be so terrible if I was pregnant?"

Helen paused a moment before responding so she

could finish chewing her fourth piece of raspberry Danish. When she spoke, she grabbed Jinx's hand across the kitchen table and looked directly into her eyes. "No, because we love you and we'd love any child you were carrying, but I know from my years of working with unwed mothers that it's very difficult to raise a child on your own."

Joyce placed her hand on top of Jinx's and Helen's and added, "Also too, it isn't always easier with a husband by your side."

Alberta wanted to join the discussion and hand holding, but couldn't. She didn't want to discuss what it was like to have a husband and a child because she didn't have many positive things to say about either so she chose to divert the conversation onto safer, albeit still mysterious, territory.

"Tell us more about this vacation," Alberta suggested.

If anyone suspected Alberta was using curiosity as a diversionary tactic, no one mentioned it, though it was most likely because Helen and Joyce were equally eager to find out what Jinx was talking about, and Jinx was even more eager to share her news.

"I may not be engaged and/or pregnant," Jinx said, "but I have a new plum assignment that is going to benefit us all. Wyck is sending me to cover the grand reopening of Icicle Lodge in Lake Ariel, Pennsylvania! And the three of you can come with me!"

"Do we have to work for it?" Alberta asked.

"Do we have to pay for it?" Helen inquired.

"Also too, do we have to do any type of outdoor activity?" Joyce pressed. "If you haven't noticed it's getting cold outside."

"Ah, *Madon!*" Jinx cried. "If I didn't love you three, I'd throttle you one after the other!"

"Listen to her, Berta," Helen said, chuckling. "She sounds just like Daddy."

Instantly Alberta, Helen, and Joyce began discussing how lovingly gruff Frank Ferrara could be. They reminisced about his foibles, his favorite sayings, and, of course, retold stories they had each heard umpteen times. Finally, Jinx had tired of the stroll down memory lane and decided to bring the conversation back into the present.

"So my editor, Wyck, asked me to cover the grand reopening of the lodge, and I thought it would be fun if all of us could use it as an excuse to get away for a week."

"A week?" Helen balked. "I can't go away for a week, the animals at the shelter where I volunteer rely on me."

"I think the shelter can find someone else to yell at the cats and dogs for doing number two in their cages," Alberta joked.

"Wait a second, Jinx," Joyce interrupted. "Isn't Lake Ariel about two hours from here?"

"More if the roads aren't plowed thoroughly," Jinx replied.

"Why would your editor be interested in the reopening of a mountain lodge that far away no matter how grand?" Joyce asked. "Isn't it a bit outside of *The Upper Sussex Herald*'s fanbase?"

"Location wise, yes," Jinx agreed. "But—and here's the exciting part—since it's the grand reopening of the lodge there's going to be a celebrity guest who has ties to Sussex County."

Hearing the word "celebrity" the three women shed decades of years from their ages and started acting as if they were teenagers again. All of a sudden, Jinx's invitation to a weeklong getaway became more interesting now that there was the possibility of rubbing elbows with a celebrity. They just needed to know how celebrated this mystery celebrity was.

"Who is it, lovey?" Alberta asked.

Not waiting for Jinx's answer, the women played twenty questions asking if the celebrity was a singer or an actress, hoping they would get the chance to be snowbound in a quaint lodge and have hot chocolate with Celine Dion or Sally Field. And then they nearly became apoplectic when Joyce wondered if it was someone who was both a singer *and* an actress like Barbra Streisand. When they finally found out who the celebrity was all hopes of a meeting with a member of Hollywood royalty were dashed and they couldn't contain their disappointment.

"Who in the world is Pamela Gregory?" Alberta asked.

"Oh come on!" Jinx shouted. "You've never heard of Pamela Gregory?"

Answering for all three women, Lola let out a huge yawn.

Shaking her head in disbelief, Jinx explained, "She just happens to be an Olympic figure skating champion like Peggy Fleming and Dorothy Hamill."

Helen's eyes lit up, "Now you're talking! I wore my hair like Dorothy's for years. I wore it in that style for so long that at the convent it became known as 'the Helen.'"

"Seriously, none of you know who Pamela Gregory is?" Jinx asked, unable to hide her astonishment.

"I'm sure she's a very nice woman," Alberta offered.

"Who cares if she's nice," Joyce said. "I want to know why Wyck is so interested in writing an article about her."

Jinx explained that Pamela grew up in Montague,

New Jersey, which was a few towns north of Tranquility, and won ladies' figure skating gold at the Olympics following in Peggy's and Dorothy's footsteps, or skate steps as the case may be. Once wildly popular, Pamela had since disappeared from the public eye, and her historic win as the only figure skater to vault from fifth place in the short program to win gold was figure-skating folklore remembered only by hardcore fans and her Wikipedia page. But after years of seclusion, Pamela had decided to come out of hiding and perform at Icicle Lodge's reopening ceremony, and Wyck thought it was the perfect feel-good piece that the *Herald* readers would devour.

"That's all very exciting, Jinx, but where does a vacation come into play?" Alberta asked. "You're going to this Lake Arlene for work."

"Lake *Ariel*," Jinx corrected.

"Like the mermaid!" Helen gushed. She didn't wait for Jinx to confirm but launched into a remarkably on-key rendition of "Part of Your World" from the famed animated film.

Jinx's jaw dropped. "You know the lyrics to a song from *The Little Mermaid*, but you've never heard of Pamela Gregory?"

"What can I say, Jinxie," Helen replied. "I'm a kid at heart."

Exasperated, Jinx realized it would be best to avoid talking about Pamela's status as a legendary figure skater and concentrate on her own status as a gift bearer.

"Yes, I'm going for work, but the Lodge gave the paper two rooms," Jinx explained. "One room is for me and the other is for Benny, our photographer, but Benny will be on assignment in Trenton to cover some rally about state cuts to affordable housing, so Wyck decided to save money and use the publicity photographer that the Lodge hired, which means I have the two rooms for myself. And since I don't need two rooms for myself, I thought the four of us could use them and go on a vacation."

Finally, Jinx got the reaction she was hoping for.

"Lovey, this sounds like fun!" Alberta exclaimed.

"I guess it isn't that cold yet," Joyce said. "It'll be invigorating to spend a few days surrounded by the great outdoors."

"Especially if the great outdoors has a great big fireplace indoors," Helen added. "I have always enjoyed reading a good book in front of a roaring fire."

Smiling, Jinx knew she had won over her family. "There are several fireplaces throughout the lodge," Jinx said. "And if you get too hot sitting by the fire there are about two hundred acres to explore."

"I'm in," Helen announced. "If the animals fall into a depression while I'm gone, I'll just have to shower them with even more affection when I get back."

"Count me in too," Joyce added. "I still have a silver and black ski outfit from the eighties that has been waiting for the perfect time to make a comeback."

Just when Alberta was about to speak and add herself to the guest list, Lola meowed loudly from the opposite side of the kitchen. Lola's aim was to remind Alberta that she needed to eat, but all it did was remind Alberta that she couldn't leave Lola alone in the house for a whole week.

"I can't go!" Alberta cried. "Who's going to feed Lola if none of us are here?"

It was a valid question and created a logical problem, but one that Jinx had already found a solution to. "Do you think I would propose a family vacation and not include Lola?" Jinx asked rhetorically as she grabbed

Lola and held her in her arms. "I made sure one of the rooms is pet friendly so Lola is coming with us."

"Looks like you've thought of everything." Alberta beamed.

"That's because when a Ferrara wants something," Jinx said, "a Ferrara doesn't take no for an answer."

The next morning while Alberta and Joyce were shopping for some vacation clothes they were reminded that the Ferraras weren't the only ones who were uncompromising.

In the fitting room at The Clothes Horse, Joyce's favorite boutique in Tranquility, which sold a mix of current and vintage styles, Alberta was trying on a Chanel brown and mustard tweed pantsuit in one of the stalls trying to figure out if it made her look stylish or sallow. Just as she decided, with much delight, that it was the former, her cell phone buzzed alerting her that she had received a text message. Reluctantly shifting her focus away from her mirrored image to the text message, her happy mood was quickly squashed.

"This isn't good," Alberta muttered.

"What is it?" Joyce asked, from the other side of the stall's curtain. "Is something wrong?"

"That kind of depends."

"On what?"

"On if you think getting a text message from the chief of police that says, 'Get to the police station now, it's urgent,' means there's something wrong."

"We better hurry," Joyce said. "Vinny doesn't usually use the *U* word in a text."

Alberta whipped open the curtain and replied, "Vinny's gonna have to wait because first I have to use the *P* word."

"The ladies' room is right down the hall," Joyce advised.

"Not that *P*!" Alberta cried. "Purchase! Urgent or not, there's no way I'm leaving this store without buying this pantsuit."

Ten minutes later, Alberta and Joyce were standing in front of a young police officer who didn't seem fazed by their desperate need to see her boss.

"If you two could please have a seat, I'll tell the chief that you're here," Tambra requested.

"No!" Alberta cried. "You need to tell him now."

"Show her the message, Berta," Joyce instructed.

Obeying her sister-in-law's command, Alberta dug into her pocketbook, searched among the clutter, and whipped out her cell phone triumphantly. She played with the keys on the phone for a bit and, finding the incriminating evidence she was looking for, held the phone up about two inches from Tambra's face.

Gently, Tambra put her palm on the top of Alberta's cell phone and lowered it until the women once again could see eye to eye.

"Like I said, I'll tell the chief that you're here."

"You did see that Vinny used the *U* word, right?" Joyce asked.

"Yes, I did see very clearly that Vinny said it was urgent," Tambra confirmed. "But at the moment he's on a call that is also urgent so if you could—"

"Maybe our urgent text and Vinny's urgent call are the same urgent matters!" Alberta cried.

"That would make things doubly urgent!" Joyce cried. "This could be very serious."

"We can't wait, we need to talk to Vinny right now," Alberta declared.

Ignoring Tambra's firm protests not to enter Vinny's closed office, Alberta did just that with Joyce hot on her heels. When they burst open the door, the ladies didn't get very far because Vinny was standing on the other side waiting for them.

"Oh my God, will you two shut up!" Vinny cried. "I could hear you both blabbering with my door closed."

Jabbing a finger into Vinny's chest, Alberta replied, "That's what happens when you make people wait, *Signor Poliziotto*. Now tell us, what the hell's so urgent that you had to interrupt our shopping spree?"

Trying to conceal his amusement, Vinny replied, "Come in and I'll tell you."

Before they all disappeared from her view, Tambra shouted from behind the front desk, "You sure you're going to be alright with those two, chief?"

Smiling, Vinny replied, "Thanks, Tambra, but I can handle these ladies just fine."

Since this wasn't Alberta's first time in Vinny's private quarters, she didn't hesitate to sit in one of the well-worn leather chairs opposite his desk that was littered with piles of papers, open files, and his computer, which, even though it was an Apple, was a few models from being up-to-date. Joyce, however, had never set foot in Vinny's inner sanctum so she was a bit more intimidated than her sister-in-law and stood awkwardly until Vinny invited her to have a seat.

Vinny gracefully maneuvered his six-foot-four hulking frame between several cardboard boxes adjacent to his desk without bumping into them or the metal filing cabinet that was only a few inches from the back of his chair. He had become used to his surroundings. On the contrary, he would never get used to Alberta's blunt approach.

"So why did you summon us here?" Alberta demanded in the guise of a question. "And what's so urgent?"

Wrinkling his handsome face and smiling impishly, Vinny shed decades from his appearance and for a moment he looked like the boy Alberta used to babysit. He would also prove to be just as mischievous.

"Perhaps I shouldn't have used the word 'urgent,'" Vinny confessed.

"But you did," Alberta corrected.

"I was trying to be funny."

"You failed."

"I'm sorry, Alfie," Vinny said, using the nickname he coined for Alberta when they were teenagers. "I have some really great news and I couldn't wait to share it with you."

"Then why didn't you tell me what the news was in your text?" Alberta questioned. "Or just call me?"

"Because I wanted to see your reaction in person when I tell you that I'm sending you on a vacation!" Vinny bellowed.

Alberta and Joyce looked at each other and both experienced a feeling of déjà vu.

"A *vacation*?" Once again Alberta said the word like it was blasphemous, but this time there was an undercurrent of disbelief. She hadn't taken a vacation in who knows how long and now for the second time in as many days someone was offering her a trip out of town. It was an odd coincidence that was about to get odder.

"I recently received an invitation to attend the grand reopening of Icicle Lodge," Vinny started. "Maybe you've heard of it, it's a few hours away in Lake Ariel."

Out of the corner of her eye Alberta saw that Joyce was about to admit being fully aware of the lodge and its grand reopening. Before she could speak, Alberta kicked her in the shin. It wasn't a subtle move, but it was out of Vinny's sight line and it did the trick. Joyce remained silent.

"The name vaguely rings a bell," Alberta white-lied.

"I'm an old friend of the owner's late husband so that's how I got invited," Vinny explained. "But I want to give the rooms to you since, well, you and your family have been such a great help to the police department and to the community of Tranquility lately. I thought it was the least that I could do as a thank-you."

Alberta and Joyce turned to face each other trying to ascertain how to play out the impromptu charade and immediately turned into giggling teenagers.

"What's so funny?" Vinny asked, put off by their reaction. "I'm trying to do something nice here."

"Don't get offended," Alberta said, unable to stop laughing. "We really appreciate it."

"We really do," Joyce added, while covering her mouth as if that would prevent Vinny from seeing her cracking up.

"Then what's so funny?"

"Jinx already invited us to the lodge," Alberta confessed. "She's doing a story on the reopening and we're her guests, Helen too."

Finally, Alberta's laughing subsided and she leaned forward placing a hand on Vinny's desk next to a photo of him and several family members who were also police officers. "But seriously, thank you for your offer and, more than that, thank you for your kind words."

Blushing, Vinny looked down at his desk to compose himself. Instinctively, the women bowed their heads as well to give their friend some privacy. When Vinny raised his head he nodded to Alberta and then

Joyce and said, "I guess I'll have to find another way to thank you for your service to this community."

"I know a way," Joyce said. "Come with us to Lake Ariel."

"There's nothing else I'd rather do," Vinny replied, his eyes lighting up. "I really wanted to go, but then I got the idea of giving the rooms to you and well, I'm sure you remember what Sister Eugenia used to say."

"Of course. 'Watch out for the flying eraser,'" Alberta replied.

"Well, yes, that," Vinny agreed. "But she always said that a true gift is the gift of sacrifice, and it would have been a huge sacrifice for me to give away this invitation."

"Are you for real, Vin?" Alberta asked, sitting back in her chair and looking at her old friend as if she were seeing him for the first time. "I've no doubt that it's a very nice lodge as lodges go, but surely you can afford to go away to a mountain retreat anytime you'd like."

Vinny's eyes lit up even brighter as he leaned forward and placed the palms of his hands on his desk. If he wasn't wearing such a goofy expression he would've looked downright menacing. "Who cares about the lodge? I want to see Pamela Gregory!"

Alberta leaned even farther back in her chair and almost tipped over. "You know that woman?"

"Everybody knows that woman!" Vinny cried. "She's one of the most famous figure skaters who ever lived."

"Never heard of her," Alberta said.

Vinny snapped his head in Joyce's direction hoping to receive a more positive reaction. He did not find one.

"Me either, Vin," Joyce said. "But I'm sure she'll love to see her number one fan."

Now that the truth of the situation sunk in, Vinny was beaming despite the fact that he was sitting across from two people who had never heard of one of his high school crushes.

"Guaranteed that once you meet Pamela you'll never be able to forget her," Vinny assured. "Dick Button once said she's the perfect combination of beauty and athleticism on the ice, and Dick Button should know, he's Mr. Figure Skating himself."

"With all your carrying on, Vinny, you sound like you could give Mr. Button a run for his money," Alberta said. "When did you become such a figure-skating fan?"

Smiling bashfully, Vinny replied, "I always loved it, but when you're my size football is a more appropriate sport. But I did take lessons."

"What?" both Alberta and Helen shouted.

Nodding, Vinny answered, "At the Ice House."

"The Ice *What?*" Alberta asked.

"The Ice House, it's an elite skating rink in Hackensack," Vinny explained. "Lots of Olympians practice there like Sarah Hughes and Johnny Weir."

"I love that Johnny Weir!" Joyce exclaimed. "He's got flair, that one."

"And I took lessons at Skylands in Stockholm and passed all my levels, I might add," Vinny declared. "You're looking at a certified level-six adult skater."

"That's amazing, Vin!" Alberta squealed. "How come I never knew this?"

"I like to keep some things private," Vinny admitted.

"Unlike that German lady skater who posed in *Playboy*," Joyce remarked. "She and Pamela must be friends."

"No!" Vinny shouted.

"Yes, you know who I mean," Joyce said. "Katarina Witt!"

"Oh my God, no!" Vinny shouted.

"*Dio mio!* What's wrong?" Alberta asked.

"Listen to me and listen to me good, whatever you do, do not mention Katarina's name in Pamela's presence," Vinny warned. "Those two get along like oil and water, prosciutto and cheddar."

"Or maybe fire and ice," Joyce added.

"It isn't funny, Joyce!" Vinny snapped. "You have to trust me on this one."

"This Pamela sounds more interesting by the second," Alberta said.

Vinny melted as if someone took a flame to his icy demeanor. "She really is, Alfie, I'm so glad you're all going to get to meet her," Vinny gushed. "Wait a second! *Everybody* should meet her."

"What are you talking about?" Alberta asked. "All of us *are* going to meet her."

"No, I mean *everybody!*" Vinny shouted. "Since you, Joyce, and Helen are going with Jinx, let's make this a real fun group outing. I'll invite Sloan, Freddy, and Father Sal to join us."

Before Alberta could protest, Vinny was already on the phone calling Sloan.

Joyce tugged on Alberta's sleeve and pulled her closer to her so she could whisper, "Are you okay with Sloan coming along? I know you're sweet on him, but a vacation is a lot different than date night."

"As long as he understands he'll be bunking with one of the boys and not me it'll be fine," Alberta said.

She didn't have to say anything more on the subject because she knew Joyce understood. Alberta had been with only one man her entire life, her husband Sammy, and even though she enjoyed Sloan McLelland's company immensely, she knew in her heart that she wasn't ready to take the leap into more intimate territory.

Although Joyce wasn't a widow or even a divorcée, she felt the same way. She was separated from her husband, Anthony, Alberta and Helen's baby brother, but she still felt like a married woman in every sense of the word. And she was old-fashioned enough to know that she would never break her vows by sleeping with another man.

"That settles it," Vinny said placing the phone back in its cradle. "Sloan, Freddy, and Father Sal are all on board. And don't worry, Alfie, there will be no fraternizing. Freddy and Sloan will share a room and I'll bunk with Father Sal."

"*Molta brigata vita beata,*" Alberta said. "The more the merrier."

"Jinx'll be thrilled Freddy is coming," Joyce squealed.

"And I cannot wait to see Helen's face when she finds out Father Sal is joining us," Alberta said.

"Maybe you should keep that a secret until we get there," Vinny said. "You don't want to ruin the vacation before it's begun."

"I think you're right about that, Vin," Alberta agreed. "But why worry? We're going to a beautiful mountain lodge for a weeklong vacation, what could possibly go wrong?"

Famous last words.

CHAPTER 3

Bella in vista, dentro è trista.

After much deliberation while devouring an entire box of Entenmann's banana iced cake and drinking a bottle of banana-flavored vodka, the ladies decided that they should drive up to Icicle Lodge in Helen's Buick LaCrosse. Jinx's Chevy Cruze was deemed too small for the two-hour road trip that would carry the ladies and their luggage, and Alberta's Mercedes and Joyce's BMW were what Helen described as "fancy cars" that wouldn't survive the trip or make driving on the rigorous mountain terrain comfortable.

"We'll wind up with flat tires or a broken axle and be stranded on the side of the road at the mercy of wild beasts and wayward men," Helen had said.

"She does realize we're not filming a spaghetti Western, doesn't she?" Joyce had whispered to Alberta.

"I love my sister, but I've never understood how her mind works."

Neither woman argued with Helen as they were happy for her to take the wheel, nor did Jinx inform Helen that the bulk of the drive to the lodge would be on a series of main throughways and paved roads.

There would be a last stretch for a few miles where they'd need to drive on roads carved into the side of a mountain, but they were going to eastern Pennsylvania and not Peru so the GPS on their phones would work if they got lost. The unspoken truth was that they all knew it made Helen feel needed to be the chauffeur so they remained silent.

"Now, isn't this nicer than being cramped into one of your cars?" Helen asked as she merged onto I-80. "It might not be an overpriced luxury car, but this Buick's got room to breathe and the peace of mind that only all-wheel drive can offer. Being practical, not fancy, is what keeps you safe and content."

"That sounds like one of Father Sal's sermons," Jinx said sitting in the back seat behind Helen while looking over her notebook filled with information she had found online about Pamela Gregory's personal and professional life before, during, and after her historic Olympic win. She was so engrossed in her reading that she didn't notice Alberta, who was sitting next to her, raise an eyebrow at the mention of the priest's name. Alberta was so surprised by Jinx's comment that she automatically squeezed Lola even tighter, making her cat squeal and jump to her freedom.

"I won't be sorry to miss hearing his blubbering for a week," Helen said.

"You won't have to, Aunt Helen," Jinx advised. "He's joining us."

If Helen weren't in the middle lane of the highway, she would've slammed on the brakes. Instead she screamed at the top of her lungs. "What?"

"Ma, che sei grullo?" Alberta asked Jinx, although she already knew the only reason Jinx would have made such a comment is because she had lost her mind.

Lifting her head from the papers in her lap, Jinx

saw her grandmother's steely gaze to her right, her Aunt Joyce leaning over from the front passenger seat looking at her in shock, and her Aunt Helen's eyes framed in the rearview mirror, and she realized this is what Rosemary Woodhouse must have seen when she checked in on her demon baby every morning.

"I'm sorry," Jinx said meekly.

"What do you mean, Sal is joining us?" Helen barked.

"Didn't you get the memo, Aunt Helen?" Jinx replied, trying to brush off the five-alarm fire with a one-note joke.

"No, I most certainly did not get the memo!" Helen shouted. "Or an e-mail, a phone call, or even a text!"

Before Helen took the first exit or tried to make a U-turn on the highway, Alberta did what all little sisters have done since the beginning of time; lied to their big sister.

"After Vinny invited Freddy and Sloan to share his rooms with him he felt bad that he left out Sal, who even you have to admit has been very helpful lately."

"If you call telling Eve where she could find the apple cart in the Garden of Eden's ShopRite helpful, then yes."

"Well, okay then," Alberta stuttered. "And so Vinny mentioned the trip to Sal and he thought it would be nice to get away with all of us since he really doesn't have any friends."

"Because he's a priest!" Helen shouted, gripping the steering wheel tighter. "Priests don't have friends, they have congregations!"

"Come on, Helen," Joyce said, deliberately speaking softer in contrast to Helen's yelling. "You may not want to admit it, but you and Sal have gotten closer lately.

He may not be your friend, but also too, you don't despise him as much as you used to."

Helen stared straight ahead as if she was trying to memorize the license plate of the car in front of her. She pursed her lips together and shrugged her shoulders slightly and said, "There might be a certain truth to that statement."

"So maybe this is God's way of helping you get to know Father Sal a little better," Joyce suggested.

"I know everything I need to know about Sal, thank you very much," Helen said tersely. "But what's done is done."

"It's a big lodge, Aunt Helen, you probably won't even run into him all week."

"*Magari*," Helen replied. "Because I'm looking forward to a relaxing week with the girls."

There was nothing relaxing about the frantic beeping from the car behind them. Everyone looked around to see what the issue was since Helen was driving at a reasonable 65 mph in the middle lane and there weren't any cars on either side of her. The impatient car could easily pass her on the left if she was driving too slow for their taste. However, it wasn't the car's speed or lack thereof that had caused a reaction, it was the car's passengers.

Turning around, Jinx cried, "It's the boys!"

Swiftly the car merged into the left lane, and, in unison, the women turned to the left and saw Vinny's white Ford Explorer emblazoned with TRANQUILITY POLICE on the side in patriotic red, white, and blue. The four passengers were smiling and waving wildly like they were schoolkids who were playing hooky to take an unsanctioned field trip.

Sloan and Freddy were sitting in the back seat grinning broadly at the sight of Alberta and Jinx in the back seat of Helen's Buick, it was perfect symmetry as the boyfriends were sitting in the same spots as their girlfriends.

In the front, things weren't as serendipitous as Vinny was, of course, driving, which meant Father Sal was in the passenger seat, and since Vinny had now matched the Buick's speed, Sal was only a few feet away from Helen.

Holding the wheel tightly, Helen glowered at the SUV, and the only reason she knew it was Sal was because he was wearing his white collar. His regular eyeglasses with the thick retro black frames had been substituted for a pair of oversized white plastic sunglasses and his thick mane of black hair was covered in a white baseball cap with the initials TPD, which stood for Tranquility Police Department, embroidered onto the front in red lettering. In Helen's mind, however, the initials stood for This Priest Disappoints.

Rolling down the window, Father Sal screamed something to Helen that was indecipherable since her window was up and on the radio Doris Day was singing, ironically as it turned out, about a sentimental journey.

"Roll your window down, Aunt Helen," Jinx said. "Father Sal is trying to tell you something."

"Two hands on the wheel, Jinx," Helen snapped. "That's my motto and I'm not breaking it to hear what that *idiota* has to say."

But Father Sal would not be ignored, and he kept screaming and waving at Helen to get her attention.

"It looks like it might be important, Hel," Joyce said. "I can lower your window from the controls on the console."

"You touch a button, Joyce, I'll turn this car right around and no one will get to see the fancy roller skater."

"Ice skater," Jinx corrected.

"Do not contradict me!"

"Basta!" Alberta cried throwing her hand up in the air and slapping the roof of the car. "Enough! Jinx, take hold of Lola so she doesn't get any funny ideas."

Jinx wasn't sure what her grandmother was talking about, but as always she did what she was told and scooped Lola up from the spot in between them where she was curled up in a ball minding her own business. Only when Jinx had her securely in her lap resting comfortably on top of her notebook did she realize what Alberta was going to do. If Mount Helen wasn't going to go to Father Muhammad, Alberta was going to move the mountain herself.

Alberta leaned forward, grabbed hold of Helen's headrest with her left hand, and with her right reached across Helen's chest to find the button that would lower the window.

"Stop it, Berta, you're gonna make me crash!" Helen yelled.

"Shut up and look at the road," Alberta replied.

Now that the window was rolled down, Father Sal's words could finally be heard. "Hi, Helen!"

With her eyes glaring straight ahead, Helen replied so only those within the Buick could hear, "Tell Sal not to distract me from driving."

"Helen says hi back, Sal, but she can't talk now, she's busy driving," Alberta yelled out the window. "Is everything okay?"

"Yes!" Father Sal yelled back, holding onto his hat as it started to billow in the wind. "Tell Helen this reminds me of when we would go on our retreats with St. Ann's Church when we were kids."

"I will!" Alberta cried back. "Now roll up your window and tell Vinny to drive safe. We'll see you all in a few hours at the lodge."

"Okay!" Sal shouted. "This is gonna be fun!"

When Alberta's window was closed she addressed her sister. "Father Sal said—"

"I heard him," Helen snapped. "And ladies, if this trip is like any of those St. Ann's retreats, get ready for the vacation from hell."

Two hours later when they pulled up the steep driveway to the parking lot of Icicle Lodge, thoughts of the fiery pits of hell were forgotten and the women felt as if they had entered the gates of paradise.

"Che bello," Alberta gasped.

And it was beautiful. Ever since moving to Tranquility and into her house on Memory Lake, Alberta didn't think she would ever see a more picturesque setting, but the view she took in now rivaled the one she saw outside her kitchen window every morning. Granted, this landscape was larger and set in a mountain region and not on the banks of a lake so it wasn't a direct comparison, but it was, as Sloan had recently remarked about Alberta's appearance when they went to dinner at Giovanni's, the new Italian restaurant in town, a knockout.

Icicle Lodge was actually comprised of three log cabins nestled into the base of Mount Ariel, a cluster of mountains that provided all sorts of winter sports activities from downhill and cross-country skiing to snowboarding, snow tubing, and snowmobiling. The largest cabin was the main house where the staff and most of the guests stayed, and where the restaurant was located. One of the smaller cabins was used for surplus guests during the busy season, and the other housed storage and a generator, and was the electrical hub of the entire operation.

Behind the main cabin and in partial view from the parking lot was the Olympic-sized ice-skating rink that offered yet another kind of outdoor winter activity and would be the stage for Pamela Gregory's comeback. There was a medium-sized shed near the rink where the Zamboni was kept along with a second, smaller generator and all the rest of the tools and materials needed for the rink's upkeep. In front of the rink and alongside the main cabin was a large outdoor hot tub built into the ground with a stone veneer. When it was in use during cold winter nights, steam would rise up into the air, giving it the appearance of being more of a natural hot spring that sprouted up from the earth instead of a manufactured item put there by man.

There was more to the idyllic setting though, which became apparent the closer the women got to the front of the main building. The parking lot was on a lower plane than the lodge so the immediate view was majestic and overpowering, it gave visitors the feeling that they were entering a kingdom. But as the women got closer to the front door of the main building, the ground leveled and they could see what lay just behind the largest cabin and what gave the area its name— Lake Ariel.

The scent of fresh water mixed with pine and spruce wafted over the landscape like a cleansing breath. The surface of the lake was silver-blue, not frozen, but already taking on a hardened sheen as if protecting its occupants from the oncoming harsh weather. Although Lake Ariel was larger than Memory Lake, it looked like it might be smaller because of its location at the base of such grandiose mountains. Where Memory Lake was surrounded by houses and foliage, giving it a wider appearance, Lake Ariel was dwarfed by the skyscraper-tall mountain range and trees that were its natural neighbors. And while Alberta appreciated this beautiful piece of nature, she preferred her lake over this one. It was a silly thought—she was hardly the owner of Memory Lake, she had just gotten lucky enough to live there—but the feeling made her happy because it meant she truly was content with her living situation for the first time in her entire life.

Cradling Lola in her arms and holding her close to her to keep her warm, Alberta didn't have to lie when she said, "Jinx, this place is *bellissima*!" She simply didn't feel the need to add, "Just not as *bellissima* as home."

"Isn't it, Gram! The lake, the snow-capped mountains, the sky! I never knew Pennsylvania was so big, it's like we're out in the Wild Wild West."

Clutching her pocketbook in one hand and her suitcase in the other, even Helen seemed impressed. "Not bad, Jinxie, not bad."

"Thanks, Aunt Helen," Jinx beamed. "I'm glad you like it. It's so much different than back home."

"Also too," Joyce started, "the temperature here is about thirty degrees colder."

"You're right about that, Aunt Joyce, let's get inside."

The women walked around the side of the main lodge and scurried up the front steps. Jinx opened the huge wooden door and they ran inside, stopping in the large entranceway and going into sensory overload. There was another flight of stairs that descended into the main room so from their higher vantage point they were able to look down and oversee the internal landscape like skiers about to race downhill. Rustic furniture, blazing fireplaces, the heady smell of balsam and cedar, not to mention the shrill, bickering voices from an unseen couple. The beauty of the backdrop outside had given way to some kind of turmoil inside.

"I told you this wouldn't work out!" screamed a man they couldn't see.

"It has to!" was the woman's reply. "It's been long enough!"

If the unseen man had a rebuttal, it wasn't heard as the next portion of the conversation was interrupted when the rest of their party entered. The women turned around and greeted Vinny, Sloan, Freddy, and Father Sal, all dressed in different types of plaid jackets and corduroy pants, hunting caps, weatherproof boots, and sporting gloves like they had stepped out of an ad for L.L.Bean, except for Father Sal, who was still sporting his white sunglasses and white TPD baseball cap. Alberta chuckled to herself at the sight and realized that boys liked to play dress-up just as much as girls did.

While the two groups were exchanging their hellos and commenting on the long and precarious drive up the winding hill that led to the lodge from the main road, the argument from the unseen couple started back up again.

"Hell would have to freeze over for it to be long enough, and then the flames would have to start to flicker again and guess what? It still wouldn't be long enough!"

When the man was finally done screaming, it was the woman's turn. "I told you before that we need this whether you want to admit it or not so stop arguing with me and *do not* screw things up!"

Before anyone could comment, one of the offstage

screamers finally made her entrance. Her expression gave no indication that she had just had a rip-roaring argument.

"Hi! I'm Cathy Lombardo, the owner of Icicle Lodge," Cathy said with a thick smile. "And you must be the folks from Tranquility. Please come in and make yourself at home."

The group made its way downstairs craning their necks to take in more of the lodge's surroundings. Alberta was the first to greet Cathy on equal footing and shook hands with her host.

"Did the cat give us away?" Alberta asked.

"No, we only have a small guest list for the reopening, mainly press and invited guests, before things really get underway next week," Cathy explained. "Plus, I recognized Vinny from my husband's old photos."

Vinny stepped forward from the back of the group and grabbed Cathy's hand with both of his.

"I still can't believe he's gone," Vinny said, his voice filled with emotion.

Cathy smiled a bit more wistfully. "Neither can I. But Mike always spoke so highly of you, Vinny, that when I found out you were the chief of police as well as an old friend, I knew he'd want you to be here."

"Thank you, Cathy," Vinny said. "That means a lot."

"And thank you, Jinx, for what I'm sure will be a wonderful article about the lodge and all the improvements we've made," Cathy said. "I'm so glad Wyck wanted to cover it."

"He insisted," Jinx replied, deliberately avoiding any mention of the real reason why he wanted Jinx to cover the event. "And now that I'm here I can understand why, it's postcard-perfect."

"We think so," Cathy agreed. "I'm delighted that you could make it, too, Alberta."

"Me? I'm just the grandmother," Alberta said. "Why would you be delighted that I'm here?"

For a second, Cathy stared at Alberta with eyes that brimmed with fear. The awkwardness threatened to take over her body like the snow that was devouring the ground outside, but she finally found her voice.

"Don't be so modest, Vinny's told me you're an honorary member of the Tranquility Police Department."

"All four ladies are," Vinny added. "They've made my job . . . and my life a bit easier lately. They've also made other parts of my life more difficult, but you can't have everything."

"Before Vinny found out that you already had rooms through the *Herald* he told me that he was going to give his rooms to you and why you deserved such special treatment," Cathy explained. "You have quite an impressive history and I look forward to getting to know you even better than I already think I do."

Alberta remained silent and smiled at Cathy. It wasn't because she was caught off guard by the praise, although it was something that she wasn't used to, it was more about the delivery of the flattery. There was something a bit too enthusiastic and rehearsed about Cathy's speech that ignited Alberta's suspicion. It was as if Cathy knew exactly what she was going to say before Alberta arrived and was determined to make sure that she had her say. Maybe it was because Alberta had heard Cathy arguing with someone seconds before they arrived and was now chipper and cheery that caused her not to believe a word that Cathy said. Before Alberta could think too long on the subject, Vinny broke the mood.

"Cathy, you must be so honored and thrilled to have Pamela Gregory as your guest. I mean, as far as figure skaters go, there's no one better!" Vinny fawned. "Which leads me to the most important question of all. When does she get here?"

Everyone smiled as Vinny beamed like a teenager, finding it endearing. Everyone except Cathy.

Her smile hardened almost imperceptibly and for only the briefest of moments, but it was there as concrete as the lodge's foundation. Something was lurking behind her smile that made it clear she was not nearly as big a fan of Pamela's as Vinny was.

"Pamela isn't due until later tonight," Cathy said curtly. "Right now, why don't we get you all settled into your rooms?"

Cathy immediately went into hotel manager mode and instructed everyone on where they could find their rooms, the restaurant menu, where they could do some hiking, the hot tub hours, and other essential pieces of information they would need to know while they were visiting.

Across the room, Helen gazed out of a window that had a spectacular view of the mountains and muttered, *"Bella in vista, dentro è trista."*

Alberta recognized the phrase—a fair face and a foul heart.

"Are you talking about Cathy or Icicle Lodge?" Alberta asked.

"Both."

CHAPTER 4

I tuoi occhi possono giocare brutti scherzi.

Several hours later and the guest of honor still hadn't shown up. Jinx wasn't sure if Pamela had changed her mind about performing at the grand opening or if she was just delaying her arrival time to make an even grander entrance. Regardless of the reason, Jinx wasn't able to conceal her frustration over the absence of her subject.

"Ah, *Madon,* Jinx," Alberta said. "Stop pacing the room, you'll wear a hole into the carpet."

"Sorry, Gram," Jinx replied plopping down on her bed in an effort to stop herself from moving. "I guess I'm a little antsy about interviewing Pamela. This is a big break for me."

"I know it is, but why don't you use this time wisely instead of giving yourself *and me* agita?"

"What do you mean?" Jinx said. "I'm here to interview Pamela Gregory, and if she isn't here there isn't much I can do."

"Why don't you interview some other people who work here and take notes about the surroundings be-

fore Pamela shows up and occupies all of your time?"
Alberta suggested.

For a moment Jinx was speechless because her
grandmother had shown true journalistic instinct and
reminded Jinx of one of the first things she learned in
writing class in college—sometimes the best way to
find a story is to get out of your own way. Stop over-
thinking a situation and trying to control it and just let
the events around you unfold.

Jinx might be here to write a story about a specific
person, but that didn't mean there weren't other aspects of the story she could uncover until that specific
person arrived. Writing a compelling feature article
was like making a five-course meal. There would be
the main course that would garner most of the attention like Grandma Marie's legendary lasagna, but even
such a beloved dish couldn't survive on its own, it
would need to be supported by smaller items like an-
tipasto, garlic bread, fried meatballs, broccoli rabe, all
of which would be equally appetizing. Alone each was
tasty, taken as a whole they became *delizioso*. That's what
Jinx needed to do: make Pamela, her as-yet-unseen
main course, as *delizioso* as possible by investigating the
side dishes. In this instance those side dishes were Icicle Lodge, its employees, and even its magnificent surroundings.

Jumping off the bed, Jinx squealed, "Thank you,
Gram, we really do make a fab team."

"Una squadra favolosa," Alberta said, translating the
phrase into Italian.

"That too," Jinx replied. "I'll see you later, I've got
some work to do."

Alberta glanced at her watch and replied, "Meet us
in the main room, Cathy said dinner is served at six
o'clock."

"Perfect! And don't worry because I told Cathy that we're all on vegan, gluten-free diets," Jinx added before closing the door behind her.

"What?"

Alberta shouted so loudly Lola jumped off the bed and scampered into the bathroom. She didn't see Jinx peek her head back in the room. "Just kidding, Gram!"

"Oh Dio mio, uno di questi giorni!" Alberta cried, unable to stop herself from breaking into a fit of laughter. She was still smiling a minute later when the door flew open. Her smile, however, disappeared when she saw a strange man burst into her room.

"Who are you?"

Since they both spoke at the same time, neither responded with an answer, but rather a demand.

"Answer me!"

Pounding out of the bathroom, Lola broke the standoff with a hiss that made the man take a few steps backward. Alberta picked up Lola, but it didn't stop the feline from continuing to hiss and do her best to protect her owner. Her performance rivaled anything immortalized on the silver screen by her namesake. Lola's actions gave Alberta even more of the courage she needed to take control of the situation.

"I said answer me now or I'll make Lola, I mean, my guard cat, attack you," Alberta warned. "And don't let her size fool you, she is vicious when she needs to be."

Holding his duffel bag in front of him as protection, the man looked at Alberta and Lola with a mixture of fear and disbelief. "I'm sorry, but I think you're in my room."

"No, this is my room," Alberta clarified.

"Isn't this the . . . um"—the man paused for a moment to look at the room key he had been holding in his hand—"snowflake room?"

"It most certainly is not," Alberta said defiantly. "It's the Snow *Bunny* room."

"I'm so sorry, I thought it was odd that the door was open," the man said. "They should really have numbers on the doors instead of giving them names."

"I like the names, I think they're cute."

"Well, sure, they're *carina* . . . sorry, I mean cute," he admitted.

"Hold on for one second," Alberta interrupted, stopping the man from leaving. "Are you Italian?"

"Yes."

"Sicilian?"

He shook his head. "No, Muffatese."

"Oh," Alberta said trying not to sound as disappointed as she felt. "I've known *some* nice Muffatese."

"I've met one or two nice Sicilians in my time," the man countered.

A worthy adversary, Alberta thought.

"I'm here with my family and some friends thanks to my granddaughter, Jinx," Alberta explained. "She's a reporter writing an article about the grand reopening and the figure skater who's going to perform here."

"Then I'll be working with her, I'm the photographer," the man revealed. "Charlie Ponti."

He wrapped his left arm around his duffel bag to hold it closer to his chest and reached out with his right hand, but his intended handshake was cut short by Lola's hiss that was even louder than the one before.

"Lola, *basta!*" Alberta scolded, patting Lola on her rump. "He's okay, he's working with Jinx. She's really very friendly once you get to know her. Lola, that is. Well, Jinx too, but she's got a fella who's here with us so don't you get any ideas."

Blushing slightly, Charlie smiled and glanced around the room, embarrassed by Alberta's comment. "That won't be an issue, I'm here on official photographer business," he admitted. "Plus I'm in the middle of a divorce that cannot be described as amicable so I have no interest in complicating my life any further."

"I'm sorry to hear that, I never got divorced, but I thought about it a couple times," Alberta added with a nervous laugh, not entirely sure why she was sharing information with a stranger that she had never shared with her family. "I'm Alberta Scaglione, though these days I feel more like Alberta Ferrara, that's my maiden name. I'm a widow so I guess I could go back to using that, but I've been Alberta Scaglione for so long I think I might confuse people. Even myself."

"I can see how you might be capable of doing that," Charlie replied.

For the second time in a short while Alberta laughed hysterically, and it felt good. Her happiness must have been contagious because Lola relaxed in her arms and even rolled onto her back so Alberta could cradle her. Charlie, exhibiting bravery that previously had not been on display, rubbed Lola's belly and with a few touches was able to turn her previous hisses into purrs.

"So much for being a vicious guard cat," Alberta chided. "But then you're not a real intruder who's out to hurt us, you're just a photographer."

"Now you sound like my wife," Charlie quipped. "'I don't know who you think you are, Charlie, you're just a photographer.' That's what she'd always say."

Alberta could see the pain behind Charlie's smiling eyes and felt like she was looking into a mirror. She didn't spend a lot of time dwelling on how Sammy used to make her feel, but forty years of marriage memories—good and bad—were hard to shed. More often than she cared to admit, her past had a way of interfering with her present. Her saving grace was that she had a present that was different than her past and she thought it might be helpful for Charlie to hear those words too.

"I don't want to stick my nose where it doesn't belong," Alberta started. "But any wife . . . or husband who puts down their spouse isn't worthy of being married. And I should know. So consider yourself lucky that your wife is going to be in your past and not part of your present."

Charlie remained silent and Alberta feared that she really had turned back into Alberta Buttinsky—as her brother, Anthony, nicknamed her when they were kids—and she had imposed her point of view on a relationship that she knew nothing about. But then Charlie's stoic mask of a face softened and he smiled at Alberta in genuine appreciation.

"Thank you," he said. "No one's said something that nice to me in quite a long time."

Thinking back on her married life, Alberta knew how that felt too. "Then you're welcome and clearly it was meant to be that you broke into my room."

"Is this guy bothering you, Alfie?"

Alberta's and Charlie's reactions couldn't have been more different. While Alberta rolled her eyes and shook her head at Vinny's obvious display of machismo, Charlie practically cowered in Vinny's presence. At five foot six and 210 pounds, Charlie was both vertically and horizontally challenged, so when he stood in front of Vinny, who was six foot four with the physique of a recently retired football player, he was intimidated. Making matters worse, Vinny was wearing his chief of police jacket and baseball cap so he was not only physically menacing, his outfit shouted power and authority.

"No, not at all," Alberta replied. "His only crime is that he confused his snowflake with his snow bunny."

"What?" Vinny replied, rightfully confused.

"He got his room mixed up with mine, that's all," Alberta clarified. "He's the photographer who's going to work with Jinx."

At the announcement that Charlie was not a threat, but also the one person who was going to get closer to Pamela Gregory than Jinx, Vinny's eyes lit up and he dropped any sense of swagger he had carried into the room either consciously or otherwise.

"If you don't take a great shot of me and Pamela on the ice together, I swear I'll have you arrested," Vinny declared.

"He's joking," Alberta said.

"I am not," Vinny corrected. "I want a glossy eight-by-ten or I'll put you behind bars. We have a deal?"

"I, um, really don't see that I have a choice," Charlie replied. "But nice to know that you're a fan too."

"I'm not a fan," Vinny declared.

"You, Vinny, are such a liar!" Alberta exclaimed.

"No, I'm not," Vinny said. "I'm a *huge* fan! Have been since Pamela won gold at the Olympics."

"Wasn't she amazing?" Charlie asked rhetorically.

"It was better than the Battle of the Brians," Vinny declared.

"Holy macaroni! Now that was a classic match-up," Charlie recalled.

"Two skaters in their prime," Vinny said. "Boitano was unstoppable."

"Yes, he was," Charlie agreed. "But Orser's proven to be one heckuva coach."

"This is how poor Jinx must feel when we all talk in

Italian around the kitchen table," Alberta muttered to herself.

"What did you say, Alfie?" Vinny asked.

"I thought you might want to show Charlie to his room and fill him in on everything you know about Pamela," Alberta fibbed. "I'll see you boys at dinner."

"That's a great idea!" Vinny beamed.

Grabbing Charlie's suitcase that had been keeping the door open, Vinny put his arm around the photographer as if they were lifelong buddies, and led him out of the room.

"Did you know that Pamela's favorite all-time program was Debussy's *Afternoon of a Faun?*" Vinny announced rather than questioned. "Now that is a master class in skating, her edges, her flow, just first-rate as Dick Button would say."

Thankfully the door closed behind the two men and prevented Alberta from hearing the rest of Vinny's monologue. It was wonderful to witness her friend so excited in anticipation of seeing one of his favorite figure skaters up close and personal, but like her Grandma Marie would say when someone wanted a third helping of her manicotti—*I tuoi occhi possono giocare brutti scherzi.* Your eyes can play tricks on you. And what you see is not always good for you.

After a long road trip and some unanticipated excitement, Alberta knew what was right for her and Lola.

"I think it's time you and I took a little catnap," Alberta whispered in Lola's ear. "Something tells me that tonight is going to be a memorable event."

A few hours later sitting around a beautifully decorated table in the lodge's main room, Alberta knew she was right. The air crackled with possibility and it wasn't just the roaring fires in the two fireplaces on opposite sides of the room. It was the combination of being around a dinner table with people she loved and truly cared about and the impending arrival of a woman Alberta had never met, but who she was suddenly very excited to see.

The table was long and rectangular and, according to Cathy, a local artisan crafted it out of an oak tree that was struck by lightning during a terrible storm a few years ago. Alberta loved that the table was made from natural resources and had a life before being brought inside to give such pleasure to everyone who stayed at the lodge. Being Italian, Alberta knew the importance of the family dinner table, it connected the generations and kept everyone grounded despite their hectic lives and the fights and squabbles that were inevitable. When a family sat down at the table to eat, all was forgotten and most sins were forgiven. It was a place of peace, comfort, and love, and Alberta felt the energy of all three emotions sitting between Jinx and Sloan.

Sloan looked as handsome as ever, his blue corduroy shirt made his own blue eyes shimmer, and he was wearing the cologne Alberta loved. She kept forgetting the name of it, but it smelled like pine and vanilla, an odd combination, but somehow it worked. She imagined it was something Gary Cooper might wear to a party.

To her right was Jinx dressed in jeans and a red turtleneck sweater, her favorite color because it served as a canvas to show off her long, wavy jet-black hair. She had on minimal makeup, but Alberta noticed that she did apply her red lipstick with a stronger brush than usual, which made her plump lips even plumper. She had beautiful skin and long eyelashes so she wisely stayed away from adding makeup to highlight her features, the excess would detract from her natural beauty.

Freddy was to her right and it was obvious to Alberta and probably everyone around the table that Freddy only had eyes for Jinx. Fashion was not Freddy's forte and he wore a simple plaid shirt and jeans, but his unkempt hair, bright eyes, and floppy ears gave him a youthful vigor that no preening could improve.

On the other side of the table sat Vinny, Joyce, Charlie, Father Sal, and Helen. They were all dressed warmly in sweaters and turtlenecks though Joyce, always the fashion plate, looked stunning in a tweed jacket, black pants, and a matching tweed cap. She looked like she'd sashayed into the lodge directly from the English countryside.

Alberta felt a tinge of pride wearing the brown and mustard vintage tweed Chanel pantsuit she recently bought, and for the first time felt like Joyce's fashionable equal. She had definitely caught Sloan's eye.

"Coco herself would be in awe of you in that outfit," he whispered.

"That's nice to hear, but I wasn't trying to impress Ms. Chanel," Alberta replied.

When Sloan grinned devilishly she knew her flirting had worked. But no matter how splendidly everyone was dressed, no one looked better than the main room itself. Above the fireplaces and the huge table, there were exposed beams on the ceiling from which hung two huge brass and metal chandeliers on opposite sides of the room. Several lived-in armchairs in plaid fabrics, two matching plum leather club chairs, and a couch with a subtle floral design that looked like the most comfortable sofa ever made were all arranged casually throughout the room.

Knickknacks and books were scattered around the

room on small end tables, and bookcases and paint-
ings of mountains and lakes hung from the walls to
create a haphazard decor, kind of a rustic happen-
stance, that was inviting and warm.

The dining table was positioned perpendicular to
the large window so no matter where you sat you simply
had to turn to the left or the right to get a breathtaking
view of Lake Ariel or the snowcapped mountains. And
if you craned your neck just a bit you could see a portion of the ice-skating rink. That was if you could take
your eyes off of the smorgasbord of food that took up
most of the real estate on the table.

The main course was a hearty beef stew, but all
around the table were baskets of bread, bowls of
mashed potatoes, plates filled with brussels sprouts
and asparagus, condiments, glasses of wine, carafes of
water. And then there were the two thick brass candle-
stick holders, each holding three green candles that
perfectly matched the green, black, and gold plaid
runner that ran the length of the table.

Alberta had thrown many a party in her day and she
knew how much work it took to make it look effortless.
She was impressed by the attention to detail that went
into this dinner, and she could tell by the happy faces
around her chatting away and munching on their
meal that she wasn't alone in her evaluation.

She was just about to make a toast to Cathy and the
staff of Icicle Lodge when the door to the main room
flung open, bringing with it a burst of cold air and a
woman who would prove to have even colder airs. The
guest of honor had finally arrived and she was not
nearly as happy about her entrance as the rest of the
people sitting around the table.

"Some welcome this is! You couldn't wait to eat until
I got here?"

Pamela Gregory stood in the entranceway at the top of the stairs and she was everything Vinny promised she would be: a diva who understood how to command attention. She was wearing a full-length fox coat and a matching fox headband, her blonde hair contrasting perfectly with the red. Her hands were balled into fists resting on her hips and she was surveying the room with eyes the color of ice cubes.

If this was even half the power and ferocity she brought to the ice during her competitive years, Alberta feared, retroactively, for the other skaters. This was a woman whom you did not want to bump into in a dark rink.

Alberta shivered and it wasn't because the cold air was rushing into the room, it was because she was remembering what her Grandma Marie had said. *I tuoi occhi possono giocare brutti scherzi.* Alberta knew in that one instant that no matter how beautiful and mesmerizing Pamela Gregory looked, Alberta could not trust her eyes. She didn't know how she knew it, but she was certain that Pamela was no good, not for her or for anyone else in the room.

CHAPTER 5

Spavoneggiearsi.

"Answer me! Is this the way you welcome the guest of honor?"

Her icy blue eyes traveled from one end of the room to the other so it was difficult to determine which person she was threatening with her question. It could have been Cathy, the owner of the lodge, or Charlie, the photographer, who should have been memorializing her entrance on film, or it could have been anyone else sitting at the table staring at her. As a result, Pamela's nonspecific, but definitely nonfriendly, query produced a hodgepodge of reactions among the guests.

Jinx and Freddy looked as if they were back in grammar school being scolded by a stern nun yielding a not-so-innocent-looking ruler. Vinny, Charlie, and even Father Sal looked like not-so-innocent teenagers who just got caught gawking at a girlie magazine, while Sloan and Joyce appeared to be amused by Pamela's not-so-innocent-sounding accusation. The remaining people in the room—Alberta, Helen, and Cathy—did not appear to be afraid, mesmerized, or entertained by Pamela's entrance. On the contrary, they seemed to be judging the woman based on the few words she had spoken. And from the looks of the steely glares and brassy sneers on the three women, the judgment was not in Pamela's favor.

Until last week, Alberta hadn't recognized this woman's name, but with only one look she knew in her gut that Pamela enjoyed being a walking cyclone causing confusion and disruption with every step she took. Alberta had met women like this before, some were even members of her family, so even though she knew very few facts about Pamela Gregory, she knew that Pamela was a woman who enjoyed every second in the spotlight even if that spotlight highlighted her not-so-innocent traits.

"Spavoneggiearsi," Alberta muttered.

She hadn't meant for anyone else to hear her one-word whispered commentary, but Helen did. And she agreed with what she heard.

"You got that right, sister," Helen whispered back. "This peacock loves to strut her stuff."

The trouble with peacocks is that while their ostentatious display can be beautiful, it can also be distracting. Even the most savvy viewers, who should recognize when they're being manipulated by a pretty image, get hoodwinked. They're so spellbound by the plumage, or in this case fur, that they can't see the ugly truth that lies beneath. Even if you're a seasoned cop who's seen a lot of ugliness.

"You must be Pamela Gregory!"

Vinny was grinning from ear to ear like a schoolboy who has found himself in the presence of his crush instead of staring at her image on his bedroom wall. The sight conflicted Alberta. A lot of tragedy had unfolded in Tranquility this past year so it was wonderful to see her old friend smile again. But on the other hand, Alberta knew that it wouldn't take much for Pamela to wipe that smile from Vinny's face.

"Of course I'm Pamela Gregory!" she snapped as a reply. "Do I look like Sonja Henie?"

Even though Pamela meant her words to be insulting, Vinny was so thrilled to see her in the flesh and not on his TV screen that he interpreted her comment as a joke. So much for his well-honed detective skills or for that matter Alberta's need to worry, Vinny wasn't going to let Pamela ruin his party.

He turned to Charlie and then Father Sal and said, "Sonja Henie! That's a good one." And the three of them burst into raucous laughter.

While Sloan and Freddy didn't join in the hilarity, they were grinning, and Alberta understood the reason all the men at the table were sporting goofy expressions—Pamela Gregory was, without a doubt, a beautiful woman.

Blonde and blue-eyed, she looked every inch the Ice Princess even if her princess days were long gone. Her pale complexion was smooth and mostly unwrinkled except for a few crow's feet around her eyes. It didn't appear that she benefitted from plastic surgery or Botox, but if she had undergone some medical procedures or chemical enhancements, the work was masterful and had left behind no visual clue that Pamela's natural canvas had been altered. Whatever method Pamela adopted to fight against the ravages of time— through scientific intervention, a healthy lifestyle, or just plain luck—the woman was winning the battle.

Standing at about five foot six, Pamela was on the tall side for a figure skater, and despite her age her body was still perfectly proportioned. Once an athlete, always an athlete, Alberta assumed.

The caramel-colored turtleneck was formfitting and

showed off her slender neck and firm breasts. Alberta wondered if the image she was seeing had some extra help and if Pamela was wearing a sports bra like the kind that she recently started wearing for her early morning jogs with Jinx. If not, she silently commented, gravity had been very kind to Ms. Gregory.

Broad shoulders tapered down to a trim waist that sat on top of lean, well-defined legs that were on full display thanks to the black leggings she was wearing. Her pants were tucked into black ankle boots with a small but thick heel that didn't make her stance look clunky but rather powerful. And matched perfectly with the sound of her voice.

"Is someone going to help me with my luggage?" Pamela barked. "Or do I have to drag it in here by myself?"

For all of Pamela's patrician, austere looks and her fancy upscale wardrobe, underneath it all lurked the soul of a Jersey girl. A woman who spoke her mind and didn't apologize if her words made anyone uncomfortable. Despite that, Alberta didn't feel a connection to this woman, and even though Pamela was the guest of honor, Alberta didn't feel she was worthy of celebration.

"Of course," Cathy said. "I can get someone to help."

When Cathy spoke, Pamela's head whipped to the right where Cathy was standing and it was like a deep freeze had penetrated every nook and cranny of the lodge. The women locked eyes and although they wore matching smiles, there didn't seem to be an ounce of friendliness emanating between them.

Alberta glanced over at Jinx to make sure she caught the exchange, and by the way Jinx's eyes were bulging and moving from one woman to the other it was clear that she was thinking the same thing. Neither Alberta nor Jinx knew if these two women knew each other, but it was obvious to them that Pamela and Cathy didn't like each other. Whether that decision had been made on sight or was based on experience, they'd have to investigate further.

Neither Alberta nor Jinx thought Pamela and Cathy were truly going to engage in a full-on death match, but the way they were staring at each other, they were definitely eyeing their competition.

Until a new competitor arrived on the scene.

"It's about time you showed up."

"Sorry, Miss Gregory, the bags are, you know, kinda heavy."

The woman standing next to Pamela was her polar opposite. She was also her assistant.

"*This*," Pamela said derisively, "is my assistant, Stephanie."

Stephanie looked nothing like Pamela. She was wearing a navy blue parka that came to just below her knees with a hood trimmed in dirty-white imitation fur. She wasn't wearing the hood, but rather a red and white knit hat with a white pompom on top that dangled weakly to the left as well as thin green knit gloves. Her appearance was colorful, but nowhere near as sophisticated or glamorous as Pamela's.

Large tortoiseshell-framed glasses covered much of her face so it was hard to tell what she looked like other than that she had long brown hair and brown eyes. At five foot two she was literally standing in Pamela's shadow so her specific characteristics and facial features would have to wait to be discovered. One revelation, however, was about to be exposed.

Plopping the two brown leather satchels on the floor, Stephanie raised a hand and waved to the group.

"Rangusso," she said. "I'm Stephanie Rangusso, Miss Gregory's assistant."

At least she's Italian, Alberta thought.

"For now," Pamela added. "If you want to keep your job there are some more bags in the car."

The women were shocked to see Stephanie actually bow a little in response to Pamela's statement; some of the men, however, only saw an opportunity to impress the queen.

"I can help."

Vinny, Charlie, and Father Sal pushed their way to the front of the group eager to act as Pamela's bell-hop, but Cathy proved that she really was a woman in charge and took control.

"No need for anyone to do that," Cathy announced, her voice sounding clear and commanding. "Icicle Lodge wouldn't leave any guest out in the cold, especially the guest of honor."

She tapped a bell on the front desk and the high-pitched sound filled the room. Immediately a man came out from the office, surveyed the area, and settled upon Pamela in the doorway. Alberta recognized the man from earlier in the day when they had arrived to be one of the lodge employees. Which explained why he was looking at Pamela not in awe or admiration, but in a workmanlike manner. She meant nothing to him except that she represented another task—getting her luggage.

"Patrick can see that all your things are brought up to your room," Cathy said.

"Well, I trust Patrick will be careful," Pamela replied. "Because my *things* are expensive."

Suddenly Patrick's expression changed from stony to smiling. "Of course, ma'am, your bags are in good hands."

And large hands to boot. As Patrick walked by Alberta she noticed that he was even taller and wider than she had originally thought. Well over six feet, so he was about the same height as Vinny, maybe even an inch taller, but considerably more muscular and his hands looked massive. They reminded her of Uncle Louis's hands without the unfortunate rose tattoo Louis got on the back of his right hand when he was a teenager.

Patrick walked directly toward Pamela and Stephanie, and just when it looked like he was going to mow them down, Stephanie awkwardly jutted out of the way to give him room to pass. Pamela stood stock-still and hardly noticed the man walk past her. She did, however, notice Cathy coming toward her, and her body started to tense up. She clutched her fur coat and closed it as if she was trying to ward off a chill that would not leave her flesh.

Cathy took up the empty space between Stephanie and Pamela and smiled at her audience.

"Ladies and gentlemen, while this woman needs no introduction whatsoever, please welcome Olympic champion and figure-skating legend, Pamela Gregory."

It was hard for Alberta to tell if Cathy's pronouncement was filled with genuine sentiment, but no one could argue that Pamela's response wasn't completely honest. She opened her mouth to speak, and after a long pause was only able to say, "Thank you," in reply. Once again Alberta glanced at Jinx and they both knew they were thinking the same thought—Pamela had so much more to say, but for whatever reason she had chosen to keep her response short and bask in the applause that was filling the room.

As the cheering grew louder and the clicking of Charlie's camera finally ricocheted throughout the room, Pamela appeared as awkward as Stephanie and raised her hands in an effort to reel in the small yet unruly crowd. A memory raced to the tip of Alberta's mind and she saw herself at her wedding reception standing next to Sammy, in front of her entire family and every friend she knew, listening to them applaud her recent nuptials, and she remembered feeling like a complete fraud. She didn't want their applause, she didn't want the marriage license. All she wanted to do was take back the wedding vows she had just mumbled in church and call a do-over. Could Pamela feel the same way about her celebrity? Could her ice queen persona be nothing more than a charade?

Patrick wheeled in a baggage cart that housed several items of luggage all matching the two brown leather pieces Stephanie had brought in earlier. There were so many satchels, duffel bags, suitcases, and hanging dress bags stacked on top of each other that it looked like Pamela was staying at the lodge for six months instead of a week.

Peeking out from the side of the cart, Patrick asked, "Where should I take them to, Ca . . . Mrs. Lombardo?"

"To the Winter Wonderland suite on the second floor," Cathy replied.

As Patrick pushed the cart to the left toward the elevator, Cathy pivoted expertly so she could face Pamela. "It's the most luxurious suite in the lodge. I think you'll be quite comfortable and find everything you need, but don't hesitate to call if we've forgotten something."

"If there is something wrong, you'll probably hear me screaming so there won't be any need for me to call."

When no one responded to Pamela's comment in

any way whatsoever, she threw her hands up dramatically and shook her head. "That was a joke, people!"

Finally, everyone laughed. Everyone except Cathy who merely pressed her lips together tightly hoping it would be interpreted as a smile.

"Do you think they hate each other as much as they appear to?" Jinx whispered to Alberta.

"It's very possible," Alberta whispered back. "They remind me of when I saw Joan Crawford and Bette Davis on an old talk show, I think it was *Dick Cavett*. They were all smiles, but oh boy, you could tell that all they wanted to do was claw each other's eyes out."

"Do you think this has anything to do with the argument we overheard when we arrived?" Jinx asked. "Maybe Cathy really doesn't want Pamela here, but feels she has no other choice if she wants to make the reopening a success."

Tilting her head back and forth, Alberta replied, "Could be, Jinxie. But maybe Cathy's just jealous. I hate to be a *pettegolezzo* . . ."

"Don't be silly, you know how much I love Gossipy Gram."

"I know you do," Alberta said, pursing her lips in reproach. "And we'll talk about that later. I hate to point out the obvious, but maybe Cathy's jealous because Pamela's so *affascinante* . . . glamorous, and Cathy's so—"

"*Sciatto,*" Jinx said, finishing Alberta's sentence.

"How do you know how to say *dowdy* in Italian?" Alberta asked.

Jinx bit her tongue because she wouldn't dare tell her grandmother that it was one of the few words she remembered her mother using to describe Alberta when she was living in Florida. Even if she had agreed with her mother's description of Alberta, she would never hurt her grandmother by explaining how she knew the word. Instead, she white-lied.

"You know I've been studying my Italian," Jinx said. "It's one of those slang words that jumped out at me."

Impressed, Alberta replied, "You're such a smart girl, Jinx. And yes, maybe it's as simple as that. Cathy could just be sensitive."

"Ow!" Cathy shouted.

Emotionally *and* physically.

"I'm sorry, Cathy, are you alright?"

Alberta and Jinx turned around and saw Joyce standing in front of Cathy, who was rubbing her shoulder.

"Yes, I'm fine," Cathy said, still wincing a bit. "I got a flu shot this morning and my arm still hurts."

"I know how you feel, I hate needles," Joyce shared. "But at my age it's important to get the shot."

"At any age," Cathy added. "I didn't get one as a kid and after one bout with the flu, you'll never forget to get it again."

Later, in the middle of the night, Lola was purring so loudly it reminded Alberta that she had forgotten something very important: Lola's milk. Every night before going to bed Alberta would put out fresh milk for Lola to drink during the night. Since she had never taken Lola to a hotel overnight before, she forgot their nightly ritual.

Alberta quickly threw on the fluffy red and black plaid bathrobe and matching slippers she bought specifically for the trip, carried Lola in her arms, and headed to the kitchen. She contemplated calling room service, but didn't want to bother the staff at such a late hour. Plus, Alberta had never met a kitchen she didn't like. Satiated by the cuddling if not having her thirst quenched, Lola was purring until they reached the dining room and Alberta noticed someone lurking in the shadows.

Only when Cathy turned around and her face was illuminated by the moonlight did Alberta know who was in the main dining room with her.

"*Mi dispiace*, I hope I didn't wake you," Alberta said.

"Oh no, I couldn't sleep," Cathy replied. "And when I can't sleep I like to take in the view."

Alberta understood why. Looking out the window, it was evident that nighttime cast a spell on the area making it even more magical than what it looked like when seen in the harsh light of day. Lit by the bluish glow of the moon, Lake Ariel and its surroundings transformed into something out of a fairy tale, ethereal, picturesque, and despite its stillness, pulsing with life. Cathy gazed out the window, and when she spoke it was almost as if she had forgotten Alberta and Lola were standing next to her.

"Life can be funny, you know," Cathy remarked. "When you least expect it you're thrown headfirst back into your past. No matter how hard you've tried to escape it, you can't, it's always there ready to grab hold of you again."

Alberta's forehead furrowed as she contemplated Cathy's quizzical comment. She didn't know what she was referencing, but she did understand the feeling.

"Did you grow up in this area?" Alberta asked.

Cathy turned to face Alberta again and this time Alberta saw the bags underneath the woman's eyes and the lines around her mouth. Stress was clinging to her face along with the past.

"No, I'm from California," Cathy replied. "But my husband, sorry, my late husband, Mike, grew up near here, closer to Tranquility actually, and his family loved going to Memory Lake every summer."

"Really?" Alberta said. "That's such a coincidence because mine did too and I live there now."

"I know."

Instinct took over and Alberta clutched Lola closer to her as a means of protection. "How do you know that?"

"Vinny told me," Cathy answered. "I hear it's a beautiful place."

Once again Alberta felt Cathy was lying. Her explanation contained logic and it was plausible that Vinny mentioned she lived off Memory Lake, but it struck her as peculiar. Alberta wanted to think she was taking this amateur detective thing too seriously, but experience had proven that her instincts were often right. So for now, she'd mentally file this bit of information for when she might need to recall it.

"Memory Lake is beautiful," Alberta agreed. "But so is Lake Ariel and this whole area. Especially at night."

"Yes it is," Cathy said, gazing back out the window. "My hope is to be here for a good long time."

Cathy might want to establish roots right here in Icicle Lodge, but Alberta was fighting a feeling of impending doom and the very real thought that she had already been here long enough.

CHAPTER 6

Gli ha piu' garbo un ciuco a bere a boccia.

There is something simultaneously soothing and dangerous about the sound of a figure-skating blade gliding over the ice. The movement is grace personified, but the mechanism helping create the movement is a deadly quarter-inch blade. It's a mesmerizing dichotomy, almost as dizzying as watching Pamela Gregory skate.

All the guests as well as some of the lodge's staff were lined up against the boards of the outdoor ice rink, eager to watch Pamela's early-morning routine. She was skating without any musical accompaniment, wearing a simple outfit of black tights, gray oversized sweatshirt, and black gloves, her blonde hair pulled back in a ponytail. She looked youthful, joyous, and despite her "look at me" actions from the night before, oblivious to the attention she was getting.

Each glide across the ice propelled her several feet in one direction, and she seemed to move effortlessly without using an ounce of muscle although anyone who knew anything about the sport of figure skating knew that was the opposite of the truth. The simpler the movement often meant the skill was that much harder to achieve. It took a lot of practice to make something look easy.

Pamela's white boots moved left, right, then backward, leaning on an inside edge, then an outside edge, all the while making soft swooshing sounds that belied the fact that her blade was cutting into the ice itself. The audience had no words to describe what Pamela was doing, and they couldn't believe the speed at which she was doing it. They didn't understand that she was performing brackets, choctaws, counters, and mohawks, all different types of turns on different edges of the blade that she had been performing and perfecting since she was four years old. They had no idea what to call the crossovers, lunges, and rockers she executed without hesitation or a break in her speed. Vinny, however, did know the name for one impressive move that required Pamela to skate across the ice with her skates facing opposite directions and on two separate horizontal planes, all the while leaning backward from the waist into a backbend.

"That is a perfect Ina Bauer!" Vinny shouted.

"I thought her name was Pamela?" Helen asked.

Laughing, Vinny replied, "The move is called an Ina Bauer, named after a famous German skater from the fifties."

"Like that Katarina Witt?" Helen asked.

Vinny's face turned whiter than the nearby snowdrifts when Helen uttered the name of Pamela's nemesis. "Please, Helen, if you know what's good for all of us, never mention that name again."

"What name?" Helen asked. "Katarina Witt?"

"Helen!"

Although Vinny was furious and furiously concerned that even though Pamela was in the middle of her routine and a bit preoccupied, she might overhear Helen speak of the German Who Shall Not Be Named, he needn't worry, Helen was playing him.

"Easy, tiger," Helen said. "I won't ruffle the ice lady's feathers. But since you seem to care a lot about this ice-skating stuff, you should get out there and join her."

A look of terror with the tiniest hint of delight filled Vinny's eyes. "That would be a dream come true, Helen," Vinny confessed. "But even with my level-six certificate, I'm no match for Pamela."

"How about you, Sloan?" Alberta asked. "Could you keep up with Pamela?"

"Oh no, I haven't skated since I was a kid," Sloan replied. "Every winter my uncle's pond would freeze up and we'd skate until my mother thought we were going to drill a hole in the ice and fall in."

Alberta imagined Sloan as a young boy bundled up to ward off the cold, skating around a frozen pond, but was soon distracted by a loud scratching sound. She thought it was a bird with a sore throat cawing when she realized Pamela was making the sound by spinning on the ice.

"And that is the perfect layback," Charlie said, snapping away on his camera.

The others may not have known it, but Charlie wasn't exaggerating. Pamela was performing what could only be described as a textbook layback spin. She was spinning on her left foot, while her right leg was bent at the knee and raised off the ice so it was almost parallel to her waist. Bending backward, her arms were lifted overhead with her fingertips a few inches apart so her limbs created the illusion of forming a semicircle. She looked like the living embodiment of a music box ballerina.

"She is absolutely stunning," Jinx gushed. "I'm half her age and I couldn't get into that position standing still."

"I don't think she has half the moves you do." Freddy didn't mean for anyone to overhear his flirtatious remark, but Sloan and Alberta did and couldn't stop from smiling. Young love was not only beautiful to watch, it was also infectious.

"You'd look pretty fetching in a skating outfit like that," Sloan said in Alberta's ear.

"As long as you're right next to me to catch me when I fall," Alberta whispered back.

This time it was Jinx who overheard the trifle.

"Do I have to separate you two?" she joked.

"You should mind your beeswax, *signorina*," Alberta chided.

"You're all missing Pamela's beeswax!" Vinny cried.

Alberta and Jinx looked at center ice just in time to watch Pamela finish her routine with a traditional scratch spin. Left blade on the ice, right skate pressed against the left, arms crossed in front of her chest, and spinning on the ice like a top. Just when the move couldn't get any more impressive, Pamela threw her head back and continued to spin so quickly that, for a few moments, it looked like she was headless. By the time she took her final position everyone, except for Charlie who was still taking pictures, was applauding.

Pamela remained in position for a few moments and looked as if she didn't know what to do with herself. Alberta wondered if this was like watching a singer on stage after performing an emotionally taxing solo—do they have to remind themselves that they're not in their own private world, but on a stage with hundreds or thousands of eyes on them? Even though Pamela only had about ten pairs of eyes gawking at her, she still looked like she was lost in some private place that no one else was privy to. Until she was rescued by an intruder.

"What the hell are you doing?" Pamela screeched.

Stephanie skated to a perfect stop a few inches from her boss holding Pamela's fur coat in one arm and the matching headband in the other.

"You, um, said that you wanted your coat and your hat thing, the moment you stopped skating," Stephanie replied meekly.

"I'm not done skating until the applause stops," Pamela croaked. "So unless you have dirt in your ears, you should still be able to hear the clapping."

The only applause Pamela could have heard was from her own mind because by this point the clapping, which had been enthusiastic and genuine, had indeed ended. Vinny's attempt to resurrect the applause on his own and prevent it from appearing that Pamela was hearing aural hallucinations only sounded embarrassing. Not that Pamela noticed one bit. Her performance on the ice may have been over, but her performance as prima donna, the well-rehearsed character that she had introduced to the group the night before, was back in all its theatrical glory.

"Why don't I hear the shutter of the camera?" Pamela bellowed.

All heads turned to look at Charlie, who was gawking at Pamela instead of clicking his camera so his photo could be published in the *Herald* and uploaded online for the world to gawk over as well.

"All I hear are the appalling sounds of nature!" Pamela cried.

After a few tension-filled moments, Charlie understood he was the target of Pamela's ire and snapped to attention. Bumbling, he grabbed the camera that was hanging feebly around his neck and began snapping away. Pamela pushed Stephanie to the side to make sure she didn't photobomb any of the images Charlie was collecting, and her assistant glided to the railing, fox apparel still in hand. This must not have been the first time Pamela engaged in such a maneuver because Stephanie didn't stumble, she merely glided to the side of the rink.

"Isn't Pamela such a strong woman?" Vinny asked rhetorically. "I'm going to see if there's any chance I can get a photo from Charlie."

After Vinny left the group, Alberta could sense Sloan wanted to say something.

"Cat got your tongue?" she asked.

"More like an ass," he replied.

"What?" was the collective response.

"I was thinking of an odd little Italian phrase I picked up while studying odd little Italian phrases online," Sloan confessed. "*Gli ha piu' garbo un ciuco a bere a boccia.*"

"Ah, *Madon!* I haven't heard that one in years," Alberta said.

"I never heard that one at all," Jinx added. "Translate please."

"He basically called Miss Olympic Figure Skater a no-good low-class . . ."

"Helen!" Alberta interrupted before Helen could finish her sentence.

"Don't look at me," she replied. "He's your boyfriend."

"The phrase translates to mean a donkey drinking from a bottle has better manners," Alberta explained.

Jinx nodded her head vigorously, thoroughly understanding: "So he called Pamela a no-good low-class . . ."

"Jinx!" Alberta shouted, once again interrupting

someone before they could finish their off-color sentence.

"I'll make sure to find out how truly low Ms. Gregory's class is once I interview her," Jinx said mischievously. "Speaking of which, I need to go prepare. Round one of our interviews starts the moment the subject can pry herself off the ice."

Sitting in one of the plum-colored leather chairs next to a crackling fire, Jinx was reveling in her first celebrity interview. She had instructed everyone in her group to fight the urge to stop by to say hello so she could have privacy, and gave Freddy special orders to keep them at bay. So far, her demands were being followed.

Jinx had already done some online investigation and learned the basic facts about Pamela. She was born in Montague, New Jersey, and was discovered during a skating lesson at a local rink when she was four years old by the man who would become her first coach. Sandy Lansing immediately recognized potential in the very young skater and was universally credited for giving Pamela a strong foundation of skating skills and solid technique that made her a darling among judges from her earliest competition. As often happens in the world of figure skating, it became evident after working with Sandy for several years that there was nothing more the coach could teach his student. Sandy suggested that Pamela move on to study with a more accomplished and acclaimed coach who could help her achieve the greatness that was in her grasp. Her search led her to relocate to the West Coast.

Within a few years she was winning major competitions and rising up the figure-skating ladder until she won the U.S. Nationals when she was only sixteen. A bevy of international medals followed that culminated in a stunning victory at the World Championships, where she ousted the favorite and returning champ from Denmark, capping off a remarkable pre-Olympic career.

But none of that really mattered. What made Pamela Gregory world famous was that she stepped onto the ice in Zurich as a contender and left an Olympic champion.

Sitting across from Jinx in a matching leather chair, her fox fur draped over her shoulders, sipping hot chocolate out of a mug, Pamela still had the mark of a champion. It was an intangible quality, the confidence knowing she was the best in her chosen field, that exuded from her and after all these years had yet to be extinguished.

But then her true self cracked through the surface.

"Stephanie! I need food," Pamela professed. "All this reminiscing is making me hungry."

Like a Pavlovian assistant, Stephanie came running up to them from where she had been sitting trying not to drop the files she was holding. "What can I get you, Miss Gregory? A protein bar? Some yogurt?"

"No, just the usual."

"A plate of nuts and cheese coming right up."

"And no cashews, you know how I despise them."

"I already put them on the UFL," Stephanie assured.

"The UFL?" Jinx asked.

"Unacceptable food list," Stephanie replied as if it should be universally known. "I e-mail it to every venue before our arrival."

"Are you allergic?" Jinx asked.

"No!" Pamela shrieked. "Cashews are disgusting!

I'm not allergic to anything. Except stupidity and dilly-dallying. Isn't that right, Stephanie?"

Stephanie paused, read between Pamela's words, and understood that her boss was talking about her and ran off. Only to run back a few seconds later.

"I'm sorry, Jinx, would you like anything?"

Feeling her stomach grumble at the thought of food, Jinx realized she hadn't eaten since breakfast. "I'd love some tomatoes and mutz."

Stephanie nodded her head, turned to leave, and once again turned right back around.

"Mutz?"

"You're kidding, right?"

"No," Stephanie replied. "What's mutz?"

"It's mozzarella cheese!"

A culinary light bulb went off in Stephanie's head. "Of course. Sorry, I have, you know, other things on my mind. Be right back."

Jinx didn't need Stephanie to spell it out to decipher "other things" meant Pamela. And Pamela didn't need to speak to render Jinx speechless. Her actions took care of that all by themselves. Pamela pulled a silver flask out from the pocket of her fur coat, unscrewed it, poured some liquid into her hot chocolate, and placed the flask back into her coat as if it was the most natural thing in the world.

"Did you just pour alcohol into your hot chocolate?" Jinx asked, trying very hard not to sound like a teenager, but knowing she probably failed.

"Yes," Pamela replied taking a sip. "Brandy, to be exact."

"I know we're secluded and in the middle of nowhere," Jinx said. "But do you think that's wise? What if someone sees you?"

"What if I don't care?"

That was not the response Jinx was expecting. Everyone in the public eye knew that every public move could be caught on camera and made even more public by being posted online. Pamela must care about her public image. Why take the risk?

"It helps ward off the chill," she explained. "Been helping since I was sixteen."

"You've been putting brandy in hot chocolate since you were a teenager?"

"How else do you think I won Olympic gold?" Pamela shrieked. "Do you think I made it this far on talent and hard work alone?"

"Yes." Jinx knew it was the wrong answer, but she couldn't think of anything else to say.

"You're either innocent or stupid," Pamela said. "Figure skating is a cutthroat sport. All those pretty little girls in their pretty little dresses that you see on TV have ice in their blood and they'd kill their own mother if it meant winning an Olympic medal of any color let alone gold. Every rumor is true, the glitz and the glamour are all a cover-up to hide the harsh reality that very few make it to the top. Most get injured or can't afford to pay for lessons any longer or they just plain suck."

Pamela took another sip of her spiked chocolate and Jinx stared at her dumbfounded, but was savvy enough to know that you never interrupt an interviewee when they're on a roll. And Pamela wasn't done spinning.

"There's not enough room at the top for all the wannabes and the hopefuls skating their little hearts out in mall rinks across America wearing the cute little outfits that their mothers embellished with cheap rhinestones and pearls so their moderately talented little girl will sparkle under the lights. If they don't crash and burn or break a hip before their fifteenth birthday maybe, *maybe* they'll make it in the chorus of some Disney on Ice show dressed up like a cartoon princess or coaching kids who are even worse than they were in some crummy rink or, God forbid, opening up a lodge like this one."

When Pamela finished she was out of breath, her diatribe took more out of her than her morning skating performance. Jinx was still in shock that she had spoken so bluntly and negatively about the sport that had made her a star and given her a lifelong career. Jinx wasn't the only one who seemed surprised.

From across the room Jinx caught Patrick staring at Pamela. She wasn't sure if he overheard Pamela's rant or if he was merely infatuated with her like most of the other men at the lodge. When she noticed Pamela lock eyes with Patrick, Jinx decided to use one of Wyck's interview tips—always try to catch your subject off guard.

"How long have you known Patrick?"

"The bellhop? Never met him before."

"Then why are you staring at him?" Jinx pushed back.

"Because that's how you garner fans," Pamela elucidated. "How do you think I built up such a huge and loyal fan base decades before social media took over the world? Look a fan in the eye and smile like you actually mean it. Works like a charm every time."

Thunderstruck yet again by the vitriol of Pamela's words, Jinx was compelled to remind her of how the relationship between a journalist and her subject works in that their conversation was being taped and everything that she said could be used against her in the pages of *The Herald*. Unfortunately, when Pamela explained the real truth of their relationship, it was Jinx who didn't have her facts straight.

"Wyck agreed to what?" she cried.

"I have final approval over the article," Pamela declared.

"That can't be possible," Jinx replied.

"If you don't believe me, go ask your funny-looking boss," Pamela replied. "I told Wyck that if he wanted to interview me, he had to adhere to my rules."

"But that's unethical," Jinx stuttered.

"That's what it takes to interview a celebrity," Pamela stated. "I told Wyck that I'm the biggest celebrity *TUSH* has or ever will interview and if he wanted my story to grace the cover of his little rag, he'd have to do it on my terms and he agreed."

Stunned, Jinx knew that *The Herald* was small, but Wyck had integrity. However, he also understood how to play the game to get a story. If Wyck had to bend the rules to interview a legend then he'd do just that, and as a cub reporter who was Jinx to judge? She just couldn't believe that every word she wrote was going to have to be scrutinized and accepted by Pamela. Her hard-hitting well-balanced interview was going to be no more than a puff piece. About a woman who did nothing but huff and puff.

"It's about time!" Pamela barked.

Stephanie placed a plate of nuts and cheese on the end table next to Pamela's chair and another plate of cut up tomatoes along with some slices of yellowy cheese that looked nothing like mozzarella.

"I hope you like cheddar," Stephanie said, a bit of fear creeping into her voice. "They didn't have any mutz."

"This will be fine," Jinx lied. "Thank you."

Pamela grabbed some nuts and threw them into her mouth. While chewing she said, "Go and draw my bath. I'll be up in five minutes. And I want the lavender bubbles, not that disgusting one you always try to make me use."

"Mustard flour is good for the muscles and breathing," Stephanie explained.

"It makes me smell like a hot dog!" Pamela shouted. "Now go!"

Stephanie ran back out and just as she was exiting the room she nearly collided with Cathy, who was entering with a tray of small vases filled with fresh flowers.

"*Prost*," Stephanie mumbled.

Stunned, Jinx turned to Pamela. "I can't even! Did you hear that? Stephanie just called Cathy a prostitute."

Laughing hysterically, Pamela corrected her. "The little dolt stutters when she's nervous, she said 'pardon.'" Still laughing, Pamela continued, "I think I'm going to have to fire her after the opening. She's only been with me a few months, but it isn't working out."

Once again Jinx was taken aback by the nonchalance of Pamela's comment as well as the seriousness of her expression. She followed Pamela's gaze across the room and saw that she was staring at Cathy.

"You really like to stare at people, don't you?" Jinx asked.

"I find people fascinating," Pamela replied. "As a reporter you must as well."

"Yes, I do," Jinx confirmed. "But I get the sense that you know Cathy and that's why you're interested in her."

It was Pamela's turn to be surprised by something her conversation partner said. "Why in the world would I be interested in Cathy? She's a nobody. The only thing that matters to me is that the check she gives me for being here at this two-bit lodge doesn't bounce."

Without saying goodbye, Pamela got up and left the room. Jinx slumped back into the leather chair and could only think of one thing—Sloan was right, a donkey engaged in any activity at all had better manners than Pamela.

CHAPTER 7

Se piovesse maccheroni, che bel tempo pei ghiottoni.

*A*n old dog can most certainly be taught a new trick. That's what Alberta thought as she strolled the grounds of Icicle Lodge with Sloan's arm around her shoulder. When he made the move it felt natural, and more than that, welcomed. She enjoyed the attention he paid to her and the physical companionship. She wasn't ready to take their relationship further and, from what she sensed, neither was Sloan, but for now she was happy where things were. Alberta was also surprised that she wasn't embarrassed knowing that her family and friends who made the trek with them to the lodge could be staring out their window watching her right now. She wasn't feeling defiant and had no intention of flaunting her relationship in their faces, she just didn't care who saw them. Ah, the benefits of growing old.

Once again the moon was shining brightly casting a glow on the landscape. The temperature had dropped several more degrees so there was a frosty mist rising up from Lake Ariel that gave it a dreamlike quality. Despite the cinematic surroundings, when Alberta looked out at the lake she felt homesick. She had grown quite fond of Memory Lake and her own magnificent setting right out her back door. Smiling, she thought, *No matter where you traveled, there really was no place like home.*

And there was also no place she'd rather be than in Sloan's arms. Unfortunately, Sloan had other ideas.

"I hate to cut our night short," Sloan said, glancing at his watch. "But I promised the boys I'd be back early to play a game of poker."

Shock came first and then laughter. Just when Alberta was starting to think Sloan was different than every man she ever knew, he proved her wrong. Had she not promised the ladies that she'd be back early to play a game of canasta, she would've berated Sloan and made him feel guilty for choosing a group of men over her, but she didn't have the heart.

"Lucky for you I have my own plans," Alberta advised.

"Really?" Sloan said, trying very hard to sound jealous.

"Yup, there's a bottle of peppermint vodka and a canasta game waiting for me in my room."

Laughing, Alberta and Sloan embraced and after only the slightest hesitation Sloan kissed Alberta on the lips. It was simple and sweet and exactly the kind of kiss Alberta was hoping for. It didn't try to erase any of her memories, it didn't try to hurl her into the future, it only reminded her of the present. A place she liked being in.

They walked in silence back to the lodge, both of them feeling the strange but invigorating sensation of being familiar and awkward at the same time, wanting to stay quite a bit, but afraid to say too much. So they remained quiet and let the natural soundscape do the work for them. Rustling leaves, hooting owls, the crunch of the dirt underneath their shoes, the raised voices coming from the office.

"Do you hear that?" Alberta asked, as they walked by a slightly opened window.

"It sounds like it's coming from the office," Sloan replied. "Are they always fighting around here?"

Walking gingerly on the balls of their feet so they wouldn't make any loud noises and interrupt whoever was arguing, it was as if Alberta and Sloan were channeling Stefanie Powers and Robert Wagner as the married amateur sleuths from the old *Hart to Hart* TV series. Sloan grabbed Alberta's hand and led her inside the lodge and, ultimately, to the edge of the front desk so they could peer into the office. When he saw Pamela and Cathy arguing, he squeezed Alberta's hand so hard she almost yelped.

Even though they could see the women clearly, they couldn't hear them as well from the inside because they were behind a glassed-in partition. But from the way that Pamela was pointing her finger and the wild gesticulations of Cathy's hands, it was clear they weren't having a friendly conversation. The snippets they did hear confirmed the women weren't engaged in girl talk.

"Leave Dee out of this," Cathy said.

"Who's Dee?" Alberta whispered.

Sloan shrugged his shoulders. He may have not had any idea, but Pamela definitely knew who Dee was.

"Dee's right in the middle of it and you know it!" Pamela bellowed.

"Have you met anyone here named Dee?" Alberta asked.

"No," Sloan replied. "Although I don't think we've met everyone."

When they heard a door slam, they knew that they

would be about to meet the one person whom, at the moment, they wanted to avoid.

Just as Pamela exited the office, Sloan pushed Alberta back against the wall and kissed her much more passionately than he did outside. Stunned, Alberta grabbed onto Sloan's shoulders not out of desire, but because she felt that if she didn't, she was going to topple over and turn their embrace into an acrobatic routine. She might not be doing any ice skating, but she knew there were other ways to break some bones.

"Get a room, you two," Pamela spat in disgust when she saw them.

Luckily the sight of them conjoined and commingling seemed to be enough to convince her that they weren't eavesdropping on her conversation with Cathy, but were making a little whoopee in the hallway.

When they heard the elevator chime and the doors close, Sloan pulled away from Alberta and couldn't wipe the smile off his face.

"I'm sorry," he said.

"No you're not," Alberta replied, a grin growing on her face as well.

"That's true, not in the least."

"I'm not sure if I should thank you or thank Pamela."

"Doesn't matter to me," Sloan said impishly. "I got more than I expected."

"*Piccolo diavolo,*" Alberta scolded. "That's what you are."

"What can I say?" Sloan teased. "You bring out the beast in me, Alberta."

There was nothing more for Sloan or Alberta to say because just then Cathy came out of the office much quieter than Pamela before her, but with a matching expression. The woman did not look happy.

"Oh, I'm sorry!" Cathy said, startled to have company. "I didn't know anyone was out here."

"We're the ones who are sorry," Alberta replied. "We were just coming from a stroll and . . . well, we heard voices and we were being nosy." Alberta wasn't sure why she was confessing to Cathy. Could be that she liked the woman or that she felt bad she had been listening in on a private conversation. Or that Pamela seemed to be making her life difficult since the moment she arrived. Turned out it was all three.

Shaking her head Cathy threw up her hands. "It was nothing. Stephanie told me that Pamela wanted a king-sized bed when in reality Pamela wanted a double bed because according to Pamela there's too much room to roll around on a king-sized bed."

"Pamela doesn't seem like the kind of woman who's ever satisfied," Sloan said.

"You're right about that." Cathy sighed. "She's been catered to her entire life. Or at least I would imagine she has since she's an Olympic champion."

"I think she could've gotten another Olympic medal for being a prima donna," Alberta said. "And I know exactly where I'd like to put it."

Cathy laughed so hard she had to hold on to the front desk. "Thank you for that, Alberta. I haven't laughed so hard in weeks. If you haven't noticed, I'm a bit stressed."

Cathy meant her comment to be a joke, but Alberta could tell she was serious. Attempting to reopen a lodge, catering to an obnoxious, needy, and petulant celebrity's every whim, and doing it without a real partner was a mammoth undertaking.

"*Se piovesse maccheroni, che bel tempo pei ghiottoni,*" Alberta said.

"Sorry, I'm only Italian by marriage, I never learned the language."

"I know a little Italian," Sloan said. "But I've never heard that one."

"It's hard to translate," Alberta confessed. "Literally it means 'if the sky falls, we shall catch larks.' Figuratively it means that having a little that's good is better than having a lot that's good for nothing. I get the feeling your husband Mike was a good man even though you didn't get to share a life with him for very long."

Cathy didn't bother to wipe away the tears that pooled in her eyes. She wasn't ashamed of them. On the contrary, she was grateful for Alberta's sentiment.

"You are a wise woman, Alberta Scaglione," Cathy said. "I really would like to chat with you just girl to girl, so to speak, at some point." She then looked at Sloan and smiled broadly. "When I can pry you away from your boyfriend, that is."

It was Alberta and Sloan's turn to laugh. "Consider it done," Alberta said. "We're not joined at the hip."

Sloan smiled like the little devil Alberta accused him of being and added, "Yet."

Fifteen minutes later Sloan was in Vinny's room being dealt in to a game of poker, while Alberta was wearing her red and black pajamas and matching bathrobe, sitting on her bed holding Lola and trying to concentrate on her game of canasta. Helen was sitting in a chair next to her wearing her long, flannel navy blue nightgown decorated with an avalanche of snowflakes, and next to her Joyce was propped up against some pillows looking resplendent in a winter white ensemble that looked more appropriate for the runway than the bedroom. Jinx was sitting cross-legged leaning against the headboard wearing a pink and black buffalo-checkered fleece sweatshirt, matching black fleece pants, and pink bunny slippers that Lola kept eyeing as either friend or foe. In the center of the bed was an Entenmann's peppermint chocolate cake and each woman was drinking peppermint-flavored vodka out of paper cups.

"I might not get to write an in-depth interview, but at least we're having a fun slumber party," Jinx declared raising her cup.

"I can't believe your editor gave that woman final approval over your article," Helen said. "Does no one have ethics anymore?"

"A businessman with ethics?" Joyce blurted. "Now that's a funny one, Hel."

"Thanks, Joy," Helen replied.

Alberta and Jinx looked at each other in disbelief and their expressions of shock deepened when they saw Helen and Joyce clink paper cups in solidarity.

"*Dio mio!*" Alberta shouted. "Call your editor, lovey, hell just froze over."

"Maybe Pamela can skate down there," Jinx joked. "I'm sure there's a rink with her name on it."

Throwing her cards facedown on the bed, Alberta said, "I'm out. And not for nothing I'm thrilled to see the two of you getting along so well."

"I'm so used to sharing a room with a bunch of women, I don't even know Joyce is there," Helen commented.

"We're having a fabulous time," Joyce declared. "Last night I was reading from the Bible that's in our room—it's a very modern, updated version—and Helen was telling me what parts they left out."

"If you're going to read the Bible, read the original!"

Helen yelled. "I mean, if you want to read *Forever Amber* you're not going to read one that has all the juicy parts deleted. Am I right?"

"So right, Helen," Joyce confirmed.

"What's *Forever Amber*?" Jinx asked.

Throwing her cards down on the bed, Helen yelled, "Canasta!" And then went on to answer Jinx's question. "It's the *Fifty Shades of Grey* of the 1940s. Total trash, but I enjoyed every scandalous page of it."

"You read that book?" Alberta asked.

"I found it in Father Sal's office one day so I knew it had to be good."

"Here's something that's even more scandalous," Joyce said, scrolling an article on her phone.

"What?" the three other women shouted in unison.

"Pamela isn't just a 'rhymes with rich,' she really is rich."

"That's not scandalous," Jinx argued. "Lots of champion figure skaters and Olympic athletes go on to very lucrative careers."

"No, I mean megarich, boo koo bucks rich, rich enough so she'd never have to work again," Joyce clarified. "Which doesn't explain why she'd come to this little out-of-the-way lodge to perform for its grand reopening."

"Or why she'd be concerned about Cathy's check bouncing," Jinx said, thinking of her conversation with Pamela.

"Maybe she feels like she wants to give back to the community where she grew up," Alberta surmised. "Or she feels it would benefit her image."

"Jinxie, what did your research tell you about her upbringing?" Helen asked.

"Nothing that really ties her to Lake Ariel," Jinx said. "She was born in a town in Sussex County, but at a very young age she moved to Delaware to train at an elite skating center with Sandy Lansing, her first coach."

"That's a tenuous connection at best," Joyce said, sipping on some peppermint vodka.

"Then after a few years Pamela and her whole family moved to California to train with an even more experienced coach," Jinx added.

"Sounds to me like Pamela's just doing it for the exposure," Joyce said. "Big fish in a little pond sort of thing."

"And don't forget the money," Helen added. "I'm not pointing a finger, but the rich always want a little bit more money. Isn't that right, Joyce?"

"I told you once and I'll tell you again, like Miss Donna Summer once sang, I worked hard for my money," Joyce shared. "So I will never apologize for being rich."

"Neither will I," Alberta said. "Even if I didn't work a day in my life to make my fortune."

As testament to their closeness, none of the women felt jealous that Alberta had inherited all of Aunt Carmela's wealth. They were happy for Alberta and even happier that she was able to joke about it.

"I don't know what I did to deserve such a windfall," Alberta confessed. "But I think that's one mystery we'll never unravel."

"I agree," Jinx said. "Let's stay on track and try to figure out this mystery first."

"We're trying to solve another mystery?" Helen asked.

"Ah, *Madon!*" Jinx cried. "Do I have to spell it out?"

All three women replied as one, "Yes!"

Jinx shook her head exasperated, sending a mass of her hair's black waves in every direction.

"The mystery of what Pamela Gregory is really

doing here at Icicle Lodge," Jinx explained. "She doesn't want to be here, Cathy doesn't want her to be here, but for some reason she's here. The clues are right in front of our eyes. So, ladies, we need to find out what secret Miss No-Class Olympic Champion is hiding."

CHAPTER 8

Essere del gatto.

The next day winter had officially arrived. Up until then it had acted like a shy boyfriend, tentative and unwilling to show its true nature, but winter, like most men, got tired of playing a game. The temperature had dropped twenty degrees overnight and snow had fallen all afternoon. It was a reminder that winter was no longer going to be coy, but aggressive. From the view inside the dining room it was also proving to be romantic.

Alberta smiled knowingly as she watched Freddy accent his conversation by touching Jinx's hand or shoulder. The young man couldn't take his eyes off her granddaughter, and from the way Jinx was beaming she was delighted to be the center of Freddy's attention.

Across the large table, once again filled with food and drinks for dinner, Alberta was also fascinated that Vinny was still enamored of Pamela even though she had proven herself to be nothing more than the adult version of a spoiled brat, criticizing the lodge and Cathy every chance she got, and treating her assistant,

Stephanie, worse than an indentured servant. Pamela might be physically alluring and strikingly beautiful, but she was not a nice person and definitely not someone worthy of Vinny's affection.

There would, of course, never be a romance between Helen and Father Sal, but sitting next to each other, the two ecclesiastic frenemies had put aside their differences and seemed to be enjoying each other's company. Perhaps it had taken near isolation for their walls to come tumbling down, but Helen and Sal were chatting about the similarities between Christianity and Mother Nature as easily as if they were discussing their favorite movie. Both of them agreed that faith, survival, and resurrection were common threads in both topics.

As for Alberta, she couldn't ignore what was happening. She was feeling the love bug and found herself smiling in Sloan's direction for no reason at all. She felt her heart swell when he returned her gaze. Alberta wasn't sure what was going on in her mind or between them for that matter, but she was enjoying the time she was spending with this man. It was a new sensation, but happily one that didn't make her feel depressed about her past, but rather gung ho for her future.

And then there was Joyce.

Alberta glanced at her sister-in-law, who was sitting to her right, and tried not to stare or to judge, but she couldn't help feeling sad for her. Joyce didn't look lonely or upset, and was, in fact, smiling like always, but there was something in her eyes that Alberta understood. She saw contentment. On its own, feeling content isn't a bad thing. There were a lot of worse feelings out there, but Alberta thought, perhaps selfishly, that Joyce's contentment had grown as a defense mechanism because it was the way Alberta had lived most of her life. But Joyce—in Alberta's opinion—had accomplished far more than Alberta ever had. A long and successful career on Wall Street, twin boys who adored her, a flourishing second-act career as an artist, and as an African-American who married into an Italian family, she was a woman who challenged racial stereotypes and broke down barriers constructed by bigotry in both her personal and professional lives. Yet all Alberta could think of was that Joyce was single and alone and something had to be done about it.

"He's a handsome fella," Alberta remarked, pointing to a man with dark features wearing a white double-breasted top and black pants exiting the kitchen.

"The chef?" Joyce asked.

"Yes," Alberta confirmed. *"Delizioso."*

Laughing, Joyce slapped Alberta's hand, "Yes, Max is easy on the eyes, and you, Alberta, are a naughty girl."

Laughing even louder, Alberta replied, "It's about time you started to be one too."

"Do I have to remind you that I'm still a married woman?" Joyce said.

"A mere technicality," Alberta replied, rolling her eyes. "You and my brother live in different states and for all intents and purposes you're divorced. You just haven't put it in writing."

"I doubt we ever will," Joyce declared.

"That doesn't mean you have to sit around with us and play canasta all the time," Alberta urged. "For all you know, my brother could be dating some old lady in Florida."

"Most likely some young gold digger who finds his comb-over attractive."

"Don't joke, I'm being serious."

"So am I," Joyce affirmed. "I have a very full life even if I don't have any romance at the moment. My

Anthony was far from perfect, but he was a very romantic man back in the day."

Growing a bit uncomfortable and trying to control her own very strong feelings about her brother, Anthony, and what she considered to be his very unmanly decision to leave Joyce and move to Florida, Alberta sighed heavily before speaking. "I don't want you to waste the rest of your life. You have so much to offer a man. Especially someone as handsome as that one."

"That's blasphemy!"

Max's outburst startled everyone at the table, but chiefly Alberta who was convinced the chef had overheard her feeble attempt at matchmaking. Her face turned almost as white as the snow falling outside until she realized that Max's eruption wasn't aimed at what had come out of Alberta's mouth, but what she was putting in it.

"Vodka should not be flavored," Max proclaimed. "It should be clean and crisp like the beginning of a storm."

Everyone at the table immediately turned their heads to look at the two bottles of cinnamon-flavored vodka and were shocked that someone could accuse something so delightful of being sacrilege. Alberta clicked her tongue and thought that this is what it must have felt like when the first Puritan decided to learn how to dance.

"Sorry, Max, but we like our storms jazzed up with a little something extra," Alberta stated.

"And there's no sin in cinnamon," Helen added.

"Also too, it's *delizioso,*" Joyce finished.

Snarling in disgust, Max swiped the air with one hand and retreated back into the kitchen. His gruff departure, unfortunately, didn't create a rippling of fear or trepidation among the lodge guests, but merely a rhapsody of a few chuckles.

"Sorry Joyce," Alberta said. "He might be handsome, but he's not for you."

"He's also not the best chef around," Helen chided. "The food's okay, but nothing like Veronica's Diner. I miss her eggs Benedict and meatloaf. Do you think they deliver?"

"It's because Max isn't Italian," Alberta claimed. "I think he's Greek, maybe Middle Eastern. There's an ingredient in the stew that he made that I just can't put my finger on."

"The stew was a misfire," Helen agreed. "But I do like these gingerbread cookies."

"They're gingerbread?" Alberta asked.

"I think so," Helen replied. "If not I don't know what they are."

"You see, an Italian chef uses ingredients you can recognize," Alberta explained. "There's no mystery, just good food."

"Berta," Sloan started. "There are some very fine chefs who aren't Italian."

"Name one," Alberta and Helen simultaneously demanded.

"Sloan, haven't you learned not to talk about food around these ladies?" Freddy asked.

"Looks like you can't talk about anything around some ladies," Jinx remarked.

For a moment it was unclear what and who Jinx was talking about until they all saw and heard Stephanie gruffly push her chair away from the table where she and Pamela were sitting. The young woman stood and glared at Pamela for a few seconds, her fists clenched into two angry balls, and finally let out an exasperated cry and stormed out of the dining room.

Pamela watched her assistant leave fully aware of
the scene she had caused, but not at all self-conscious
enough to be embarrassed. On the contrary, she once
again reveled in the attention.

"My assistant thinks she's Julie the cruise director
and wants to control everything including me! Re-
stricting my diet? Give me a break! I've had dessert my
entire life, even when I was training, and I've never
gained an ounce!" Pamela spoke so loudly she could
be heard throughout the entire dining room. After a
pause, she added in an even louder voice, apparently
hoping that Stephanie could hear her from up in her
room, "Hey Julie, remember what happened to the
real *Love Boat*!"

"What happened to the real *Love Boat*?" Jinx whispered.

"I think it went the way of the *Titanic*," Joyce replied.

"If only somebody would sink the ice queen, then
we'd finally get some real entertainment around here,"
Helen said.

Overhearing the barb, Pamela, still seated alone at
her own table, side-eyed everyone like the Grinch plot-
ting revenge on the unsuspecting inhabitants of Whoville
while everyone sitting around the larger table raised a
glass of chef-unapproved cinnamon-flavored vodka in
solidarity and full support of Helen's comment.

A few hours later more glasses were raised in honor
of a much more worthy tribute—Alberta and Helen's
father.

The sisters walked arm in arm down the hallway to
their rooms, and together raised their glasses of red
wine filled with fond memories of the patriarch of the
Ferrara family—Frank.

"I can't believe Daddy would've been ninety-four today," Alberta recalled.

"Of course you can't believe it, because it isn't true. He'd be ninety-three," Helen corrected.

"Really? Are you sure?"

"He was twenty-six when I was born and I'll be sixty-seven this year."

Alberta did the math in her head. Then she did it again to make sure her first answer was correct. "*Dio mio,* Helen! You do know everything."

"It's about time you figured that out," Helen said. "I've been aware of that fact my entire life." She then added in a dramatic sotto voce whisper, "What I don't know is what Stephanie is doing sneaking down the hallway."

Helen pushed Alberta to the side so they wouldn't be seen, but given the way Stephanie was racing down the hallway in her pajamas, bathrobe, and slippers, she looked to be determined to reach her destination as quickly as possible and without any interruption. It was a safe bet that Stephanie wouldn't turn around and strike up a conversation. But where exactly was Stephanie headed at eleven thirty at night?

"Looks like the klutzy assistant may have found a playmate," Helen surmised.

Eyes bulging, Alberta started to giggle at the thought of mousy Stephanie sneaking around for a clandestine rendezvous with someone else at the lodge. But who could it be? The guest rooms were in the opposite direction of where Stephanie was heading so if she was hotfooting it to a rendezvous in a stranger's room it would have to be a member of the staff.

"Do you think she and Max are having an affair?" Alberta inquired.

"They both seem to be preoccupied with limiting a

person's diet," Helen remarked. "Maybe they bonded over their dislike for anything sweet?"

"We're probably jumping to conclusions and Stephanie just forgot something in the main room or she needed to ask Cathy a question," Alberta suggested.

As they turned another corner they saw Stephanie wasn't the only restless guest at the lodge. Pamela was sipping red wine out of a real glass and staring pensively out the window wearing a long sleeveless nightgown made of gray silk that looked more appropriate for a vacation in the south of France than one in eastern Pennsylvania. It was startling how different she looked, still beautiful, but for the first time vulnerable and even troubled.

Pamela didn't acknowledge the presence of the women until they were less than a foot away, and when she spoke she didn't alter her gaze, but kept peering out the window as if Lake Ariel would unlock all the mysteries of the world.

"I should never have come here," Pamela said quietly. "Too many memories."

The comment sparked confusion as neither Alberta nor Helen thought Pamela had ever been to this area before. They were right, and Pamela's comment was more figurative than literal.

"I haven't skated in public for quite some time, and I think it's a mistake to start up again."

Perplexed by the much softer tone of Pamela's voice, Alberta was trying to process what she was hearing and seeing as this was not the Pamela they had witnessed since she arrived. Was this the real Pamela? Was the other hypercritical, demanding, and downright nasty woman an imposter? Or were they two sides of the same person, one unable to exist without the other? Pamela didn't seem to know the answer herself.

"I don't know who I am anymore," Pamela lamented. She said the words out loud, but it was almost as if she didn't want them to be heard. What she did want was redemption. "You're a nun, aren't you?" she asked, finally turning to face her intruders.

"I used to be," Helen admitted.

"How do you make amends for past sins?" Pamela asked.

Alberta was glad Pamela was speaking to Helen. She didn't want to try and answer that one. Helen, however, had no problem replying.

"There are many different roads to salvation," Helen began. "But they all start with taking responsibility for what you've done, owning up to the actions that originally led you astray."

Looking both lost and grateful, Pamela replied, "What if your actions didn't create the sin? What if you were just an innocent bystander?"

"Dear, none of us can be innocent if we stand by and watch a sin be born."

Helen's words were spoken softly and with empirical observation, not arrogant judgment, so they landed with a much louder thud than Helen anticipated. Pamela turned away from the women and once again stared out at the landscape and announced, "Then I'm doomed."

Without saying another word Pamela turned and went into her room, which was the first door on their left.

"The night keeps getting *strano*," Alberta remarked.

"And it isn't over yet."

"Freddy, what are you doing with Lola?"

When they got to Alberta's door, they saw Freddy sitting on the floor holding Lola, who was affectionately rubbing the side of her face against Freddy's red velour bathrobe. She was in heaven even though Alberta was in a state of confusion.

"I got a craving for those cookies Max made," Freddy confessed.

"The gingerbread ones?" Helen asked.

"Yes, they're almost as good as Entenmann's," Freddy confirmed. "So I snuck into the kitchen for some and on my way back I found this little whippersnapper roaming the hallway. For some reason she was trying to get into Stephanie's room."

"Stephanie isn't there," Helen said, raising her glass of wine and winking. "If you get my drift."

"I know. I knocked and no one answered," Freddy replied. "I thought maybe you or Jinx might be inside your room, but you're here and Jinx must be in a coma because I knocked a few times on your door and no one answered."

"*Molto strano,*" Alberta said.

"Exactly what I was thinking," Freddy said, standing up from the floor. "Or would be if, you know, Italian was my first language."

"Let's see what's going on," Alberta said as she unlocked the door to her room.

Inside the lights were off, but they could see Jinx asleep in her bed, the moon shining a ray of light across her face and making it glow. At the sight, Freddy smiled so brightly it made Alberta's heart sing.

She took Lola from Freddy's arms and whispered to her cat, "*Essere del gatto.* Stop getting into trouble, *signorina,* and no more traipsing around in the middle of the night for you, that's how you get a bad reputation."

"I better get back to bed myself," Freddy said. "I want to make sure I get up early to see Pamela skate. She's doing her entire routine tomorrow morning."

Alberta tried to reconcile the thoughtful, almost broken woman she just spoke to with the fiery, dynamic athlete Pamela was while on the ice and couldn't believe the two women were the same. "That'll be something none of us will want to miss."

The next morning there was a third Pamela Gregory on the ice. This one unmoving.

"Looks like we missed everything," Helen commented.

Lying facedown on center ice with both arms spread out in opposite directions was the former Olympic champion. All around her body were curlicues and swirls on the ice that resembled figure eights, only these were made out of blood.

"Oh my God!" Alberta cried. "She's dead!"

Once again Pamela Gregory had scored perfect marks. Sadly this time it was for being a corpse.

CHAPTER 9

Chi mal pensa, mal abbia.

Everyone knows that ice is slippery. It was now common knowledge, at least to those at Icicle Lodge, that ice was also deadly.

As a result it was pandemonium in the rink when everyone tried to get close to Pamela's unmoving body in the center of the ice, because no one except the deceased was wearing ice skates. Despite how slowly or gingerly they moved, people kept slipping and some even fell onto the surface of the ice on the short, but risky, trip from the safe ground outside the rink to the precarious surface that was the crime scene.

Vinny led the group and walked steadily to where Pamela was lying facedown, his work boots with their grooved soles giving him some traction on the slippery surface. Right behind him was Alberta and Sloan, who held on to each other and took small steps to minimize their chances of falling, and Helen and Joyce, who despite their combined efforts were taking more slips than steps.

Trailing behind was Jinx who, filled with a reporter's curiosity and youthful energy, kept finding her feet slip out from underneath her because she was walking too quickly. Luckily, Freddy was right behind her and picked her up each time she fell. His athleticism and sports background gave him a natural ease to glide across the ice even without the benefit of wearing skates.

Straggling behind and to the sides of them were Stephanie, Charlie, Cathy, and Max. Cathy and Max were holding hands and seemed to understand the best way to maintain their posture from the waist up was to use their feet to glide across the ice, followed by Stephanie, who, even though she took more measured steps, fell twice. Bringing up the rear, Charlie fell so many times he finally gave up and crawled on his hands and knees until he joined the group that had formed a circle around Pamela's dead body.

Vinny knelt beside Pamela and with his gloved hand gently pulled her right shoulder allowing the body to turn onto its back. The result caused more than one member of the group to shriek in horror.

The left side of Pamela's face was glistening from the ice it had been resting on, while the right side was powdered with snow, making her look like the titular star of *The Phantom of the Opera*. Her eyes were still open and were alive with shock and confusion, she didn't seem to know why or how she had died any more than the observers around her did. While her face was alarming, it wasn't the body part garnering the most dreadful responses. That honor went to her wrists. They were covered in blood.

"No!" Cathy shouted. "This can't be happening!"

Max held her back from getting any closer to Pamela, although it wasn't clear if he was reacting in order to protect the crime scene or prevent his boss from giving in to her emotions and doing something impulsive she'd later regret like shaking the dead body until it came back to life.

Cathy finally stopped screaming, not because of Max's intervention, but Patrick's. Coming out of the shed where the Zamboni was housed, Patrick hopped over the wall of the ice rink and expertly glided to where Cathy was standing. When she saw him, she broke free from Max's grip and glided with similar ease into Patrick's arms. Whatever he whispered to her couldn't be heard by the others, but it resulted in Cathy becoming calm and in total control of her emotions. His words, whatever they were, worked.

Helen's words worked to bring everyone back to reality. "Who has a phone to call 9-1-1?"

As everyone started to reach into their pockets, Vinny brought them to a halt. "I already did that and I spoke to my buddy on the force in Jefferson Township, which has jurisdiction over this area. There's a massive accident on I-80 so it'll be a while until someone can get here. Until then, I'm in charge."

"Then it looks like it's up to you to find out who would've murdered her," Freddy said.

"And who *could've* murdered her?" Sloan added. "Without being seen, I mean. The lodge is a couple hundred feet away."

Wearing an exasperated expression perfected from years of police work, Vinny shook his head and warned, "Don't jump to any conclusions, we don't know that Pamela's been murdered."

"Yes we do."

Alberta's quiet proclamation caused everyone to face her, eager to hear how she could substantiate her claim. But they'd have to wait a bit longer.

"No, Alfie, we don't," Vinny corrected. "This has all the markings of a suicide."

"Except that the markings are wrong," Alberta confirmed.

"What are you talking about?" Vinny asked. "A blind man can see that she's got slash marks on her wrists."

"And if the blind man were also smart he'd know that the marks were slashed in the wrong direction," Alberta replied.

"Berta, how do you know that?" Joyce asked.

Holding on to her sister-in-law's arm for security, Helen bent forward to get a better look at Pamela's bloodied cuts, and answered, "It's quite obvious, actually, if you know what you're looking for."

"Do you wanna clue the rest of us in?" Vinny asked, his temper beating out his professionalism.

"I don't want to steal my sister's thunder," Helen said. "Go for it, Berta."

"If someone is trying to commit suicide by slitting their wrists they'll cut vertically to open up the veins and arteries more fully so the blood flows faster," Alberta explained. "They won't make horizontal cuts like the ones on Pamela's wrists."

"Oh my God, Gram!" Jinx cried. "How do you know that?"

"Vicky DeGrasso, God rest her soul," Alberta said softly. "Distant relative on my mother's side killed herself that way."

"Well, thank you for that enlightenment, Alfie, but that doesn't completely rule out suicide," Vinny affirmed. "Pamela might not have known the right way to do what she was trying to do."

"Looks like she succeeded anyway," Freddy added.

Cathy gasped, but before she could let out another scream Patrick buried her face into his chest so her cries were still heard, but muffled.

Jinx tried to bring the conversation back from an

emotional and inflammatory discourse and to a more mundane and logical route. "Howsabout we search for the murder weapon?"

"Only if you all understand that if we find a weapon it might have been used to commit murder," Vinny cautioned. "But it could also have been used by Pamela herself to commit suicide."

Vinny watched the group nod in agreement and was even satisfied by the shrug of Alberta's shoulders and the tilt of her head.

"Work in teams of at least two and do not touch anything, even with your gloves," Vinny instructed. "If you find something, call for me."

"Wait! Don't move."

Once again Alberta had shifted the focus from Vinny to herself with a simple announcement.

"What now?" Vinny asked, openly perturbed.

"We're ignoring another very important clue," she said. "Look around the ice."

Everyone turned their heads to the left and the right searching for whatever Alberta was talking about, but came up empty.

"What are you talking about, Alfie?" Vinny asked. "There's nothing on the ice."

"Exactly!" she replied excitedly. "The only marks on the ice were created by Pamela's skates, there are no other grooves anywhere, which means that whoever killed her wasn't wearing skates."

"Or someone killed her off the ice and she somehow tried to skate away," Jinx suggested, adding to her grandmother's theory.

"Or there was no murderer and she killed herself," Vinny concluded.

"Stop it!" Stephanie's cry echoed loudly gaining power with each repetition until it grew as large as the mountains surrounding them. Everyone turned to see her, crying and shivering and looking much younger than her years. Even though Max was standing close to her, he didn't reach out to comfort Stephanie, it was as if he was paralyzed by her outburst. Alberta, however, understood when a person needed nothing more than a hug.

Walking slowly toward Stephanie, Alberta managed to make it to the young woman without falling. She didn't say a word, but wrapped her arms around Stephanie, who began to sob in Alberta's arms. Whatever kind of dysfunctional relationship she had with Pamela, her unexpected and very public death greatly upset her. Alberta didn't waste any time dissecting the relationship or trying to understand it, such examination could wait until later. Right now all Stephanie needed was to be held.

Without the strong maternal instinct of her grandmother, Jinx focused on her strengths and utilized her own skills to start questioning those around her.

"So Patrick," Jinx started. "What did you hear this morning?"

Caught off guard, Patrick didn't have an immediate answer, but rather a question. "What do you mean?"

"You were in the shed, presumably when Pamela was being killed—"

"Allegedly," Vinny interrupted.

Jinx disagreed with Vinny's hope that Pamela was her own murderer, but knew she'd be wasting her time arguing until it could be proven that she was indeed murdered, so she acquiesced to his point of view and amended her question. "Did you hear anything when Pamela died?"

"We don't know exactly when she did die." This time it was Sloan who pointed out a flaw in her questioning. Before she could alter her approach yet again, Patrick answered.

"I cleaned the ice with the Zamboni early this morning around seven o'clock knowing that Pamela would want to take the ice around eight," he explained. "Then I drove it back into the shed and stayed there working."

"On what?" Jinx asked.

"If you haven't noticed we're in the middle of a major snowstorm and according to the reports it's only supposed to get worse," Patrick shared.

No one could question that statement as the snow had fallen even harder during the short time they'd been outside.

"So I wanted to make sure the generator and snowblowers were all in perfect working condition."

"What time did you get into the shed after cleaning the ice?" Jinx questioned.

"Probably no later than 7:15," Patrick replied. "It only takes about ten minutes on the Zamboni."

"And you were in the shed from that time until you heard the commotion outside?" Sloan interjected.

"Yes."

Jinx didn't mind having help while questioning a potential witness, but she wanted to remain in control of the inquiry. "And you didn't hear anything suspicious?"

"The equipment can get pretty loud so I closed the door so it wouldn't disturb anyone, and the windows, of course, were shut," Patrick conveyed. "Even if there was a disturbance I doubt I would've heard anything."

"And yet you heard Cathy scream."

Sloan was much more a librarian than a detective so he was not yet the master of subtlety. His forte lay in facts. The result was that his comment sounded exactly like an accusation, which is how he meant it to be interpreted. Sloan didn't believe Patrick's claim, and Patrick's stony glare was proof that he was not happy with his thinking.

"I finished my work just as Cathy started screaming," he stated. "Got lucky, I guess."

"You're also lucky that you didn't break your neck racing over to Cathy," Freddy said. "Dude, you ran over that ice like you owned it."

Patrick maintained his blank expression for a few moments before shrugging his shoulders to confess, "Must've been adrenalin. I'm not very good on the ice."

Alberta and Jinx exchanged glances and they each read each other's minds—they weren't sure if Patrick was telling the truth, but they sure were impressed by their boyfriends' detective work. They both had to conceal smiles since an air of joviality in the presence of a corpse would be harder to explain than the reason for the presence of the corpse in the first place.

Two hours later that reason had still eluded the group. After Vinny and the men wrapped Pamela's body in a large plastic bag that typically was used to haul mulch to the recycling center half a mile away as a sort of makeshift body bag and placed her in one of the lodge's freezer units until an ambulance could arrive to take her to the morgue, the group conducted a thorough search of the area. It was a search that proved futile.

No one had found a knife or sharp object that could've been used as a weapon to commit murder or suicide. The group checked the area surrounding the ice rink and even the grounds near the banks of Lake Ariel and the start of the mountain trail, and not only came up empty,

but they didn't see any footprints in the snow or bla-
tant attempts to cover up any footprints that would
suggest someone had walked to the lake or the mountains to dispose of the weapon. And considering that
however Pamela died it was done within a small window of time between 7:15 and 8:00 that morning, after
Patrick drove the Zamboni back into the shed and before people started to arrive to catch Pamela practice
her skating routine. All they knew was that her death
had to be quick and quiet since it didn't arouse anyone's suspicions nor did it attract anyone's attention.
It was ironic that Pamela had died so differently than
she had lived.

"Maybe her death was symbolic," Vinny offered.

The fire in the fireplace crackled violently in response to Vinny's comment, and to Alberta it sounded
as if Pamela was laughing at Vinny from beyond the
grave. "What do you mean, Vin?"

"If it was suicide, maybe Pamela wanted to embody
her death with meaning," Vinny hypothesized. "The
Ice Princess who lived for the ice dies on it."

"That's fancy talk, Vinny," Joyce said. "But I don't
think it holds water *or* ice."

"Why not?" Vinny asked.

"Because Pamela was rich and successful and didn't
show any signs of being depressed."

"I'm not so sure about that," Alberta said.

"Why?" Cathy asked. "Did Pamela say something to
you?"

"As a matter of fact she did, to me and Helen, just
last night."

"Well, don't keep us in suspense, Gram, what did
she say?"

Before Alberta spoke she surveyed the faces of the

people sitting in the main living room of the lodge and tried to see if she could read their faces. She wanted to see who was worried by what she might reveal and who was merely curious. Unfortunately, no one looked obviously nervous so she couldn't vamp any longer.

"Pamela told us that she regretted something from her past and that the harder she tried to run from it the harder her sin clung to her."

"Who among us is unblemished by sin?" Father Sal scoffed.

"That's right, we all have regrets," Cathy said. "She didn't get any more specific than that?"

"No," Helen replied. "Only that she thought coming here might have been a mistake."

"Here?" Patrick repeated. "Why would she say that? She was about to skate in public for the first time in years. That's what we . . . all of us wanted. I mean, isn't that what skaters do? They skate."

"I don't think it was necessarily Icicle Lodge that she regretted coming to," Alberta clarified. "It was returning to the ice."

"That's ridiculous," Stephanie declared. "She loved the ice. She lived for it. And whoever killed her knew that."

"*Chi mal pensa, mal abbia,*" Vinny muttered.

"What?" Stephanie asked.

"Sorry, a bit of Italian," Vinny said. "Don't attribute something to malice that can be explained some other way."

"You can hide behind your fancy sayings," Stephanie replied angrily. "Someone murdered Pamela and that someone is sitting right here."

Silence permeated the room like an invisible airborne

disease. It couldn't be seen or heard, but everyone felt its closeness and its threat. And everyone knew Stephanie was right—they were in danger of being infected.

Intuitively knowing that fear and panic could swiftly become the new unwanted guests at Icicle Lodge, Vinny had to take action and assert his power.

"You might be right about that," Vinny agreed. "But until we can find a murder weapon and a motive to dispute what looks like an apparent suicide, let's try to keep the accusations and finger-pointing to a minimum. There is absolutely no reason to jump to any unsubstantiated conclusions. Everything will be fine and as the chief of police back home and the person in charge of this investigation for the time being, you have my word on that."

When the rest of the group had cleared out and retreated to their rooms, Vinny sounded much less convincing.

"Alfie, I think it might be time to resurrect the Ferrara Family Detective Agency."

This was the last thing Alberta had expected to hear. "So all that bluster and bravado back there was all for show?" Alberta questioned.

"Let's just say ever since you've come back, I've understood the true meaning of 'backup.' "

Alberta hoped their services wouldn't be needed and foul play would be ruled out, but she was bursting with pride that Vinny was willingly reaching out and asking for their help. She would not let an old friend down.

"Never fear, Vinny," Alberta replied. "If we find ourselves in the middle of another murder mystery, you can rest assured that the Ferraras will solve it."

CHAPTER 10

La morte non prende mai una vacanza.

Despite the fact that death had come to Icicle Lodge and contaminated the bucolic scenery, Jinx could not suppress her enthusiasm. Not because she disliked Pamela enough to wish her dead, she was as upset by the loss of human life as everyone was. But the fact remained that Pamela's death made Wyck like Jinx even more.

"The hell with your nickname, Jinx, you're my good luck charm!"

Jinx pressed her cell phone closer to her ear hoping to muffle the sound of Wyck's cries of delight from the people milling about the common area of the lodge. She didn't think people would understand her editor was merely separating his personal emotions from his professional ambitions, and since Wyck was her mentor, Jinx was trying to do the same thing. She was surprised, though not greatly, to discover that she was having an easier time with it than she thought possible.

Her compartmentalized view of the recent tragic events could be due to her having more experience covering murder cases, but she thought it more than likely had to do with the fact that she didn't know Pamela very well and the former champion figure skater had no ties to anyone she knew. It might sound callous, but Pamela Gregory was nothing more than the subject of her article. And one added benefit of the skater's demise was that Jinx no longer had to get Pamela's approval to publish her interview.

It was a devious thought, Machiavellian almost, but it was the truth. And if Jinx wanted to be an investigative reporter, the truth always had to come first.

"The truth needs to be told, Jinx," Wyck declared, sitting behind his desk, his ears as bright red as his hair, which is how they always looked when he got excited about a story.

"That's exactly what I was thinking!" Jinx cried. "I know it's terrible that Pamela was possibly murdered, but my emotional response doesn't matter. All that matters is uncovering the truth behind her death."

"Oh yeah, well, sure, that too," Wyck stuttered. "I was talking about my journalistic instincts and how good they are. I knew sending you to Icicle Lodge would pay off!"

"And here I thought all I'd get to do was write a fluff piece about some over-the-hill skating star," Jinx admitted.

"That's why I love this business," Wyck confessed. "You literally never know what the next minute is going to bring."

"I won't let you down, Wyck," Jinx promised. "I'll get to the bottom of this and I'll send you the first article within the hour."

"I'm standing by!" Wyck shouted. "Wait! I almost forgot the best news of all."

Jinx wasn't sure what could top her being at the

scene of a celebrity crime in the middle of nowhere, but she was willing to take the bait.

"How could the news get any better?"

"Calhoun is stuck in Trenton reporting on state-wide budget cuts. Some fluke snowstorm coming from the Midwest got him stranded. I think it's coming your way, too, so be careful, but boy is he gonna flip out when I tell him you scooped him!" Wyck shouted. "I told you it was only a matter of time before you'd best the best of 'em!"

As Wyck's laughter bellowed into Jinx's ear, she couldn't help feeling proud of herself. But pride was quickly replaced with insecurity—she hadn't done anything yet. Her only accomplishment was being in the right place at the right time. She still had to write an article that conveyed all the facts while creating a picture of a woman readers would want to know more about and, most importantly, a woman with whom readers would connect. Jinx needed to make *The Herald*'s readers empathize with Pamela and care that she was killed or possibly took her own life, but everything she knew about Pamela up to now did not paint a picture that would elicit sympathy. Jinx definitely had her work cut out for her. If she was ambivalent about her own success-to-failure ratio, Wyck had enough belief in her ability for the two of them.

"Now, go start banging on that keyboard and make us both proud!"

"I will!"

Jinx's exclamation interrupted the pall that had been cast on the lodge ever since Pamela's dead body was found. It wasn't an entirely unwelcome interruption, some of the group needed a distraction and were relieved to talk about the situation instead of pretending that everything was still normal or that they had to mourn. No one knew Pamela very well, and some like Vinny and Charlie had only admired her from afar. Sadly, since the only interactions they had with her at the lodge were caustic, argumentative, and uncomfortable, there was only one person who truly missed her company.

"I can't believe she's dead!" Stephanie cried. "And I can't believe she's been stuffed in a plastic bag and thrown in a freezer to rot!"

"Actually, the freezer is preventing her body from rotting," Sloan offered.

"I don't care!" Stephanie cried even louder. "It's disrespectful. She should be sent to the morgue so she can at least rest in peace."

"The side roads haven't been cleared yet from last night's ice storm," Sloan explained. "And that accident on the highway is making it even worse so it's going to take some time before an ambulance can get here."

Stephanie didn't even bother to respond this time. She simply whipped off her glasses and covered her face with her hands, before bursting into a new jag of sobbing.

"I know you're trying to be helpful, Sloan," Alberta commented, "but I think *silencio* should be your word for today."

"Sorry," Sloan replied. "It's the librarian in me, I like to help."

"Nobody can help us now, it's a lost cause." Alberta knew Cathy wasn't talking about Pamela, but rather herself. Ever since they had come inside, she, Patrick, and Max had been silent and kept staring at each other like they wanted to say something, but thought the better of it and remained quiet. Alberta assumed they were all in shock, what was supposed to be the beginning of a new adventure for them—the grand re-opening of the lodge—had suddenly turned into a nightmare. The paying guests hadn't even arrived yet and already they were in crisis control mode.

A downright ghoulish memory from Alberta's childhood resurfaced and she shuddered reliving it. A family friend, Mr. Della Bella, went fishing with his two sons one weekend in the Delaware River. The full details were never known, but somehow their small boat capsized. After Mr. Della Bella made sure his sons were safe he went back in the river to retrieve the container filled with their food and safety supplies. He drowned before he completed his mission. When Alberta's mother told her what had happened, she added a most helpful and insightful saying that Alberta had never forgotten, *La morte non prende mai una vacanza.* Death never takes a holiday. Or a vacation.

"I know this must seem *disperato* . . . hopeless," Alberta said. "But remember you still have all of this. Icicle Lodge is beautiful."

"And already a lodge of death," Cathy retorted.

"It's all my fault!" Stephanie cried.

Alberta caught Helen's eye and they both sighed. Alberta had been waiting for this. It was the natural instinct where death was concerned to blame yourself for not preventing the death in the first place.

"How could Pamela's death be your fault?" Helen asked.

"I was supposed to be at the rink with her this morning, but I overslept," Stephanie confessed.

"Did you maybe go out last night and stay up too late?" Helen asked.

Most everyone thought Helen was being facetious since they were essentially stranded at the lodge, there was nowhere for Stephanie to go, but Alberta and Freddy knew otherwise. They didn't know where Stephanie had gone, but they knew she wasn't in her room the previous night or at least during some portion of it. Neither of them thought it the appropriate time to bring up that fact so they didn't correct Stephanie when she said that she was overtired from all the traveling she'd been doing recently and slept through her alarm.

"I should've kept a better watch on her," Stephanie said. Her voice was filled with such self-incrimination it was almost like a confession. "How could I be so stupid?"

"You didn't do anything wrong, Stephanie," Alberta said. "You shouldn't blame yourself."

"Of course you'd say that, you're a dumb old woman," Stephanie yelled. "Like everyone else in this crummy lodge. None of you people get it. Helping Pamela was the only job I had."

The word "old" may have stung, but the word "job" sprung Alberta into action.

"Shouldn't you have been doing *your* job, Charlie?" Alberta asked. "As the lodge's photographer for the event, why weren't you taking photos of Pamela? That is your only responsibility, isn't it?"

Awkwardly, Charlie opened his mouth, but when he tried to speak his voice was so dry no one heard him. His second attempt fared slightly better.

"I wanted to shoot her, I mean *photograph* her while she warmed up, but she refused," Charlie explained. "She left me a note last night specifically telling me not to take any photos until she performed her routine at eight o'clock or else she'd . . . well, let's just say she wouldn't have been happy if I went against her wishes."

"Very convenient," Helen replied.

A few others agreed with Helen and shared their opinions loudly. Charlie put his hands up in front of him as if to ward off the not-so-figurative onslaught of questions and accusations that had begun. His defensive body language only created more questions.

"What happened to your hand?" Jinx asked.

On the palm of Charlie's left hand was a small bandage, the center of it was a pinkish color, the result of bleeding.

"This?" Charlie said inspecting his own bandaged wound. "I cut myself."

"Obviously," Jinx replied. "How?"

Once again Alberta was impressed by Jinx's confidence and her ability to push forward and not back down. It was a trait it took Alberta almost a lifetime to learn and Jinx was already mastering it at her young age. It made a grandmother proud, but it made the photographer nervous.

"What?" Charlie asked, searching the room to find some support. "I mean, why are you so curious about my cut hand?"

"I don't know, Charlie," Jinx started. "Maybe because a woman was found dead with wounds of her own on both wrists. Kind of a coincidence that you have a cut, too, isn't it?"

Charlie resembled one of those old cartoon characters in the throes of anger, all he needed was puffs of steam to waft out of his ears.

"This morning I reached into my medicine bag and accidentally grabbed hold of my razor," Charlie explained. "I forgot to put it in its case last night. Does that answer your question and satisfy your curiosity?"

"Not really," Jinx replied. "Nothing will satisfy my curiosity until we find out how Pamela died."

Just then Vinny walked into the room with an announcement of his own. "I've got more bad news."

"Is someone else dead?" Alberta asked, praying she was wrong.

"No, there was a water main break on one of the side roads last night that turned the hill leading up to the lodge into a sheet of ice, so we have to wait a bit longer for the ambulance and the police to arrive," he shared. "Until then I need to remind you all that this is an active police investigation and you have to remain silent and not share this information with anyone."

"Anyone we can tell is here and already knows what happened," Alberta said.

"He's talking about texting and e-mails and that thing called the Internet," Stephanie bellowed, her hands gesticulating wildly. "How freakin' old are you?"

Alberta shot Jinx a warning glare just in time before she tried to defend her grandmother's honor. She felt it best to allow Stephanie and the rest of the suspects to speak freely, and if Jinx told Stephanie off like Alberta knew she wanted to, one of the prime suspects would clam up. Before Sloan or one of her relatives could come to her defense, Alberta showed them all just how old an old lady could sound.

"I hate the Internet!" Alberta cried. "It's ruined everything. And don't get me started on texting. No more talking, no more family time. *Pericoloso!*"

"Everybody better share Alfie's point of view because I don't want this leaking out before we can get some answers," Vinny declared. "And that means you, too, Jinx."

Jinx wasn't surprised that Vinny had singled her out. She was a member of the media, after all, but she was surprised again by her response. She didn't reply verbally, but remained silent so if she did post an article online later or submit a story to Wyck, she couldn't be accused of defying police orders. She'd deal with that later. For now, she wanted to brainstorm with the rest of the Ferrara ladies, plus one very special guest.

When Cathy and Patrick left the main room to take a walk around the grounds to clear their minds and Max returned to the kitchen to start making lunch, Jinx grabbed Alberta, Helen, Joyce, and Freddy and signaled them to move into a corner of the room near the crackling fireplace. They spoke quietly, but not in a whisper so they didn't attract any visitors or attention.

"I think we're all in agreement that Pamela didn't commit suicide," Jinx started. "But in order to prove she was murdered, we need to find a motive."

"Isn't it enough that Pamela was a rhymes with switch?" Helen asked.

"You mean witch," Joyce corrected.

"She was that too," Helen said.

"*Basta!*" Alberta cried. "Enough with the name-calling."

"Am I wrong?"

"No, but that doesn't make it any better."

"But also too," Joyce said, "Pamela was a bitch."

"Okay, yes, Pamela wasn't a very nice person," Jinx conceded. "But there has to be a better reason than that to turn someone into a killer. And since the murderer is more than likely still among us, the clues must be here too."

"You really think one of us killed her?" Freddy said.

"Well, I'm sure it isn't one of us," Jinx asserted.

"Or Vinny or Sloan," Alberta added.

"And I guess you can take Father Sal off the suspect list," Helen said.

"That's very big of you, Helen," Joyce remarked.

"I'm finding it easier to be magnanimous in my old age," Helen confessed. "So who does that leave?"

"Cathy, Patrick, and Max," Jinx said.

"Don't forget Stephanie and Charlie," Alberta added.

"It has to be one of them. I mean, it's highly doubtable that it's someone we haven't met yet since the roads have kind of secluded us here since last night, making it impossible to escape," Freddy surmised.

"We'll make a Ferrara lady out of you yet, Freddy," Helen joked.

"Thanks, Aunt Helen," Freddy replied. "Sorry, is it okay if I call you Aunt Helen?"

All eyes were on the former nun to see if her magnanimity would continue. When she answered Freddy's question, they were all relieved and amused.

"For now."

"So to sum things up, we have five main suspects: Cathy, Patrick, Max, Stephanie, and Charlie," Alberta said. "I think it's time we started investigating."

Taking advantage of the two main suspects' absences since Cathy and Patrick had not yet returned, Jinx and Freddy waited until no one was looking and then walked into Cathy's office. It was a daring move, but Jinx had already come up with an alibi—if they got caught she would say that she was waiting for Cathy to return to interview her for her article and make sure she was able to put a positive spin on the tragedy. Journalism really was a helpful profession.

When they saw what was lurking behind a cubicle wall at the back end of Cathy's office, Jinx knew the five *W*s weren't going to save them because they had entered Crime Scene Central.

The wall, which was made out of material like a bulletin board, contained newspaper and magazine clippings that chronicled Pamela's entire career. There were photos and articles of Pamela as a young girl just starting out as a figure skater through her journey to Olympic champion and beyond to her professional career on and off the ice as a spokesperson for a variety of products from all types of skating equipment to beauty products and even organic ice cream. It was frightening to see such a collage of a person's life, especially since that person's life had just violently ended. Fear clung to Jinx like the snow clung to the ground outside because she knew if Cathy found them the violence would continue and it was very possible that more corpses would join Pamela's in the walk-in freezer.

"Dude! This is like something out of *Law & Order*, just pick your franchise," Freddy said.

"You're right about that, Freddy," Jinx agreed, calmed by Freddy's funny take on their current circumstances. "And not that I like to harp, but seriously, you've got to stop calling me 'dude.' "

"Sorry, du . . . Jinxie."

Ignoring Freddy's verbal faux pas, Jinx took out her cell phone and started taking photos of the memorabilia. The more times she clicked the button on her phone, the more the gravity of the situation got to her.

"This really is creepy, Freddy. I mean, why would she have all of this?"

"Maybe she was doing prep work," he suggested. "You know, gathering info on the skater before she arrived."

"When did she start planning her arrival? The eighties?" Jinx asked. "If she was just doing research, she could've done that online. This collection has been amassed over decades, starting almost at Pamela's birth."

"You think Cathy's some kind of stalker?"

"This is the hallmark of a stalker," Jinx said waving her hand at the ephemeral montage before them. When she got to one particular article, she gasped.

"What's wrong?" Freddy asked.

"Look at that," Jinx said pointing to an article dated six months ago. "I don't know who those people are in that one picture, but the one next to it, that's Pamela."

Underneath the headline there were two photos, one of people gathered around a table at some kind of fancy gathering, but the photo next to it was a photo of Pamela in her heyday wearing her ice-skating costume with her gold medal draped around her neck. The two photos had to be connected, but how?

The headline was made up of only two words— "Death Cruise"—which didn't explain anything about why the two photos were placed side by side. But when Jinx read the first paragraph of the article, she found out everything she needed to know.

"Six months ago Dimitri Vasilievsky died under mysterious circumstances while a passenger on a cruise ship," Jinx read out loud.

"What does Dimitri whatever his name is have to do with Pamela?" Freddy asked.

"According to this article, everything!" Jinx revealed. "He was Pamela Gregory's figure-skating coach."

"Dude!" Freddy squealed. "No way!"

"Two mysterious deaths in six months. We don't have a murderer, Freddy," Jinx announced. "We have a serial killer!"

CHAPTER 11

Se all'inizio non ci riesci.

Back in the main room Alberta needed to kill two birds with one stone as well or else more blood was going to be spilled.

First, she needed to prevent Cathy from going back to her office, where she was heading, so she wouldn't find Jinx and Freddy rummaging through her personal space. And second, she needed to prevent Stephanie from embarking on her own quest to find Jinx or Freddy so she could speak with someone her own age instead of the old farts she was forced to cohabitate with. So, Alberta minimized all risk by zeroing in on both targets with one slingshot.

"Cathy, Stephanie, please won't you join us for some tea?" Alberta asked.

Taking the seat next to her at the table near the smaller fireplace in the main room, Joyce added, "Also too, we have peach-flavored vodka. Max might not approve, but I promise it goes perfectly with these gingerbread cookies he's so fond of making."

Cathy hesitated and glanced toward her office. Alberta disguised her involuntary gasp by forcing herself to cough. Once she was confident that Cathy hadn't seen either Jinx or Freddy, she insisted Cathy join them.

"I simply won't take no for an answer, Cathy," Alberta said, pouring tea into a cup and placing it in front of an empty chair. "You've been working tremendously hard, we've all had a horrible shock, and you need to rest."

"But I should really . . ." Cathy started to protest.

"Basta!" Alberta replied. "I insist."

Either Cathy wasn't strong enough to continue to resist or she really was looking for a reason to sit down and ignore her responsibilities because without any further argument she sat down and joined the tea party. Stephanie was a harder sell.

"No offense, Miss Ferrara," Stephanie said.

"It's actually Mrs. Scaglione," Alberta corrected.

"Right, sorry," Stephanie apologized. "And I'm sorry about the cracks about your age before, but I was really hoping to find Jinx so she and I could talk."

"No offense taken, we are getting old," Joyce interrupted. "But Jinx is off with her boyfriend Freddy, and I got the impression they wanted some private time."

"Of course, I should've known that," Stephanie replied, blushing. "I mean, if I had a boyfriend and I was away at a place like this, I'd want some private time too. Even if, you know, someone had just been murdered."

"Something always gets in the way, doesn't it?" Joyce's comment didn't quite get the reaction she had anticipated, and Cathy and Stephanie looked at her as if she herself had just committed homicide right in front of their eyes.

"That sounded rather callous, didn't it?" Joyce said.

"I only meant that tragedy always happens unexpectedly so it can be very difficult to know how to handle it."

Cathy let out a laugh, an excess of nervous energy, not out of place given their current situation, but in fact, a rather common response. It was absurd that they should have found Pamela's dead body in the center of the ice rink and that she was resting in peace in a walk-in freezer because the storm was worse and not subsiding like the local weatherman had advised, but that was their reality. It didn't matter what anyone did because how could things get worse?

"I really can't believe this is happening," Cathy admitted. "This was supposed to be a celebration, a rebirth, and instead—"

"It's a funeral," Stephanie finished. "Except that no one is mourning."

"I think everyone is still in shock," Alberta suggested, handing a cup of tea to Stephanie. The girl teetered between acceptance and running away, but ultimately took the offering and joined the other women at the table. Although she had agreed to join the group, she was hardly agreeable.

"If you believe that you must be in denial," Stephanie argued. "Nobody liked Pamela. You saw firsthand how she could be. She yelled, insulted, alienated people, acted like a spoiled diva, and that's when she was in a good mood."

Both Alberta and Joyce opened their mouths to speak, but no words came out. It wasn't as if they couldn't think of something to say, they just couldn't think of something to contradict Stephanie's assessment of Pamela's personality. So, when in Rome . . .

"You're right, I mean, not for nothing, she really wasn't a very nice person," Alberta stated. "I don't like speaking ill of the dead and I hardly knew her, but except for the last conversation Helen and I had with her last night, she was always barking orders and putting people down. Especially you, Stephanie. Why did you stand for that?"

Taken aback by the direct questioning, Stephanie's youthful face seemed to de-age and grow younger and more innocent by the second. It was as if Alberta had spoken in a foreign language that Stephanie didn't speak and therefore couldn't translate. Finally, the words started to make some kind of sense.

"Pamela was like my mother."

"And who does that make you?" Cathy asked. "Cinderella?"

Once again Stephanie seemed surprised by the comment even though she was the one who mentioned Pamela's less-than-hospitable character flaws. Alberta got the uneasy impression that Stephanie sounded like a battered child. She remembered Helen once telling her that an abused child will often be terrified of the parent who is the abuser, but will always defend that parent for fear of retaliation. Maybe Stephanie was doing the same thing—protecting Pamela because she was afraid of some kind of beyond-the-grave retribution.

"I know that must sound odd," Stephanie agreed.

"More like ridiculous!" Cathy shouted. She looked around and saw that the women were shocked by her outburst. "Sorry, it's just that from everything I overheard and the few conversations I had directly with Pamela, she did not exude motherly warmth."

Alberta caught a glimpse of Stephanie's expression just before it changed to something a bit more neutral and saw her nostrils flare and her jaw clench, telltale signs that she was working overtime to conceal her anger. When she spoke, she sounded as if she had perfected the art of hiding her true feelings.

"Pamela definitely wasn't touchy-feely," Stephanie conceded, "but she had many wonderful qualities."

"Such as?" Cathy challenged.

"For starters, she was incredibly helpful in getting me to find my focus when working on a task, and she helped me streamline my goals and turn my ambition into more than just an ideal, but a game plan," Stephanie shared. "She helped me figure out what I want to do with my life."

"That sounds very motherly to me," Alberta said, taking a sip of tea.

"Being around Pamela was never unicorns and rainbows," Stephanie said, "but it was always interesting and always filled with learning lessons. I really am grateful for everything she taught me."

Cathy swallowed half of her glass of peach vodka and closed her eyes as the burning liquid traveled down her throat. When she opened her eyes, they were as hungry for information as they were dark brown.

"So tell us, Stephanie, what is it that you want to do?" Cathy asked.

"I want to be as successful and famous as Pamela Gregory."

"You want to be just like her?" Joyce asked.

"Yes," Stephanie immediately replied. "But a whole lot nicer."

This time Cathy's laugh wasn't the product of feeling awkward or a nervous reaction to their circumstance, it was nothing more than a reaction to finding something downright hilarious.

"That should be the easiest thing you ever attempt to do in your entire life!" As Cathy continued laughing, Alberta surveyed Stephanie's reaction, and as she expected, the young and now out-of-work woman was not finding the humor in Cathy's observation nor was she finding laughter contagious. Sensing that their impromptu tea party was about to become a scandal, Alberta stared at Joyce, raised her eyebrows, and tilted her head in Stephanie's direction. Joyce understood the physical cues and knew what she had to do.

"Stephanie, why don't you and I go and try to find Jinx?" Joyce suggested. "She can't be very far."

Her eyes were still seething, but somehow Stephanie managed to add a smile to her countenance. Alberta was impressed. This young woman had truly learned the art of the facial masquerade. But in the next moment, Alberta was alarmed. How many other secrets was Stephanie hiding? She'd have to wait for her answer since Stephanie had taken Joyce's bait.

"That sounds like a great idea," Stephanie said. "Let's go."

Without exchanging any further goodbyes, Joyce and Stephanie got up and left the room. Alberta saw Joyce lead the way and walk in the opposite direction of Cathy's office so there would be no chance of Stephanie bumping into Jinx when she finally made her exit. Alberta just wished that Jinx would do that soon. She didn't know how much longer she could keep Cathy seated.

"More tea?" Alberta asked.

"No thank you," Cathy replied.

"More vodka? A cookie?"

"I'm good, thanks."

Alberta wracked her brain to come up with a reason to convince Cathy to continue the conversation. She didn't have to work very hard as Cathy proved to be a willing participant. It was the location that would prove problematic.

"Alberta, I'd like to talk to you in private. Could you come with me to my office?"

Ever since she had turned amateur detective, Alberta understood the importance of moments like these, when a murder suspect announces she would like to have a private conversation since the word "private" implied confession. But this was the absolute worst time to hear such magical words. *Dio Mio*, Alberta silently cried, *how do I get out of this one?*

There was no way she could say yes to Cathy without being led directly to her office and directly into the path of Jinx and Freddy. The only solution she had was to persuade Cathy to speak privately, but elsewhere. Before she could suggest they go to her room or for a walk on the grounds, Cathy turned and started walking toward her office expecting Alberta to follow.

Mechanically, Alberta did follow, but silently recited a Hail Mary that grew more desperate with every step she took. It worked. Just as Cathy was about to turn the corner toward the front desk Jinx and Freddy bounded down the hallway that wrapped around the back of Cathy's office. That wasn't the most surprising thing, however. They were both wearing bathing suits and had towels flung over their shoulders.

"Gram, go put your suit on and meet us at the hot tub," Jinx commanded, thrusting a bathing suit and a long, plush towel into her grandmother's hands.

"What?" Alberta said, duly confused.

"Things have been very stressful around here and we all need to decompress, wouldn't you agree, Cathy?"

Cathy's pinched smile said no, but her lips said yes.

"Of course, go and relax before the storm gets worse," Cathy replied. "Alberta, I'll find you later and we can have that talk."

Calmer than she was before, but still baffled by the turn of events, Alberta answered, "Yes, I'd like that very much."

"Cool!" Jinx squealed. "Now go change and meet us in the hot tub."

A few minutes later, Alberta was standing in front of the glass door that opened to the trail leading to the hot tub and couldn't believe she was about to run outside in her bathing suit while it was snowing. Not just snowing, but snowing really hard.

Ah, Madon, Alberta thought, *I really must be pazzo.*

She might be crazy, but she was also trusting, and she knew that Jinx had a reason to want her to defy the cold temperature barely naked when she'd rather be sitting by the fire sipping vodka. When she reached the hot tub, her heart skipped a beat when she realized her granddaughter was playing matchmaker.

"Sloan!" Alberta cried. "What are you doing here?"

"Enjoying a soak in the tub," he replied with a rascally smile. "What brings you here?"

"My granddaughter's urgent demand," Alberta replied testily. "But now I see there was no urgency required."

"Gram, shut up and get in here before you freeze to death!" Jinx yelled. "And I'll explain everything!"

Self-consciously Alberta stepped into the hot tub still clutching her towel around her shoulders and chest to ward off the cold, but also to prevent Sloan from seeing her in her bathing suit. It was the first time he had seen her wearing so little, and Alberta was unsure if she wanted to throttle Jinx for not warning her Sloan would be present for the hot tub festivities or hit Sloan on the side of the head for wearing that smirk on his face.

Alberta stepped onto the first rung of the ladder leading into the hot tub and Sloan immediately stood up to take hold of her hand. He might look like a rap-scallion, but at least he was a gentleman. As Alberta lowered herself into the bubbling water, she knew that if she took one more step she'd get her towel soaked, which would not help dry her wet body on her retreat back into the lodge, so reluctantly she tossed the towel on the railing surrounding the hot tub, thereby expos-ing herself in her full bathing suit glory.

"Don't you look beautiful, Alberta," Sloan said, his mouth and eyes smiling.

Blushing, Alberta couldn't find her voice to reply, but merely smiled back and submerged into the hot water up to her neck. It was an odd sensation to feel warmth from the neck down and cold from the neck up, but a completely enjoyable one. Another first! Until of course she caught pneumonia, but she'd blame Jinx for that later. For now, she wanted to know why they were all sitting out here and how Jinx and Freddy got out of Cathy's office without anyone seeing them.

"There's a back door that leads out into the hall-way," Jinx explained. "After we broke into Cathy's of-fice and found what we were looking for, we thought it best to leave that way than risk being seen by Cathy or anyone else."

"You broke into Cathy's private office?" Sloan asked.

"Don't worry about that now," Alberta replied. "What did you find out?"

Jinx and Freddy explained to Alberta and Sloan

about the collage of newspaper and magazine clippings chronicling Pamela's life and career on and off the ice as well as the cryptic article about her coach, Dimitri, dying under equally mysterious circumstances.

"Two people who used to work so closely together dead within six months of each other?" Alberta asked rhetorically. "That's more than mysterious, it proves that Pamela was murdered."

Sloan scrunched up his face the way he did when he had to burst Alberta's bubble. "Don't yell at me, but it doesn't prove anything. Both deaths could be unrelated and neither death could've been the result of murder."

"Sloan might be right," Jinx added. "According to the article, Dimitri died of cardiac arrest while on a cruise, although he was in excellent physical condition and had no history of heart disease."

"Which proves that he was murdered too!" Alberta exclaimed.

"Sorry, Gram, it only proves that like the coroner's report said, Dimitri died of unknown causes."

Alberta shook her head and threw her hands up in the air splashing the others with warm water. "Everybody knows that unknown causes really means murder! And Pamela's death wasn't just a death either, we all know somebody killed her. *Se all'inizio non ci riesci.*"

"What's that mean?" Freddy questioned.

Before Alberta could answer, Jinx interrupted, "I know that one! If at first you don't succeed."

"Ooh, Mrs. Scaglione, I like that one!" Freddy squealed.

"Thank you, Freddy," Alberta said, wiping some snowflakes off her eyelashes.

Once again Sloan's face got scrunchy. "Or Pamela did commit suicide because she was depressed after finding out her old coach died. He was her coach almost her entire life, and those relationships are sometimes closer than family."

The first instinct Alberta had was to remind Sloan that no relationships are closer than family and then remembered her own relationships both with her husband and daughter. Lisa Marie had left years ago, and she and Alberta hadn't spoken since then. And even though Sammy died with Alberta by his side, they hadn't spoken about important matters for decades. Sadly, she knew very little about either of them so perhaps Sloan was right, perhaps the bond between a coach and a student was stronger than familial relationships.

"This isn't good at all," Alberta stated.

"I know," Jinx replied. "If it's true and both Dimitri and Pamela were killed, it's likely they were killed by the same person."

"Looks like we're dealing with a serial killer," Freddy added.

"A serial killer with restraint," Alberta said.

"What do you mean, Gram?"

"If this is true, we're not talking about plain old premeditated murder," Alberta explained. "We're dealing with someone filled with so much hate and rage that they were willing to wait six months to strike again. That's not everyday murder, lovey, that's downright evil."

CHAPTER 12

Cogliere in castagna.

The murderer might have exhibited patience, but the weather was a different story.

The heavy snowstorm was now an all-out blizzard, which meant the scenery looked like something out of *The Sound of Music* had the movie taken place during the winter, but it also meant that the inhabitants of Icicle Lodge were officially cut off from the rest of civilization.

Snowdrifts were being built almost in fast motion, the pine trees on the grounds that were skyscraper tall now had clumps of snow on their branches so high they looked like little white hills, and the air seemed to be breathing snowflakes. The ice in the rink was completely covered by several layers of snow, and some crescent moons were already starting to appear on the window panes. It was every vintage Currier and Ives Christmas card come to life, and it would have been joyously received if only there wasn't a homicide investigation underway.

"How am I supposed to find a murder weapon with all this snow?" Vinny shouted.

"We already checked the grounds and came up empty," Jinx replied.

"Which is why we need to check them again!" Vinny shouted yet again.

The front doors burst open and along with Freddy and Sloan came a mini-cyclone of snow, howling wind, and frigid air. The two men pushed against the strong wind to close the door behind them and then began to shake off the snow that clung to their hats, parkas, and boots. They created such a mess that it looked like the blizzard was creeping indoors.

"Folks!" Freddy yelled. "We got ourselves a blizzard!"

"Really, kiddo?" Charlie yelled sarcastically. "We hadn't noticed."

Charlie was sitting by himself in a corner of the main room drinking whiskey from a wineglass. As he had told Jinx when she asked why he wasn't using a tumbler, he said that he wasn't a choosy drunk. She quieted the investigative reporter within her and decided not to pursue the subject, but let the man be with his drink. She assumed he was drowning his sorrows now that his celebrity crush and paycheck were dead.

"We checked the shed with the Zamboni again and there doesn't seem to be a tool out of place nor do any of them have blood on them," Sloan informed the group.

"Don't you think the killer would've wiped his weapon clean of any blood before putting it back from wherever he found it?" Stephanie asked.

"He might have," Vinny replied. "Or *she* might have as well. I think it's important that until we know who the murderer is we keep it gender neutral."

"That's very progressive of you, Vinny," Jinx said.

"I've had my sensitivity training," he replied. "Now listen up, we've done as much as we can outside, it's time that we check inside for a weapon. First place I want to look is the kitchen so we'll need to shut it down for at least an hour."

"That's ridiculous!"

Everyone heard the exclamation, but no one knew whose voice it belonged to. Jinx looked around the room and tried to figure out who was contradicting Vinny. She, Freddy, and Sloan were standing near the front door, Charlie was sitting in the main room, Patrick was at another table trying to compose an e-mail to send out to the guests advising them that the grand reopening was being postponed without revealing why, and Stephanie was sitting next to the fireplace by Vinny. The voice wasn't female so that excluded Alberta, Helen, and Joyce, who last Jinx knew were all in Alberta's room, or Cathy, who was in her office. So that left only Father Sal or Max. Knowing Father Sal retired already blaming his early departure on a headache that left only one possibility.

"Max!" Jinx cried. "Don't you want us to find the weapon that killed Pamela?"

The only response was the sound of knives and forks being thrown onto a metal platter. When Max entered the main room from the kitchen, he looked as angry as he sounded.

"Of course I do, you stupid girl!" Max bellowed. "But I don't want my kitchen disrupted."

"I get it, Max, but we don't have any other choice," Vinny said calmly hoping to ease the tension that was starting to swallow the lodge whole. His tactic didn't work.

"How would you like strange people invading your office and touching everything you own?" Max asked.

"If it meant finding a clue to solve a murder, I'd be all for it," Vinny answered.

Max stomped his foot like a child and thrashed his fists in the air. "I don't care! I won't allow it!"

No one saw Patrick stand up until he was in the center of the room standing directly in front of Max. Both men were roughly the same size and build so neither would be intimidated by the physicality of the other, but Patrick outranked Max. In the pecking order, the owner's second-in-command definitely trumped the cook.

"We don't have a choice, Max," Patrick affirmed. "If we want to get to the bottom of who killed Pam, this is what we have to do."

Breathing deeply, it looked like Max might scream or throw a punch at Patrick. Luckily it wasn't the latter or else the main room might have turned into a boxing ring. "You might not have a choice, but I do!"

"No you don't, Max," Patrick replied. "None of us have a choice with Vinny around. He's a cop, remember, the chief of police, he's in charge and he's got a job to do. So don't make this any more difficult than it needs to be and let him search the kitchen. Okay?"

Nodding stoically, Max replied, "Fine."

Upstairs there was a different kind of commotion going on, this one of the feline variety.

"Lola! Don't you dare run away from me!"

Alberta watched as Lola scampered down the hallway and took a right at full speed as if she had lived at Icicle Lodge her entire life.

"Lola! *Torna qui!*"

"Even if that cat could hear you, she's not going to

listen to you," Helen said. "Let her roam around and have fun."

"With a killer on the loose? Don't be such a *stunod*!"

"I keep forgetting that the person who killed Pamela might be right under this roof," Joyce said.

"Why do you think I put the chair in front of our door?" Helen asked.

"I just thought it was one of your crazy quirks," Joyce replied.

"For a smart woman, Joyce, you can be clueless sometimes."

"Will you two knock it off and help me find Lola before she becomes victim number two."

"Berta, nobody's going to touch your cat, trust me," Helen said. "She has a worse disposition than Joyce. Now come on, if we're going to find her, let's go."

Helen walked briskly down the hallway, turning right in the direction Lola was last seen. In a matter of seconds they saw a door to one of the guest rooms ajar.

"I think that's Stephanie's room," Alberta said.

"Maybe she's paying the kid a visit," Helen suggested.

When they entered the room they saw that Lola wasn't paying Stephanie a visit, but she was quite interested in the contents of her duffel bag. Lola was pawing at the inside of the bag and was sniffing one item in particular with such fervor it was as if it was her favorite toy mouse stuffed with catnip. Alberta picked Lola up, much to Lola's displeasure, and found the source of her cat's curiosity.

"Stephanie uses the same hair dye that I do."

Alberta held up a bottle of Clairol's Shade 2 Blue Black as proof.

"Isn't she a bit young to dye her hair?" Joyce asked. "I mean, she's only twenty-five or so."

"Could be a new fad all the kids are into," Helen suggested. "It's a lot less permanent than piercing random body parts."

Alberta tossed the bottle back into Stephanie's bag and proceeded to leave the room with Helen and Joyce in tow. She kissed the side of Lola's head and scolded her at the same time. "You're a bad girl, *signorina*."

"She's not the only one," Joyce said.

Alberta and Helen looked up and saw Cathy leaving Father Sal and Vinny's room. Joyce closed the door so only a sliver of the hallway could be seen, and they all waited to speak until Cathy rounded the corner and they heard her walking down the stairs. When they were sure they wouldn't be overheard, Alberta finally said what she was sure was on all their minds.

"*Per l'amor di Dio!* Cathy's having an affair with Father Sal!"

"Berta, I don't think Sal would do that," Joyce gasped. "I mean, he's a priest."

"He's also a man," Alberta reminded.

"Sal DeSoto is many, many things, but an adulterer?" Helen said, "Never."

"There's only one way to find out," Alberta said.

She marched right up to Father Sal's door with Helen and Joyce scurrying behind her and knocked loudly three times. It took less than three seconds for the door to open.

"Are you ready to tell me everything?"

"No," Helen replied. "But you better be."

The women barged into Sal's room despite his flustered refusal to see anyone due to his splitting headache and backed him into a corner until he plopped into the red, beige, and black club chair in the corner of his room, the same as the one that was in Helen and Joyce's room.

"Now, spill the beans, Sal," Helen demanded. "What was Cathy doing in your room?"

"C-Cathy who?" the priest stuttered.

"Kathy Selden from *Singin' in the Rain!*"

"I love that movie!" Father Sal squealed. "Let's see if they have the DVD downstairs."

"There'll be no movie watching for you until you fess up! *Cogliere in castagna!* You were caught redhanded," Helen declared. "Now tell us, what was Cathy doing in here?"

As usual it took very little time for Sal to crack. It wasn't that he was a bad priest who disrespected clergy-practitioner confidentiality, he just knew that when Helen wanted to know something it was futile to try to fight her because he'd always lose.

"She's been coming to me for some counseling and confession," Father Sal confessed.

"She confessed to killing Pamela?" Alberta gasped, squeezing Lola tighter.

"I didn't say that she confessed to killing anyone!" Sal exclaimed. "She came here to talk about . . . things."

"What *things*?" all three women asked at the same time.

"There's a man in her life who is causing her trouble," Sal explained. "She's deeply concerned and afraid that he's done something terrible."

"Like kill Pamela?" Alberta asked.

"Boy, Berta, you've really developed a one-track mind," Sal commented.

"So who's this man?" Joyce questioned.

When Father Sal paused, Alberta knew that he knew who the man was, but when he spoke she knew that he was going to keep that secret to himself.

"May I remind you that while some of you . . . and by 'you' I mean Helen . . . might not think I'm worthy of wearing my collar, I am still a priest and I take my confidences seriously so I am not going to tell you the name of the man who is causing unnecessary drama in Cathy's life, just like I'm not going to tell you that she also talked quite a bit about Alberta."

"Me? Why was she talking to you about me?"

"Oh, Anna Maria Alberghetti in a taxi, honey!" Sal shrieked. "That's a secret so forget I said anything. Now get out of here. You women drive me absolutely bonkers."

Just before the door slammed in their faces, Helen replied, "The feeling is mutual!"

The next morning Alberta woke up before sunrise because her mind was racing with thoughts of who the mystery man in Cathy's life could be—Patrick, Max, Charlie—or someone else who was unknown to her. She also didn't understand why Cathy was confiding in Father Sal. They hardly knew each other and Cathy didn't appear to be an overly religious person, although the moment she had that thought she knew it was silly since a person doesn't have to look religious to be religious.

Alberta dressed quickly in the dark so she wouldn't wake up Jinx and quietly went downstairs to the main room and made herself a cup of coffee. Sitting by the window, she was happy to see that the snow had lessened from last night, but she was surprised to see something even more unexpected outside.

About twenty minutes later, Alberta was on her second cup of coffee when Patrick entered the room.

"Hi, I didn't think anyone would be up yet," he said, pouring some coffee for himself.

"Looks like I'm not the only one who couldn't sleep," Alberta replied.

"I wanted to get the Zamboni out and clear all the snow off the ice," Patrick explained. "It might snow again, but it's not good to let the snow settle in onto the ice like that."

"You were doing more than that, I see you've got the bug."

"I'm not sick," Patrick protested. "I got my flu shot, did you?"

"No, I know I should, but I hate needles."

"Don't be a fool, Alberta, it can ruin your career."

"What career? I'm retired."

"Your life then," Patrick clarified. "As you get older the flu can be dangerous."

"Yeah, I know, but I wasn't talking about that, I meant the skating bug," Alberta said. "I saw you out there before you started the Zamboni, you're really good."

Patrick's face went as pale as the landscape outside and his left eye started to twitch. Alberta didn't know what to say, but she feared that Patrick was going to have a panic attack.

"You can't say anything about that," he finally said. "Cathy . . . she doesn't like her employees to be using the rink and it's supposed to be closed because of, you know, what happened to Pamela. I was just letting off some steam. Please don't say anything."

Alberta wasn't convinced by Patrick's performance as Nervous Nellie, but she thought it best to play along. "Don't worry, your secret's safe with me."

Patrick exhaled slowly and said, "Thank you, I really appreciate that."

As he was walking back to the front office, Alberta wanted to see if he would share another secret. "Did you see Charlie the morning Pamela was found dead?"

"No, like I told everyone, I didn't see Charlie or anyone outside that morning."

Huddled around a table in the dining room an hour later, Alberta whispered to Jinx, Helen, and Joyce. "This place should change its name to Secret Lodge because it's got more secrets clinging to its walls than icicles."

"Stop talking in riddles, Berta," Helen said. "I haven't had my morning coffee yet so it's hard for me to concentrate."

"This morning I saw Patrick skating like a whiz on the rink. He even did a few jumps, and when I complimented him he begged me not to say anything to Cathy or else he'd get in trouble."

"For ice skating?" Joyce asked. "Cathy's tough, but she's no prison warden."

"Maybe not, but she's got her own secrets too," Alberta said.

"Gram, I can't believe she was meeting Father Sal on the sly! Aunt Joyce filled me in on everything."

"And then there's Stephanie," Alberta added. "There's something off with her and with that Charlie too. He's hiding something, I know it."

"Or he's just some crazy superfan," Joyce suggested.

"We might not know all their secrets, but we do know what the common denominator among all of them is," Helen said.

"We do?" Alberta asked.

"Of course we do, Berta!" Helen cried and then added in a whisper, "It's Pamela Gregory."

"You're pretty sharp for someone who hasn't finished her morning coffee yet, Aunt Helen."

"I just need a few sips to get my motor running, Jinxie."

"Well, our next step is clear," Jinx announced. "It's time we visited Winter Wonderland."

"I'm not going outside," Alberta protested. "There's about ten inches of snow out there."

"I'm not talking about an outdoor adventure, Gram, I'm talking about the Winter Wonderland suite," Jinx replied. "It's high time we broke into Pamela's room."

CHAPTER 13

Como Dio comanda.

At times, life is simply unfair. That's exactly what the women thought when they finally picked the lock to Pamela's room. Yes, the former celebrated athlete was dead, but boy, were her last days spent in the lap of luxury.

Made up of three separate rooms, the suite was more than double the size of their individual accommodations. And unlike the rest of Icicle Lodge that was decorated in a traditional rustic mountain resort palette, this Winter Wonderland was decidedly more urbane pioneer than country bumpkin.

The first room was a sitting area complete with a camelback sofa in a black and beige tartan plaid with a mahogany frame, two wing chairs in black flannel upholstery, one of them accented with a gray lamb's wool pillow, and an end table and cocktail table both lathered in black lacquer paint. The lamp to the right of the sofa was a six-foot-tall arcing floor lamp with an Edison bulb trapped in a large silver mesh shade.

Above the couch was an abstract painting, large and rectangular, that was a depiction of the Olympic rings, distorted in shape, but floating on a black and gray canvas and set aglow by the red flames of the Olympic torch that seemed to rise up from the lower right-hand corner. The painting was obviously put there in honor of its medal-winning guest, but now that she had met her untimely end, the painting gave the room an eerie quality of dark foreshadowing. A flat-screen TV mounted on the wall opposite the couch hung above a mirror-topped credenza adorned with some metal knickknacks, which balanced out the room.

To the left of the sitting area was an en suite bathroom consisting of a walk-in shower, double vanity, and separate water closet with its own door. The bathroom walls were made of distressed white shiplap that rose a quarter of the way up the room and was then taken over by wallpaper depicting columns of white birch trees against a black void. The decor reminded the women of bathrooms they had seen in the reveal of their favorite HGTV show, *Fixer Upper*.

"It's a bit too *cupo* for my taste," Alberta remarked. "But I have to admit it's beautiful."

"It isn't gloomy, Berta," Helen contradicted. "The white paneling brightens it up."

Shaking her head and dismissing her sister's comment, Alberta replied, "But that Sanitas, *Madon!*"

"Sanitas?" Jinx asked. "What's that, Gram? I never heard of that word."

"It's like wallpaper," Alberta explained.

"Very easy to clean, Sanitas is," Helen added.

"Remember the Sanitas in your mother's kitchen?" Joyce asked. "All different kinds of yellow flowers. It was all so happy and cheery."

"I loved Mama's kitchen!" Alberta exclaimed. "But this, it's like we're lost in some wicked forest and the evil queen is about to rip our heads off."

"Which is probably what the evil ice queen would do to us for invading her personal space right now, you know, if she were still among the living," Joyce added.

"You might want to come over here and check out the boudoir," Jinx shouted from the bedroom. "It really is fit for an ice queen, evil or otherwise."

Alberta, Helen, and Joyce retreated into the back room to join Jinx and were even more shocked to see how elegantly decorated it was. Although the bedroom was only slightly larger than the sitting room and its walls were painted a glossy jet black, the room appeared immense thanks to two tried and true tricks of the decorator trade. The crown molding was thick and had an intricate multilayered silhouette, but was painted the same milk white as the baseboard and corner moldings that framed the room. The result was that the white architectural accents made the black walls appear like floating masses that cradled the room instead of suffocating it. But what really supersized the bedroom was the panel of floor-to-ceiling windows that ran the entire length of the back wall.

Pamela's suite was above and to the left of the main room on the first floor of the lodge, which meant it had the same spectacular view of Lake Ariel and the surrounding mountain region. Even though it was snowing and the cloudy skies cast a grayish-blue glow on the landscape, the room was still filled with natural light that bounced off every piece of furniture in the room. The occupant might be dead, but the room was filled with life.

The white upholstered headboard appeared to glow against the darkness of the wall, and the rest of the furniture, all in shades of creamy white, mimicked the snowdrifts outside. Each piece seemed to sprout up from the wooden-paneled floor so the texture and organic design of the room could shine through instead of sitting heavily on its foundation.

Jinx plopped on the bed and spread her fingers through the pearl gray throw that was folded in half and lying at the foot of the bed. It felt as soft as the powdery snow outside.

"Geez Louise, this suite is gorgeous!" Jinx exclaimed. "I mean, I thought our room was nice, but compared to this it's like we're living in a shack."

"I don't know, lovey," Alberta said. "I think our room is much cozier."

"And the furniture's sturdier," Helen added. "The things in here are nice, don't get me wrong, but they're kind of flimsy."

"*Como Dio comanda,*" Joyce murmured.

"What did you say, Aunt Joyce?"

"It means 'like God commands.' " Helen translated.

"Which in English means 'it's the way things are supposed to be,' " Joyce elaborated. "Pamela was meant to live a glamorous lifestyle. We were meant to live with each other."

"That's a beautiful sentiment, Joyce," Alberta gushed.

"Also too, there isn't much closet space in here," Joyce said. "Look at this. I would need at least five of these to hold my wardrobe."

"That's because you're too vain and have too many clothes for a woman your age," Helen chaffed.

"If God is okay with my love for fashion, Helen, you should be too," Joyce chided. "But seriously, look how small this closet is."

The women stood behind Joyce who had opened the door to the small closet opposite the bed. Still hanging from the bar were Pamela's coats and a long black gown that she presumably was going to wear to the grand reopening party that now had been postponed. On the floor was a mound of shoes and sneakers and an odd-shaped black duffel bag.

"Aunt Joyce, look at this!"

Jinx pulled out the bag from underneath the pile of shoes and held it up for display.

"What's so special about that, honey?" Alberta asked.

"This is Pamela's skating bag!"

Excitedly, Jinx placed the black bag on the bed and laid it flat so it spread out to its full size and looked like a simplistic drawing of London Bridge, high on the ends with a dip in the center. A zipper traveled the length of the bag's straight end, and after Jinx unzipped it she reached in and revealed two white ice skates.

"*Dio mio!*" Alberta cried. "You're right, those are her skates."

"I'm guessing they were her backup skates," Joyce clarified.

"Why would you say that?" Helen asked.

"The leather is scuffed up and the laces are dirty," Joyce explained. "A diva like Pamela wouldn't be caught dead on the ice in a pair of skates like that."

"You're right, Aunt Joyce, the skates she was caught dead in were brand new, like she was still breaking them in."

Jinx picked up one of the skates and held it perpendicular to the floor, holding the neck of the skate with one hand and with the other grabbing hold of the long rectangular piece of black plastic that was clamped to the blade.

"What are those things?" Alberta asked.

"Those are the blade guards," Jinx replied. "Skaters

put them onto their blades when they come off the ice so they don't get dull and damaged by walking on a regular surface. They just clip on and off."

Jinx turned the skate upside down and peeled back the plastic guard to reveal the sharp blade underneath. Her movement revealed a bit more as well.

"Something fell out of the skate," Alberta said. She bent down to pick up the piece of paper that had fallen to the floor and opened it up. "Ah, *Madon!* It's a note."

"A suicide note?" Helen gasped.

"I'm not sure."

"Read it, Gram! What does it say?"

" 'I'm so sorry for everything I've done. I had no idea the pain I caused you,' " Alberta said. "It's signed 'Pam.' "

Silence crept into the room as loud as the wind that occasionally roared against the windowpanes. Could Pamela really have left a suicide note? Could she actually have taken her own life? The women weren't sure the note was proof of that, but they were certain the note was proof of one thing.

"I don't know what this note means, but Pamela was definitely not writing a farewell note to the world," Alberta said. "She was writing to someone specific. She says, 'I had no idea the pain I caused *you.*' "

"Not only that, Gram, she wrote it to someone here at the lodge."

"How do you know that, Jinxie?" Helen asked. "She could've written the note a long time ago, shoved it in her skate, and forgot about it."

"No, she wrote it after she got here," Jinx said. "Look at the logo on the back of her note, it's the logo for the lodge."

Alberta turned the note around and they all saw Icicle Lodge's logo. The name of the lodge was in ice blue lettering and underneath, as if it were the words' shadow, was a row of icicles, each a slightly different size and thickness. Pamela had written her note on the back of the paper at some point after she arrived.

"So who was she apologizing to?" Joyce asked.

"It has to be someone here," Jinx answered. "Cathy, Patrick, or Max."

"Or Charlie," Helen added. "You can't forget him."

"But if Pamela did kill herself, which I still don't believe," Alberta said, "why would she come all the way here to do it?"

"Publicity." The women wished they could appear shocked by Helen's comment, but they realized she was more than likely right. Pamela had been a celebrity all her life so like most celebrities she craved attention. It was a macabre thought, but not a far-fetched one to think that she would have staged her suicide under the public eye. What better way to guarantee attention and, by extension, adoration, than by committing suicide at the moment of her return to the limelight?

"If that's true, shouldn't she have waited for the day of the reopening to kill herself for maximum publicity?" Jinx asked.

"Maybe something pushed her over the edge a few days early?" Helen suggested.

"Or someone," Alberta added. "I just don't buy the suicide scenario. Pamela wasn't very nice, but she was passionate, and passionate people don't typically take their own lives."

"Sadly there are a lot of reasons why people take their own lives," Helen remarked. "But regardless of how she died, the fact remains that she did leave behind a note written to someone here at the lodge. Who do you think that is?"

Jinx and Joyce shrugged their shoulders, but Alberta replied with only one name. "Cathy."

"Really, Gram? Why do you think Pamela was apologizing to Cathy?"

Alberta placed the skate back on the bed next to its partner and replied, "Remember that Cathy's late husband, Mike, grew up in this area so there's a very good chance that he knew Pamela. Plus, Pamela moved to California, where Cathy grew up. Now I know it's a long shot that the two of them knew each other, but maybe it isn't such a random connection after all."

Jinx was impressed with how Alberta was starting to think like a real detective, and was even more impressed with her own investigative skills that were becoming more fine-tuned as well.

"What we really need to do is get inside of Pamela's head," Jinx instructed. "First and foremost she was a figure skater. She lived and literally died on the ice. So where do figure skaters go when they put themselves on display? When they're at their most vulnerable and can't hide? The kiss and cry."

"The kiss and what?" Alberta asked.

"The kiss and cry," Jinx repeated. "It's the section of the rink where skaters go to while they're waiting for the judges' scores."

"But why is it called a kiss and cry?" Alberta asked.

"Because if you do well you get a kiss from your coach, and if you suck you cry on his shoulder," Jinx explained.

"That sounds like a confessional to me," Helen commented.

"I have a hunch!" Alberta said. "Follow me."

"Oh God," Helen muttered.

"What's wrong?" Alberta asked.

"I hate your hunches," Helen said.

"Why?" Alberta asked. "Because they're always right?"

"No, because they always put us in danger."

Fifteen minutes later, the women were trudging through the snow and cursing the fact that they only put on boots and threw on jackets before heading outside. They were so eager to act on the clue they had found they forgot that accessories like a hat, gloves, and scarf were rather necessary when forging into the mouth of a snowstorm. Shivering, they finally made it to the small kiss-and-cry area next to the ice rink. It was a smaller version of the ones seen on television or at skating competitions and consisted of a small bench with a curved clamshell wall behind it. The bench seat was heavy-duty plastic in a bright blue, and the bench's base was covered by a white curtain made out of a fiberglass material like the kind industrial-strength shopping bags are made out of.

A burst of wind erupted with such vigor it flipped up the back of the curtain so it fell over the top of the bench. When Alberta saw what was underneath the bench, she almost fell over herself.

"*Dio mio!*" Alberta cried, clutching her chest and pressing her hand into the gold crucifix underneath her jacket. "We found the murder weapon!"

CHAPTER 14

Dolor comunicato è subito scemato.

In an instant everything changed. Any lingering thoughts the women had about Pamela possibly taking her own life were squashed by what they were looking at hidden underneath the bench. They had found indisputable proof that Pamela Gregory did not succumb to depression, anxiety, or some unknown personal demon, she had fallen victim to the hands of a murderer. They also found a reason to be truly afraid. Someone currently residing at Icicle Lodge was a killer and, worse, a killer with an ironic sense of humor.

Hidden from view behind the curtain covering the underbelly of the bench in the kiss-and-cry area was a lone white figure skate. Well, most of it was white, the blade and some of the boot itself were covered in dried blood.

Instinctively the women made the sign of the cross and reached out to hold each other's hands. Seeing the blood-stained skate and knowing that Pamela had been killed by some vicious predator instead of her own fragile, yet determined, hand, somehow made it seem as if Pamela died all over again. When they had first found her body they were in shock and their mourning was marred by the unsettling nature of the unexpected. Finding the bloodied murder weapon was a further shock, but one that brought with it a finality, at least now they knew how she died, the next thing they needed to do was find out why.

"Someone really did kill her," Jinx whispered. "I know it was always the logical assumption, but until now there was still the possibility she had done this on her own."

"Now we know that she had help," Joyce added.

"Whoever killed her was somehow able to slit her wrists with the blade of the figure skate while she was on the ice because no blood was found anywhere else," Alberta conveyed.

"Also too, the killer wasn't wearing ice skates because we didn't see any other marks on the ice," Joyce said. "The ice was Zamboni-smooth and the only scratches were from Pamela's skates."

"So after the killer got off the ice he—or she—hid the skate under here," Jinx said. "Which is pretty risky, don't you think?"

"The killer was short on time," Alberta replied. "Remember, Patrick was in the shed locking up the Zamboni and the rest of us were about to come out to watch Pamela perform her routine so the crime scene could've had an audience at any moment. It isn't the most secure hiding spot, but it worked."

"Until now," Jinx finished.

Jinx crouched down on her knees and started to reach underneath the bench to pull out the skate.

"What are you doing?" Alberta cried.

"Retrieving the evidence," Jinx replied.

"Do it like that and you'll contaminate it too."

"Sorry, Gram, I forgot my gloves."

"We all did," Alberta said.

"Not all of us." They all expected Helen to pull out a pair of leather gloves from her pocketbook or at least some knitted mittens, but instead she pulled out a different kind of glove, one of the latex variety.

"What in heaven's name are you doing with latex gloves in your pocketbook?" Alberta demanded.

"Because you always seem to need them, Miss Murder Mystery Detective Lady!" Helen shouted. "And, unlike you, I like to be prepared."

Helen passed a glove to Jinx, who tried to slip it on, but was having difficulty getting her fingers into the openings.

"*Madon,* these are tight!" Jinx exclaimed.

"Just shove your hand in, lovey," Alberta urged. "That's how the doctors do it on TV."

"I don't want to break a nail, Gram."

Jinx waved her hand in the air and showed off her freshly polished inch-long nails, painted a deep shade of burgundy that eerily resembled the color of the dried blood that covered the skate blade. Not that Jinx noticed that. All she cared about was the survival of her nails.

"Jinxie, sometimes in this life we have to make sacrifices," Helen started. "If I can walk around with a pocketbook filled with latex gloves, you can risk breaking a nail."

"Thanks, Aunt Helen, you always do put things in perspective."

"Someone around here has to," Helen quipped.

Finally, Jinx got the glove on, reached underneath the bench, and pulled out the bloodied skate by the boot's tongue. She held it as far from her body as possible so she didn't accidentally make contact with it and destroy any evidence the skate might contain and declared, "I guess it's time we shared our booty with the fuzz."

The victorious feeling that had been pumping through their veins since they made their discovery was snuffed out like candlelight in a windstorm the moment they entered the lodge. They could see into the dining hall and saw Vinny at a table. Before they could scurry up to their room, he saw them and called them over. They weren't scared to meet with him. Vinny was the person they were looking for. They just didn't want to share their evidence with the people Vinny was sharing his table with.

Sitting across from him with her back to the front door was Cathy, next to Vinny was Charlie, and standing in the doorway of the kitchen trying to shake the curiosity from his expression was Max. The only other person in the room they were happy to see was Freddy who was reading his favorite comic book, *The Legion of Super-Heroes*, curled up on a window seat. Unfortunately, they had no choice because Vinny not only saw them, he saw what they were holding and he wanted to know how it had come into their possession.

"Where did you get that?"

When they walked into the dining hall, their feelings of pride were quickly replaced with feelings of apprehension. They had wanted to share their evidence with Vinny privately and take their investigation to the next level without alarming anyone else with what they were up to, but now they were forced to disclose what they had uncovered with suspects. Vinny and Freddy they trusted implicitly. Cathy, Charlie, and Max, not nearly as much. Worse, since they were isolated at the lodge until the storm let up and the roads cleared, if one of them was the killer, learning that the murder weapon and a mysterious note left behind by the deceased had been found could cause him or her to become desperate. And everybody knows that desperate people do dangerous things. Unfortunately they had no choice but to play show-and-tell.

"Exhibit A is a woman's figure skate for the right foot stained with blood," Alberta announced. "Aka the murder weapon."

"I can see that, Alfie!" Vinny barked. "Where'd you find it?"

"We found it underneath the bench at the little kiss-and-cry area near the ice rink," Jinx explained.

The only one who needed that phrase explained was Freddy.

"The what?"

"The place where skaters go to after competitions to find out their scores," Vinny advised. "If the score is good they kiss, if the score is bad they cry."

"Really?" Freddy said, intrigued. "Do they do anything more than just kiss?"

"Freddy!"

Jinx's cry reverberated through the room until Vinny cut it short with his next question.

"Is there an Exhibit B?"

Helen pulled out Pamela's note from her pocketbook and handed it to Vinny. "Yes, not as gruesome as Exhibit A, but just as interesting."

As Vinny read the note out loud, Alberta kept her eyes on Cathy, examining her face for any telltale signs that she understood the true meaning of the cryptic message.

"'I'm so sorry for everything I've done. I had no idea the pain I caused you,'" Vinny read. "Signed 'Pam.'"

Just as Alberta thought she saw a flicker of recognition ignite in Cathy's eyes, Charlie jumped up and stood in front of her.

"That's the logo for the lodge," Charlie announced pointing at the back of the note. "She must've written that after she got here, which means . . ."

"We're one step ahead of you, Charlie," Jinx said, not able to disguise her dislike for the man. "She wrote it to someone who's staying here."

"But what was she apologizing for?" Charlie asked.

"She did mention to Berta and me that she had regrets," Helen reminded everyone.

"I don't know, something's not right about this note," Vinny declared.

"What do you mean?" Jinx asked.

"Are you sure she wrote it?"

"I assume she did," Alberta replied. "But I don't know her handwriting."

"I do." Up until now Cathy had been silent so her voice sounded foreign for an instant. It took everyone a few seconds to realize she spoke. "She signed some photos for me that I was planning on auctioning off, and of course she signed the contract that I sent to her. I should be able to recognize her handwriting."

Vinny placed the note on the table and with his fingertips gingerly turned it around so Cathy could see.

"I can't be one hundred percent certain, but it looks like it's authentic."

"Even though it's signed 'Pam'?" Vinny asked.

"That was her name!" Charlie scoffed. "Of course she'd sign it like that."

"No, Vinny's right," Alberta interrupted. "Her name was Pamela, not Pam. I never once heard her or anyone refer to her as Pam."

"I did." With all the commotion and theorizing they had forgotten Max was standing on the outskirts of the room. When they turned to look at him, his large presence seemed to grow exponentially and take up all the oxygen in the room.

"When?" Vinny asked.

"I overheard her talking to Stephanie a few times," Max explained. "They were Pam and Stef when they were by themselves."

"I guess that isn't so odd," Cathy said. "Pam is the obvious nickname for Pamela."

"It is, but . . ."

"But what, Vin?" Alberta asked, egging Vinny on to finish his thought.

"It's uncommon to the casual ear," Vinny said. "It's like Alberta just called me Vin, but only because she's known me almost her entire life. No one else would do that. So whomever Pamela was writing this note to, it was someone she's known for a very long time, someone whom she's very close to."

Max laughed so loud and long the sound quickly moved from entertaining to disturbing. "I don't think that woman was close to another living being," he announced. "Bitches don't usually travel in a pack."

After making that colorful comment, Max whipped the towel he was holding over his shoulder and marched back into the kitchen to start preparing dinner.

"I hope his sarcasm doesn't drip into the stew he's making," Joyce quipped. "It would make it rather salty."

While the others basked in the uncomfortable silence brought about by Max's politically incorrect comment, Alberta noticed that Vinny, in addition to growing quiet like everyone else, was staring out the window, and the only thing in full view was the ice rink.

Alberta knew he was thinking about Pamela's final moments, but she wanted confirmation.

"What're you thinking, Vinny?"

"Is it possible that Pamela used the skate to slit her own wrists?" Vinny asked out loud, but really to himself.

"No way," Jinx answered.

The decisiveness of her comment made Vinny turn around. "How can you be so sure?"

"Because there wasn't any blood trailing from the ice rink to where we found the skate," Jinx said. "Nor was there any other blood on the ice itself except around Pamela's body."

"As disturbing as it is, Jinx is right," Joyce added. "If Pamela did slit her own wrists, she would have had to do so, then hide the skate underneath the bench, go back on the ice, and not let any blood drip onto the surface until she got to her final resting place in the center. That's a pretty hard feat to accomplish even for an Olympian."

"Plus, we found Pamela's spare skates," Alberta informed. "So these can't be hers."

"Where'd you find her spare skates?" Vinny asked.

"In her room," Alberta replied. "The note was stuck in one of the skates."

"You went in her room?" Vinny shouted. "Without asking permission?"

"Why would we need permission?" Helen asked. "It's not like Pamela needs the room anymore."

"So you didn't find the note by the bloodied skate?" Vinny asked.

"No, two separate clues, two separate locations, one conclusion," Alberta announced.

"Which is?" Cathy asked.

"That unfortunately Pamela was murdered by someone using the skate we found outside," Alberta replied. "The only thing we don't know is who the skate belongs to."

"Well, we do know that the skate doesn't belong to Pamela," Vinny said, looking at the heel of the boot.

"How can you be so sure?" Jinx asked.

"The initials on the bottom of the skate are CO and Pamela's initials are PG."

"The initials could be something other than the abbreviation of a name," Joyce suggested. "Could it be a state? Did Pamela have any connection to Colorado?"

Without realizing it, the women and Freddy turned to Cathy knowing that she had held her own private investigation into the life of Pamela Gregory. Cathy felt the stares and didn't question them, but she did feel compelled to answer. "I don't believe so. Her official bio online doesn't list anything about Colorado—well, at least nothing that I can remember."

"Could be that's where the skate was made?" Charlie offered. "Let me see."

Charlie reached out to grab the skate from Vinny's hands, but Vinny pulled it away and said, "I don't want any prints on this."

In his attempt to keep Charlie's hands off the skate Vinny almost dropped it. He got it settled in his arms, but then he started shaking it around.

"Are you expecting it to play music?" Helen asked.

"I thought I felt something jostle inside," Vinny explained.

"Dude!" Freddy yelled. "Maybe there's something hidden inside that skate like there was something hidden inside the other one."

Jinx beamed at Freddy's suggestion even though she was a bit embarrassed that he kept calling everyone dude. She couldn't remain upset for long because Freddy was right. Vinny pulled out an object that would become their third clue. Although few people in the room knew the intricacies of the sport of figure skating very well, they all knew a championship medal when they saw one. Vinny placed the round medal on the table and smoothed out the red, white, and blue ribbon attached to it that the receiver would wear around her neck as if he was displaying a rare artifact.

"This proves this isn't Pamela's skate," Vinny declared. "The woman never won a bronze medal her entire life."

"Come on, Vin," Alberta said. "She won lots of medals."

"Yes she did, tons of gold and silver," Vinny replied. "But never a bronze."

"He's right," Cathy agreed. "You must have followed her career quite carefully."

"For the most part," Vinny admitted. "But I remember I was watching some holiday skating show on TV years ago and one of the hosts, the short guy who won a gold medal at the Olympics and survived cancer?"

"Scott Hamilton," Cathy replied.

"Yeah, him!" Vinny confirmed. "He said Pamela never came in less than second place her entire professional career, even when she was just starting out in the junior ranks."

"Who knew the chief of police was such a fan of figure skating?" Helen remarked.

"And how did you know Pamela never got less than a silver medal, Cathy?" Alberta asked. She tried to make the tone of her voice sound innocent, but she could tell by the way everyone in the room except Cathy looked at her that she failed.

Stuttering slightly, Cathy took a few seconds before she replied. "Online research, of course. I wanted to find out as much as I could about her before she got here to make her feel as comfortable as possible since I knew it had been some time since she performed in public."

"Did you do all your research online?" Jinx asked, sounding even less innocent than Alberta had. Luckily Cathy didn't seem to hear the accusation in her voice.

"Is there any other way these days?" Cathy replied. Without missing a beat or taking a breath, Cathy changed the subject. "You know, Alberta, it would be great if we could have that chat now. There really is something I've been meaning to talk to you about."

Before Alberta could reply, they heard a loud crash coming from the kitchen followed by Max's voice shouting something not entirely decipherable.

"Did he just say 'yept'?" Alberta asked.

No one answered her because everyone rushed into the kitchen to see what had happened and stopped when they saw several broken plates on the floor between Max and Stephanie.

"Where'd you come from?" Jinx asked.

"I was jonesing for one of Max's beet salads, they're so fresh," Stephanie said. "And I got in Max's way and made him break some dishes. I'm so sorry, I'll pay for them."

"I have more things to worry about than some broken china, honey," Cathy said. "Don't give it a second thought."

Cathy was satisfied, but Jinx wasn't.

"I mean, how did you get in the kitchen? We didn't even see you come in."

"I came through the back entrance so I wouldn't disturb you," Stephanie explained. "It looked like you were having an intense conversation."

"They found some clues about who killed Pamela," Max answered.

"Really?" Stephanie exclaimed. "Do you know who did it?"

"No," Vinny said. "But we're getting close."

"That's the best news I've heard all day," Stephanie said, her eyes watering a bit.

"What exactly did we hear you shout, Max? 'Yept'?" Alberta asked.

"It was probably 'yikes,' right, Max?" Cathy asked.

"Yes," Max confirmed. "Yikes."

"This is a family-friendly lodge so I've instructed the staff to use 'yikes' instead of anything more colorful," Cathy explained.

Alberta didn't believe a word Cathy or Max had just said, but decided it wasn't the appropriate time to reveal her suspicions. "Well, isn't that clever of you. I may have to try that at our next canasta game."

"Let me help clean up this mess," Cathy said, immediately crossing the kitchen to the closet and getting out a broom and dustpan.

While Cathy and Max were making noise picking up the debris, Vinny whispered in Alberta's ear, *"Dolor comunicato è subito scemato."* A problem shared is a problem halved. In practical terms, it was a cry for help.

"I don't know if Cathy killed Pamela, but I don't trust her," Vinny said. "And I think she knows more than she's letting on."

"My thoughts exactly," Alberta whispered back.

"I may never say this again, Alfie, but I'm giving you

and the rest of your lady detectives free rein to find out anything you can."

Alberta felt a rush of power run up her spine and didn't even try to hide the smile beaming on her lips. "Vin, that's the best decision you've made in years."

CHAPTER 15

Nessuno è solo.

Ten minutes later pacing the floor of her room with Lola in her arms, Alberta was still smiling. She couldn't help it, she felt as if she had just scored a huge victory, not only for herself but all womankind.

Alberta couldn't remember exactly when it started, but early on in her life she resented the fact that her gender automatically forced her to play a subservient role. In her family, in her relationship with her husband, in the world around her women were treated as second-class citizens. Sometimes the treatment was obvious and unapologetic, other times it was more subtle, but no less hurtful. That's why when Vinny gave Alberta permission to lead her own investigation her brain understood that it was the act of one friend asking another friend for help, but in her heart it was validation of her worth.

Alberta closed her eyes and silently recited the Hail Mary, her go-to prayer for any occasion, and gave thanks for a friend like Vinny and for the blessings that came with it. Thanks to him she felt empowered and was reminded that not all men were created equal.

She laughed out loud when she realized the same goes for women.

"Le donne sono come gli uomini," she whispered. "We don't come in one-size-fits-all either."

Sitting in the plaid club chair next to the window, Alberta thought of the women right here at Icicle Lodge and had to admit that no two were alike. Just like in her own family, the women were different. Of course Alberta didn't know the other women in the lodge as well, but she knew enough to understand they were all cut from different cloths.

Cathy was a smart businesswoman and seemed to have taken a tragedy like the untimely death of her husband and used the curveball life threw at her to her advantage. She didn't wallow in the shadow of her dead husband, she honored his memory and proved to him and herself that she was a capable woman, who didn't need a man to survive. But she also seemed to be incapable of telling the truth. Her words were carefully chosen, her expressions monitored, and her emotions kept under wraps.

Stephanie seemed to be timid and shy, but underneath the insecurity and lack of confidence, Alberta detected a strength and determination not unlike Jinx's desire to climb the journalism ranks to glory. Alberta suspected that something from her past, whether a specific incident or a long-term pervasive treatment from her family or an authority figure, taught Stephanie that being submissive and silencing her own voice was the safe route. Alberta hoped that now with Pamela gone from the picture Stephanie might break free from her own self-imposed prison.

And Pamela. Alberta had found the woman to be rude, brusque, vain, narcissistic, and opinionated. Pamela was definitely not someone who Alberta had wanted in her company, she didn't want to spend time with her, and yet after Pamela revealed a part of her soul to Alberta, she desperately wanted to get to know the troubled athlete better. The only thing Alberta knew was that something from Pamela's past was haunting her, and it was probably the same something that had gotten her killed. If she could uncover what secret lay in her past, she would most certainly be able to uncover who killed her. But like every smart woman, Alberta knew she wouldn't be able to do it on her own, which is why she sent text messages to the rest of the Ferrara ladies to meet in her room for a strategy meeting.

By the time Jinx and Joyce arrived, Alberta had already turned the desk in the corner of the room into a buffet table. Two bottles of vodka—one peppermint twist, the other cherry—were in the left-hand corner of the table next to a stack of plastic cups. In the center were an Entenmann's cherry strudel and a special limited edition peppermint loaf cake, which Alberta had brought with her in case she didn't approve of the lodge's menu. Plastic utensils and napkins filled out the rest of the space and were swooped up within seconds after the women entered the room.

"Thank God!" Jinx declared just as she cut herself a hunk of cherry strudel. "I'm starving."

"Make sure there's enough for all of us, lovey," Alberta said. "You know how my sister gets."

"Do tell, how does your sister get?" The door slammed behind Helen and she stood there, pocketbook dangling from the crook of her left arm, and a crooked smile dangling from her lips.

"Like a crazy ex-nun who wants to make up for all the years she was forced to eat convent food!" Alberta yelled.

"If you had to eat Sister Scholastica's meatloaf every Thursday night, you would've turned Jewish after the first month," Helen scoffed. "Kosher may be bland, but it's edible."

"Have a piece of strudel, Helen, it's cherrylicious," Joyce said. "So's this vodka."

"I think I like Entenmann's more than I like Max's food," Jinx announced, shoving a forkful of strudel in her mouth.

"I agree with you on that," Alberta concurred. "Some of his dishes are good, but others . . . there's something not right."

"He's a bad cook, that's what it is," Helen said. "He's like you, Berta, when you try to bake."

"No, that isn't it," Alberta disagreed. "It's almost as if he uses the wrong ingredients on some meals that makes them taste . . . *different.*"

"Luckily we have our secret stash," Joyce said.

"Hear, hear!"

The ladies raised their plastic cups and clinked them together before taking sips of their vodka. Once they had gotten settled and were satiated, Alberta thought it time to get the impromptu meeting started.

"I called you all here because I have news," Alberta announced. "Vinny gave us the go-ahead to handle our own investigation into Pamela's murder and the potential suspects."

"Gram, that's great and all, but we weren't waiting around for Vinny's permission to get to work. We never do."

"And not for nothing, but we usually don't need Vinny's help either," Helen added.

"Also too," Joyce said. "That isn't the point."

All three women looked at Joyce as if she was the one who didn't get the point. They had no idea what she was referring to. But Alberta was thrilled when she finally understood.

"Of course we weren't waiting for Vinny to give us permission to snoop around, just like we wouldn't wait for any man to allow us to do something we felt we had to do," Joyce explained. "But how wonderful that Vinny finally understands that we are more than four nosy ladies who interfere. We're formidable women who have the skills and smarts to get the job done."

"That's exactly right, Joyce," Alberta said. "It means that Vinny trusts and respects us, and as far as I'm concerned, that's what is called a game changer."

Swallowing the rest of her vodka, Jinx said, "I keep forgetting that you three grew up in a different time. I'm so used to feeling like an equal to men, I have to remind myself it wasn't always that way."

"It still isn't in some places," Helen said. "Lots of men around the world don't understand a woman's worth. Who knew Vinny was so enlightened?"

"Especially for an Italian," Joyce joked.

"Watch it, Joyce, you're only Italian by marriage," Helen replied.

"Which makes me even more Italian than you," Joyce surmised. "I chose to embrace my Italian side, you had no choice in the matter."

"She's got you there, Hel," Alberta said.

"I've also got some interesting news about Cathy I'd like to share," Joyce announced.

"What is it, Aunt Joyce? Tell us!"

"Right after we found out that Cathy was seeing Father Sal for counseling, I realized that if she had personal secrets, she might have professional secrets as well so I made a call to a former Wall Street coworker and asked him to do a credit check on her," Joyce explained.

"Is that legal?" Alberta asked.

"Stop asking silly questions, Berta," Helen said. "Of course it isn't legal, but I still want to know what this Wall Streeter found out."

"Nessuno è solo," Joyce replied.

"They speak Italian on Wall Street too?" Jinx asked.

"It means that no one is alone," Joyce explained. "My contact discovered that Cathy has a silent partner in the lodge."

"So what?" Helen scoffed. "That isn't important."

"Yes it is, Helen," Alberta corrected. "Cathy told us that she was on her own and made it very clear that she's the only owner of the lodge."

"Maybe she needed front money to buy the lodge, but she's still the sole proprietor," Jinx hypothesized. "That's what she might have meant when she said she's on her own."

"That's possible," Alberta acquiesced.

"But you don't buy it, Gram?"

Alberta let out a long sigh. "I don't. There's something about Cathy that makes me think she's lying about almost everything. I think she wanted us to believe that she's running the lodge by herself, but she secretly has a partner."

"Did your big-shot coworker tell you who this silent partner is?" Helen asked.

"No."

"So much for all your connections," Helen replied.

"But he did tell me that Cathy and her silent partner used a separate company to buy the lodge called Boyodell, Inc."

"Any idea what that means?" Alberta asked.

"None, but if you're thinking like I'm thinking, you're thinking it means something."

"That's exactly what I'm thinking," Alberta said.

"I have no idea what the two of you are thinking or talking about," Helen added. "But maybe that's why Cathy wants to talk to you, Berta."

"That's right. She keeps mentioning that she wants to tell you something in private," Jinx said. "But never gets around to telling you."

"I know," Alberta said. "At first I thought it was just a tactic to divert the flow of conversation or end it altogether, but now I think she might actually want to tell me something, though I can't imagine what in the world it could be."

"Before you do that, I think we need to come up with a surefire game plan so we can expose the killer before he strikes again," Joyce announced. "I don't know about the rest of you, but I'm starting to get nervous stuck here in this storm knowing one of the other guests might be a homicidal maniac."

"Freddy was just saying the same thing," Jinx said. "He told me the first break in the weather and we're out of here, and I don't disagree with him."

"Well then, ladies," Alberta announced. "We've got some work to do. Our prime suspects in no particular order are Patrick, Stephanie, Cathy, Max, and Charlie. Why don't we split them up among ourselves and trail them to see if they make any suspicious moves."

"That's a great idea, Gram! I'll take Stephanie."

"And I'll take Cathy and Patrick," Alberta said. "I get the impression that they're some kind of team."

"Like a couple?" Joyce asked.

"I don't know about that," Alberta admitted. "But there's some connection between the two of them. So that leaves Max and Charlie."

"I'll take Max," Joyce said.

"Of course you would, he is the more handsome of the two," Helen said.

"I'm old, Helen, but I'm not dead," Joyce replied.

"You're also married," Helen reminded.

"Don't worry, I already tried to get her to go after Max, but she won't cheat on her husband," Alberta explained.

"Who happens to be our brother! You want Joyce to cheat on our brother, Berta? Is that what you want?"

"Why not? Our brother cheated on Joyce," Alberta said. "What's fair is fair, am I right?"

"Remember, two wrongs don't make a right," Helen replied. "I'll take Max and Joyce'll take Charlie."

"Fine with me either way," Joyce said.

"Then it's settled," Alberta declared. "See what you can find and we'll report back here tomorrow. Until then remember what Joyce said, *Nessuno è solo*."

"Why do we have to remember that, Gram?"

"Because a killer is on the loose. We always have to be with someone we can trust," Alberta said. "Which is all of us plus Vinny, Freddy, Father Sal, and Sloan."

"Are we sure we can trust Sloan?" Helen said with a smirk. "I mean, he is after your virginity."

Alberta and Jinx both spit out their vodka at the same time, the scent of peppermint and cherry filling the air. "If that's his mission, he's about forty years too late," Alberta said. "Now finish your food and let's play a quick round of canasta, I have a feeling tomorrow will be an exciting day."

The next day Alberta was using one of the computers in the small business resource center off the main room at the lodge. The windowless room contained one large table with four computers, two on each side of the table with their backs facing each other. A watercooler and a framed poster of Lake Ariel fleshed out the space. Sitting at a computer searching the Internet for information on the company that owned Icicle Lodge, Alberta was so focused on her search she didn't notice she had company.

"I've been looking all over for you," Sloan said.

"I'm doing some research," Alberta replied.

Sloan sat in the chair next to Alberta and peered at the computer screen. "You're speaking my language. What kind of research?"

"I'm trying to find information on Boyodell, Inc."

"What's that? It sounds like Chef Boyardee, and I know you wouldn't be caught dead with a can of that in your house."

Laughing, Alberta took a moment to stare into Sloan's eyes and was delighted to find that he was staring right back into hers. Blushing slightly, she said, "It's the company that owns the lodge."

"I thought Cathy was the sole proprietor."

"We did, too, but Joyce found out she has a silent partner and their company is Boyodell, Inc. I'll be damned if I can find anything about them online."

"I'm sure something will pop up, but in the meantime I did solve one mystery," Sloan said.

"Which one? The mysteries around here seem to be growing by the minute."

"Max uses beetroot in his recipes," Sloan announced proudly.

"That's the strange ingredient we keep tasting!" Alberta cried. "I'm impressed, Sloan."

It was Sloan's turn to blush. "Thank you."

"How'd you find that out?" Alberta asked.

"I asked him."

"That's certainly a novel approach." Alberta laughed. "I have no idea what beetroot means, but if it helps solve Pamela's murder, I'll give you full credit."

When her cell phone rang, Alberta was also intrigued. She thought it odd that Vinny would call her
since they were only a few hundred yards from each
other, but then she thought he might have gone outside on the grounds of the lodge to talk in private.

"Hello."

"Hey, Alfie," Vinny said.

"Vinny, what's wrong? Why are you calling me?"

"I have to deal with an emergency in Tranquility
and I'm leaving."

"Leave? Have you noticed there's a blizzard outside?" Alberta cried. "What could be so important in
Tranquility that you have to risk your life to get there?"

Alberta waited for Vinny's reply, but it never came.
The line had gone dead.

"He hung up on me," Alberta said.

"Did he really leave?" Sloan asked.

"He said there's an emergency back home, but that
doesn't make sense. He's got a whole police force back
home to handle emergencies, and we have our own
emergency right here."

"Why don't you call him back? Maybe the storm in-
terfered with the cell towers and dropped the call."

Alberta dialed Vinny's number, but it went straight
to voice mail. Just as she was about to call him again,
another visitor entered the business resource center. It
was officially the most crowded it had ever been.

"Father Sal, what brings you here?" Sloan asked.

"This."

Sal held up a note and passed it to Alberta. "It's from
Vinny, and I found it in our room, but the last part is
for you."

"*Il cielo lo aiuta!*" Alberta cried.

"Why does Vinny need heaven's help?" Sal asked. "I

know the roads are bad, but he wouldn't leave if they were that dangerous."

"He didn't leave on his own, Sal, this note is a cry for help," Alberta said.

"Berta, what are you talking about?" Sloan asked, taking the note from Alberta's shaking hand and reading it. "He said exactly what he told you on the phone and that the investigation is now in your hands. It says so right here."

"That's right," Father Sal confirmed. "The note says the investigation is in your hands, Alfee."

"Don't you see? He spelled my name wrong. He always spells it like the movie *A-l-f-i-e,* and on this note he's spelled it with two *E*s. It's a clue."

"If that's the truth," Father Sal said, "what's Vinny trying to tell you?"

"That his life is in danger!"

CHAPTER 16

Tutto torna alla famiglia.

Alberta's heart started to race. She knew Vinny was in trouble and needed her help. She was incredibly moved and honored that her friend would reach out to her, but she was also terrified that she would fail him and not find him in time. Or was it already too late? Was Vinny already dead and past the point of saving? *No!* Alberta thought, *I can't allow myself to think that way. Vinny put his trust in me and I will not let him down.*

But to save her friend, Alberta had to take action, and she had no idea what to do. She felt paralyzed and physically had to shake her body to break free from the emotional shackles that were suffocating her. Alberta wanted nothing else than to turn back the clock ten minutes so she could be free of the knowledge she currently possessed. It was a fanciful thought, but not a practical or realistic one. She needed to use the information she had and move forward, she had no other choice because Vinny's life depended on it

"Alberta, what should we do?" Father Sal's question was simple, but it triggered a complex series of emotions within Alberta that she had not expected. For almost her entire life—as a daughter, a girlfriend, and a wife—she had allowed men to make decisions for her. First out of respect for her father and then out of necessity when dating and then later married to Sammy because it made life so much easier. If she didn't allow her husband to be in control, there would be consequences, arguments, tension, drinking binges, and Alberta learned early on that it was easier to avoid those things from happening if she just gave in to her husband. It took her years to realize that giving in to Sammy meant giving him huge chunks of herself and leaving her with nothing, turning her into a hollow shell.

Even in her role as a mother where she should have been in total control of how to raise her children, Lisa Marie and Rocco, she often took a back seat to the opinions, rules, and sometimes the whims of those around her. Sammy, her parents, and Sammy's parents all had strong voices that demanded to be heard and would hold grudges if Alberta went against their wishes. So again, instead of asserting herself and not caring how others reacted to the decisions she felt were in the best interest of her and her family, she bent, she cowered, she ignored her own instincts to follow the path carved out by others. It was a rhythm and a pattern she was used to, ingrained in her brain like a muscle memory, and now she was asked to break it. Someone was asking her what to do in connection with an incredibly important issue, and she wasn't sure what to do. Until Sloan spoke.

"Berta, please, we need your help. Tell us what to do."

Alberta wasn't sure she heard correctly, *a man needs my help.* She stared into Father Sal's and Sloan's eyes and saw things that almost made her burst into tears. Respect, need, and hope.

One cleansing breath followed another and Alberta felt her spirit rise. She felt years of doubt and insecurity and even apathy strip away from her mind, heart, and soul as easily as the skin of an onion to reveal her true self underneath. And that self was not going to let down the three men who were reaching out to her for help. The time for self-doubt and standing in someone else's shadow was over. It was time for Alberta Ferrara Scaglione to take action.

"The first thing we need to do is confirm my suspicion is correct," Alberta announced.

"How do you plan on doing that?" Sloan asked.

"By calling the source," she replied, pulling her phone out of her pocketbook.

"You're going to call Vinny?" Father Sal asked. "That doesn't make sense, if he's in danger, he's hardly going to be in a position to answer his phone."

Alberta ignored Sal and scrolled through the contacts of her phone until she found the number she was looking for. Once she did, she initiated the call and waited for someone to pick up.

"I'm not calling Vinny," Alberta said. "But I am calling the one person who will know if he told us the truth and if I'm making this whole Vinny's-in-danger thing up."

Sloan and Sal exchanged confused looks, unsure as to what Alberta was talking about, but since neither one of them had a better alternative, they kept quiet and waited for Alberta to speak to whoever was about to pick up on the other end of the line.

"Tambra, hi, this is Alberta Scaglione, how are you?"

"Hi, Mrs. Scaglione," Tambra replied, "I'm doing well, how about yourself?"

"Please call me Alberta."

"Of course, sorry. How are you . . . Alberta?"

"I'm doing fine, thank you, enjoying the wintry scene out my window here at Icicle Lodge."

"That must be beautiful. I go skiing up that way and love it up there," Tambra said. "I will admit I was a bit jealous when Vinny told me he was going and left me here in charge. I mean, don't get me wrong, I'm honored he left Tranquility in my hands, but a week at that lodge sounds kind of perfect."

Alberta wasn't sure Tambra would consider the week perfect if she filled her in on all that had happened, but she didn't want to get off track from the reason she was calling. Better to stick to her real intention.

"I'm sure Vinny will give you some time off for good behavior," Alberta joked. "Speaking of Vinny, have you heard from him?"

"Not since early yesterday," Tambra replied. "Why, is anything wrong?"

"I thought I overheard him mention something about an emergency back home," Alberta fibbed. "Is there anything going on that we should be worried about?"

"No, all's quiet on the Tranquility front, nothing at all to be concerned about," Tambra confirmed.

"Wonderful news!" Alberta replied, a bit too enthusiastically. "And you're sure you haven't heard from Vinny? He didn't call to check in?"

There was a pause on the other end of the line and Alberta could hear Tambra's police officer mind kick into high gear. She knew she had to end the conversation; otherwise she could tip her hand and put Vinny in even further danger than he was already in.

"Is there anything going on at the lodge that I should know about, Mrs. Scag . . . Alberta?"

"Oh no, nothing at all," Alberta said, this time out-and-out lying. "We're just getting ready for Pamela's exhibition for the grand reopening. It should be quite something."

"It would be quite something to see Pamela skate in her present condition."

Alberta slapped Father Sal on the shoulder and shushed him to keep quiet so Tambra wouldn't overhear.

"Sorry, Tambra, my granddaughter is calling me to join her for a bit of a nature hike around the lake . . . I'll be right there, Jinx!" Alberta yelled to no one in particular. "Thank you so much, Tambra, and I'll see you when we get back."

"Alberta, are you sure—"

Alberta didn't hear the rest of what Tambra was going to say because she disconnected the call.

"Berta, what's wrong?" Sloan asked. "You look like you've seen a ghost."

Alberta instinctively made the sign of the cross, kissed her gold crucifix, and replied, "Father Sal, I know my sister Helen likes to give you a hard time, but you better pray harder than you've ever prayed before that Vinny is alright."

"I hate to say this, but I don't think prayer alone is going to save Vinny if he really is in harm's way," Sloan advised.

Swallowing hard, Alberta nodded in agreement. "You're right, we need to take action. Follow me."

With more obedience than her children ever displayed, Sloan and Father Sal followed Alberta out to the parking lot. The wind was blowing from the east so the roofs of all the cars were covered in snow, but only their right sides, the left sides were virtually uncovered making it easy for them to see the body of each car and for them to realize that Vinny's car was no longer in the lot.

"Maybe he really did go back to Tranquility," Sloan said.

"Could he be working on some top secret case that he wouldn't share with his detectives?" Sal asked.

"Or did he go investigate a break in Pamela's case?" Sloan suggested. Alberta wanted to accept this as a possible theory, but couldn't—it went against everything she knew about Vinny's character.

"No," Alberta said. "Vinny's cops are like members of his family, and if there was an emergency back home the first call he'd make would be to them to make sure they were alright. He would never not check up on them."

"So that leaves only one explanation," Sloan said.

Reluctantly, Alberta agreed. "Wherever Vinny is, he isn't there because he wants to be. He was taken against his will."

"This is getting serious," Father Sal said. "We have to tell the others."

"No," Alberta declared. "There's no reason to worry everyone. Plus, there are only a few of us here that I trust."

Two of those trustworthy members were about to have their personal time rudely interrupted.

Alberta, Sloan, and Father Sal swooped into the main room of the lodge like a SWAT team on a mission. They sat in the chairs on either side of Jinx and Freddy, and from the looks on their faces, Jinx immediately knew something important was going on.

"What is it, Gram? You have intense face, the same expression you get when you can't figure out a recipe."

"This is much worse than screwing up a lasagna," Alberta admitted.

"Dude!" Freddy cried. "This must really be serious."

"You both have to promise me that when I tell you, you won't scream," Alberta said.

"Now you're scaring me, Gram."

"Sorry, lovey, but it's important that you act natural."

"Okay, what's going on?" Jinx asked.

"Vinny is missing."

Jinx and Freddy couldn't conceal matching shocked expressions, but they did obey Alberta's orders and remained silent so no one else in the room or the kitchen heard them.

"Please tell me that 'missing' means 'missing' and isn't a euphemism for something much more permanent," Jinx begged.

"Not as far as we know," Sal answered.

"But we don't know much," Sloan added.

"Except that Vinny left a note that he had to handle an emergency back home, but when I called the police station Tambra said there wasn't any emergency and she hadn't heard from Vinny," Alberta explained.

"Plus, Vinny spelled Alfie wrong," Father Sal added.

"As a journalist I know that spelling is important," Jinx replied. "But what does that have to do with Vinny's disappearance?"

Before Alberta could explain the importance of that specific clue, her phone beeped and she received a text message from someone that made her scream.

"It's Vinny!"

"Gram, I thought you wanted us to remain hush-hush about the Vinny thing?"

"He just sent me a text!" Alberta cried.

The other four replied in unison, "What does it say?"

Alberta turned her phone around so they could all read the text. Unfortunately, they didn't fully understand it.

"Help br," Jinx said, reading the text out loud. "What does 'br' mean?"

"Could it be a town?" Sloan suggested.

"Basking Ridge?" Sal replied. "That's a very nice town in Jersey, but it's nowhere near Tranquility."

"Maybe it's a person," Freddy said.

"Whose initials are BR?" Alberta asked.

Jinx tried to visualize the contact list on her phone. "No one I know."

"Could it be Bruno Bel Bruno?" Alberta asked.

"Why would Vinny need a public defender?" Jinx asked.

"He's the only one I could think of who has a *B* and an *R* in his name," Alberta said.

"Why don't you text him back, Berta?" Sloan advised.

"*Ovviamente* . . . of course."

Alberta typed out a text to Vinny and hit the Send button. Then the five of them waited. After about ten seconds, Alberta sent another text message asking Vinny to respond to her. Another ten seconds later she sent another text demanding that he not ignore her earlier text. Before she could send a fourth message, Sloan grabbed her hand and told her to stop.

"Clearly, Vinny is unable to send another message," Sloan advised. "If he could he most certainly would."

"What are we going to do?" Alberta whined. "We might not know what 'br' means, but it isn't hard to decipher what 'help' means. Vinny's in trouble."

"Hold on," Jinx ordered. "Wyck always reminds me that sometimes the most obvious answer is the correct one."

"That sounds as cryptic as a psalm," Sal said.

"It means that maybe 'br' means just what it means," Jinx replied. "Say it out loud, 'brrrrr,' it means cold."

"You think Vinny is somewhere cold?" Alberta asked.

No one replied, they merely looked out the main window and saw that it was snowing heavier than it had been, if that was even possible. They all realized at the same time that Vinny could be anywhere within a ten-mile radius and be freezing to death. Although Alberta didn't trust everyone currently taking up residence at Icicle Lodge, she had no choice but to call in the rest of the troops. The more people involved in the search party, the better the odds of finding Vinny before frostbite set in.

The wind howled all around them and lifted and swirled the snow in the air so it looked like they were caught inside a snow globe. It was beautiful, but it made for minimal visibility and precarious movement. Helen and Joyce kept slipping on the snow and held on to each other so they wouldn't fall as they walked around the entrance to the woods. Alberta silently remarked that the women probably touched each other more these past few days than they had in the past decade.

Max, Jinx, and Father Sal trudged past the skating rink, and it took both Max and Father Sal pulling open the door before they could enter the Zamboni room. When they were inside they were immediately assaulted by a cacophony of sounds from the generator and other machines that were running.

"It's louder than a congregation reciting a responsorial psalm on a high holiday," Father Sal remarked.

Splitting up, Sal looked in the front of the room while Max and Jinx retreated into the back behind the Zamboni. The wind roared and the natural and mechanical sounds combined to create something overwhelming.

"The storm is really picking up!" Jinx yelled. "Thankfully it's a lot warmer in here."

"Why don't you check the office over there?" Max suggested pointing to a door behind her and toward the entrance of the room. "Before the storm gets so bad that we get trapped in here, regardless of how warm it is."

Jinx hesitated and started to peer behind the Zamboni just to satisfy her own curiosity that Vinny wasn't a few feet away tied and bound or, God forbid, dead, when she heard another sound that wasn't created by Mother Nature or machinery, but man.

Jinx turned around and saw Sal lying on the floor. "Father Sal! Are you alright?"

Trying to push himself up from the floor, but not having much success, Father Sal replied, "I think I slipped. Or I passed out. Or both."

"Passed out?" Jinx asked. "Are you sick?"

"I've been a little light-headed, but nothing serious," he admitted. "I do think I need to get back to my room and lie down."

Jinx helped Sal up and he threw his arm around her neck until he was standing upright. He put pressure on his left foot and before he could step forward on his right, his left knee buckled and Jinx had to grab Sal's waist to prevent him from falling once again to the ground.

"You must've sprained your ankle," Jinx deduced. "We need to get you back to your room."

They tried to take a few more steps, but it was obvious that they were going to need additional help.

"Max!" Jinx cried. "We need you."

A few seconds later Max came out from behind the Zamboni, wiping his hands on his thighs, and shouted, "I'm coming."

He grabbed Sal around the waist and practically lifted his feet off the floor.

"Did you see anything suspicious back there?" Jinx asked.

"Nothing," Max replied. "Wherever Vinny went, he didn't stop here first."

On the border of Lake Ariel, Alberta, Sloan, Helen, and Joyce were surveying the area, not really knowing what they should be looking for, but scouring the landscape nonetheless. Even though they were all wearing parkas, hats, and gloves, they were still shivering from the cold and wind and were having a hard time seeing anything beyond snow. Until Alberta saw something on the banks of the lake that piqued her interest.

"Do they look like tire tracks?" Alberta asked.

They moved to the edge of the lake to inspect the ground closer.

"They look like the trailer tracks at Memory Lake that are used to haul boats out of the lake during the winter," Joyce explained.

Curious, Alberta knelt down to get a better look, but became distracted by the echo of voices wafting on the wind. She turned around and saw Cathy and Patrick on the back porch of the lodge. Patrick had his hands in his pockets, while Cathy was gesturing wildly.

"What's going on over there?" Alberta asked.

Sloan looked up and said, "Looks like those two are arguing about something."

"Why do you always act like such a fool?" Cathy asked. "You seriously never learn."

"Really? You might want to look in the mirror," Patrick replied.

"Me? You've never taken responsibility for anything you've ever done," Cathy retorted. "It's always *his* fault! Or *her* fault! You're a broken record."

"You should know!" Patrick yelled. "I have never heard someone more in love with the sound of their own voice than you. It's like you just can't shut up!"

Alberta listened to their words, but she was much more interested in the tones of their voices. There was something she was hearing that made her feel as if she knew the both of them much better than she truly did.

"Listen to them, Berta," Helen said. "They sound like you and me."

That's it! Alberta thought. That's why they sounded so familiar. *"Tutto torna alla famiglia,"* Alberta gasped.

"Of course everything starts with family, Berta," Helen remarked. "But what are you talking about?"

"The reason they sound like you and me, Helen, is because they're not *like* family," Alberta said. "It's because they *are* family."

Shocked, they all looked at Alberta and she knew they needed her to spell it out for them.

"Cathy and Patrick aren't employer and employee," Alberta stated. "They're sister and brother!"

CHAPTER 17

L'ultima Cena.

No matter how far you travel, no matter how old you get, you are never far from your family.

That's what Alberta was thinking as she watched Cathy and Patrick continue to argue with each other, their hands opening and closing, their arms punching and swooshing the air, their faces contorting into expressions that they both had seen millions of times before. She imagined the words they were saying to each other were words they had repeated on countless previous occasions so they could finish their sentences.

It appeared as if Cathy and Patrick were quite upset, but Alberta couldn't tell if they were disgruntled about something miniscule or life changing. She almost laughed out loud as she watched them because she was reminded of how she and Helen must look to people. They might be bickering about the simplest of things, like how much salt to add to pasta sauce or which cousin forgot to attend someone's funeral, but to an uninformed viewer it might look like they were a few seconds away from causing bodily harm. Cathy and

Patrick could be having a typical fight or it could be cataclysmic.

Alberta knew from experience, however, that siblings had a way of reconciling. In all the fights she'd had with Helen and her brother, Anthony, none of them caused irreparable damage. Because siblings are inseparable. And Cathy just proved that.

"Did you hear what Cathy just said?" Sloan asked the second she and Patrick stormed back into the lodge.

Alberta opened her mouth to reply, but Joyce beat her to it.

"Yes! And I assume you're thinking what I'm thinking."

"I have a feeling I am," Sloan said excitedly. "What about you, Alberta? Are you thinking what we're thinking?"

Again Alberta opened her mouth, but someone else's voice spoke before hers.

"What about me?" Helen asked. "Doesn't anyone care if I'm thinking what the rest of you are thinking?"

"Of course we do, Helen," Sloan said. "What are you thinking?"

Scowling, Helen replied, "I don't know, what are you all thinking?"

"*Basta!*" Alberta cried. "Cathy just gave us the clue we were looking for."

"Sorry, with the wind howling and my bad ear I'm lucky I can hear myself think," Helen remarked. "Let alone hear a clue."

"You have a bad ear, Helen?" Sloan asked.

"Yes."

"Which one?"

Alberta and Joyce answered Sloan's question at the

same time, but Alberta said it was the left and Joyce
said it was the right.

"I told you," Helen started. "No one pays attention
to me."

"*Dio mio!*" Alberta sighed. "Cathy called Patrick 'boyo'
and then stormed back into the house. That's another
piece to the puzzle."

Alberta, Joyce, and Sloan continued to chatter excitedly about the clue they were just given and how it
solidified the theory that Cathy and Patrick were siblings. After about a minute of frenzied discussion, one
by one they realized Helen was still silent and was staring at them wearing a highly perturbed expression. Alberta didn't know why her sister would be mad at them
until she realized her sister felt left out because she
had no idea what 'boyo' meant.

"It's short for their company," Alberta divulged.
"Boyodell."

Helen's expression turned from dismissive to deri-
sive. "How do you know that?"

"Because the name of the company that owns the
lodge is called Boyodell, Inc., and Cathy just called
Patrick boyo," Alberta said.

"So where's the dell in Boyodell, Inc., come from?"
Helen asked.

"That we don't know," Sloan admitted.

"Maybe Dell is their last name," Joyce suggested.

"Only one way to find out."

Alberta led them back to the business center of the
lodge, and when they entered they saw Charlie was sitting behind one of the computers. They immediately
slowed down their pace to a languid stroll so it didn't
look like they were on an important mission.

"What brings you four in here?" Charlie asked.

"What's it to you?" Helen replied.

"Helen, don't be so rude," Alberta chastised. "Sorry, Charlie."

When she replayed those two words back in her mind, Alberta started to laugh and then, realizing she was the one who was now being even ruder, she tried to cough to hide her laugh, which only made her laugh harder.

"Don't worry, everyone thinks it's hilarious," Charlie said. "Especially my wife, I mean soon-to-be ex-wife. She'd say it to me every day when I would try to give her a kiss. She'd say, 'Sorry, Charlie,' and crack up laughing. I really miss the sound of her laughter."

After his disclosure all thoughts of laughter were sucked out of the room. Alberta felt bad for Charlie and wanted to offer words of encouragement and compassion, but seeing his doe-eyed expression, she didn't think any words would help him. He was lost in the past, which was where Alberta needed to be as well. Not her past, but Cathy and Patrick's.

As nonchalantly as possible Alberta sat behind one of the computers as Sloan, Joyce, and Helen stood around her. Even though Charlie didn't seem to be paying attention to what Alberta was doing, the group—without discussing it—decided it would be best to distract Charlie so he didn't ask Alberta what she was doing.

"I can't believe it's still snowing out there," Sloan said to Charlie.

"My wife, I mean soon-to-be ex-wife, told me a storm was brewing," Charlie replied. "I thought she meant our divorce proceedings, but she was talking about the weather."

"Is she a weather girl on the news?" Joyce asked.

"No, she's just a doomsayer," Charlie clarified. "Always thinking the worst of every situation. But I don't think she would've guessed how things have turned out here. I mean we really are stranded up here with a dead body in the freezer. Doesn't that give you the willies?"

"In my former line of duty you acquire a different perspective where death is concerned," Helen said.

"I mean no disrespect when I say this, Helen," Charlie started. "But unless you're a medical examiner or perhaps God himself, knowing there's a dead body in a walk-in storage unit where they keep the rest of the meat is the definition of how to give somebody the willies."

"I have to agree with you on that one, Charlie," Sloan said. "The more I try to push it out of my mind, the more I see Pamela's frostbitten face."

"Also too, her bloodied wrists," Joyce added. "I don't think I'll ever get over seeing that."

"That's the other thing," Charlie said. "Not only is there a dead body hibernating on the premises, there's also the dead body's killer."

"Dammit!" When Alberta shouted they all thought she was responding to Charlie's comment and had forgotten that they had come to the business center with a purpose, to find out Patrick's last name.

"Berta, what's wrong?" Sloan asked.

"I can't find it."

"Find what?" Charlie inquired. "I'm almost as good with a computer as I am with a camera."

Alberta turned right to look at Joyce and Helen and then to the left to look at Sloan, trying to silently gauge their opinion on whether she should speak freely in front of Charlie. She thought Sloan's and Joyce's eyes were saying yes, while Helen's were saying no, so she chose the safe route and went with the majority.

"I'm trying to find out if Patrick's last name is Dell and the only thing that pops up is O'Dell, which is close, but doesn't fit as neatly if the name is a combination of the words boyo and Dell," Alberta explained. "You see, we're pretty certain Cathy and Patrick are siblings and they own Icicle Lodge together under the name Boyodell, Inc. We overheard Cathy call Patrick "boyo," which is why I thought Patrick's last name was Dell, but I guess it's close enough, which means that Cathy and Patrick's last name is O'Dell."

"Oh for God's sake!" Charlie shouted.

"I know Alberta can ramble," Helen said. "But really, is that a good reason to use the Lord's name in vain?"

Ignoring Helen, Charlie continued, "I can't believe I didn't figure it out before! Cathy and Patrick are more than brother and sister, they're a brother and sister ice-skating team!"

"A what?"

The announcement was so startling that even Helen joined in the group shriek.

"That can't be," Alberta scoffed.

"It is!" Charlie continued. "They're a former ice-skating pairs team."

"Are you sure?" Sloan asked. "That would've been a long time ago."

"I'm positive," Charlie argued. "In the back of my mind I always knew there was something familiar about them, like I always knew even while on my honeymoon—don't ever go to Venice in the rainy season, by the way—that my wife would want to leave me someday, but I thought it was just that I was overexcited about seeing Pamela."

"I think you're overimagining things as well," Helen said.

"I have to agree with my sister," Alberta said. "I've seen Patrick and he can skate very well, but I don't think he's an Olympic-caliber skater."

Charlie didn't respond but banged on the computer keyboard frantically until he found what he was looking for. "If you don't believe me, take a look at this."

The group gathered around Charlie and peered over his shoulder to gawk at what was on his computer screen. When they saw it they felt they had each walked through some kind of time warp. On the screen was a decades-old photograph of Cathy and Patrick O'Dell when they were teenagers and they were either on their way to a costume party dressed up as figure skaters or that's exactly what they were.

Cathy's forehead was covered in bangs and her blonde hair was pulled back into a ponytail and tied with a teal ribbon, the same color as her eye shadow. Her skating outfit was the same color, only several shades brighter, with a deep pink skirt that fell in the briefest of ripples and only covered the tippy top of her thighs. The bodice was embellished with silver and pink rhinestones in the shape of an inverted triangle that began around her neck and plunged into a point at her belly button.

Standing next to Cathy with his right arm around her waist and his left hand holding hers was Patrick. His outfit was the same color combination, but only the collar and cuffs of his long-sleeved shirt and his belt were pink, the rest of his form-fitting jumpsuit was teal.

The caption underneath the photo read, "Cathy

and Patrick O'Dell, United States Pairs Team bronze medalists on their way to represent their country in Zurich, Switzerland, at the Olympics."

"Zurich!" Alberta cried. "That's the Olympics Pamela was in."

"So, Cathy, Patrick, and Pamela must have all known each other," Sloan surmised.

"Is there any other information about them online, Charlie?" Alberta asked. "Did they win a medal too?"

"According to Wikipedia, they came in dead last."

"Last!" Alberta gasped. "*Madon,* that's heartbreaking. To travel all that way and come in last with the whole world watching."

"According to this they withdrew from the Olympics after the short program," Charlie said.

"Withdrew?" Helen cried. "Why in the world would anyone withdraw from the Olympics?"

"Maybe they sustained an injury?" Sloan suggested.

"I can't remember," Charlie confessed. "But it had to be incredibly serious for them to withdraw at the biggest moment in their professional lives."

Each of them grew silent trying to imagine what could have happened to make a young and presumably ambitious figure-skating pair travel halfway around the world to compete in the Olympics and then give it up halfway through. None of them could come up with a viable scenario that would explain such a drastic decision. Then again, none of them were elite skaters so how could they know?

"I don't know about you, but I'm starving," Charlie announced. "I'm going to see if Max has whipped up anything for dinner."

As he was exiting the room he nearly collided with Jinx and Freddy, who were entering.

"Sorry, Charlie," Jinx said and immediately started laughing. Unlike Alberta, she didn't try to cover her laughter with a coughing fit.

"Your grandmother beat you to it, kid," Charlie said before bounding down the hall in search of something to eat.

"What did he mean by that?" Jinx asked.

"I laughed at the same joke before."

"Does anyone else find that guy creepy?" Freddy questioned the group.

"Creepy as in a creep?" Helen asked. "Or creepy as in a murderer?"

Freddy pondered and then replied, "I haven't decided yet. Perhaps we should put it up to a group vote."

"Before we do that, why don't we share the photo I found with everyone?" Jinx proposed.

"What photo, lovey?" Alberta asked.

Jinx reached into the back pocket of her jeans and pulled out a folded piece of paper. She unfolded it, smoothed it out, and placed it on the table between two computers.

"I printed this out earlier," Jinx said. "It's similar to the photo that we found pinned up in Cathy's office, but with a few more people. It's Pamela's coach, Dimitri, sitting around a dinner table on the cruise right before he died."

Alberta picked up the photo to get a better look and let out a low whistle. *"L'ultima Cena."*

"You could be right about that, Berta," Joyce said.

"Sorry, the last . . . what?" Jinx asked.

"The Last Supper," Helen translated.

Sitting next to Dimitri was a beautiful dark-haired woman dripping in fine jewelry, and standing nearby was a blond-haired man sporting a full beard, in a shirt and tie, holding some kind of white cloth in his hand. A few of the people had their backs to the camera so their faces couldn't be seen including one woman with luminous blonde hair and a tattoo of some kind of symbol on her left shoulder. The design couldn't be made out because her hair was in the way, but it looked like Poseidon's trident.

"This is quite possibly the last photo ever taken of Dimitri, other than, you know, the photos of him in the morgue," Jinx said. "He died at some point after this picture was taken and before the ship returned to dock."

"Do you know what this means?" Alberta asked.

"I am never going on a cruise?" Helen remarked.

"It means that Cathy and Patrick probably knew Dimitri as well."

"How do you figure that, Gram?"

Alberta quickly relayed the information they just uncovered to Jinx and Freddy so they were all now up to speed. "So if Cathy and Patrick were in the Olympics with Pamela, and Dimitri was Pamela's coach at the Olympics, they had to know him," Alberta explained.

"He's Dee!" Joyce blurted out.

"Who's Dee?" Sloan asked.

"The person Cathy and Pamela were arguing about," Joyce explained. "We overheard them saying something like 'Keep Dee out of this' and 'Dee was always in this,' stuff like that. Dee is short for Dimitri."

"Then they definitely knew each other," Alberta agreed.

"Maybe Dimitri was Cathy and Patrick's coach too," Sloan suggested.

"Would a singles skater and a pairs team have the same coach?" Freddy asked. "Don't figure-skating coaches specialize in one particular discipline?"

Everyone looked at Freddy as if he was speaking in hieroglyphics.

"You're like one extreme or the other, Freddy," Jinx remarked. "You either call everyone 'dude' or you're really smart."

"I like to keep everybody guessing."

"Well, I'm tired of guessing," Alberta said. "Cathy and Patrick have been lying this entire time. They're siblings, business partners, and former competitive figure skaters. They've known Pamela and Dimitri almost their entire lives and now both of them have died under mysterious circumstances. It was no coincidence that Cathy asked Pamela to come here and be the celebrity guest performer for the grand reopening of the lodge."

"Are you saying what I think you're saying, Gram?"

"*O Dio mio!*" Helen cried. "Not that again! Just say what you're thinking."

"Do you think Cathy lured Pamela here to kill her?" Jinx asked.

Once again the room grew silent, this time because they were each contemplating if Jinx's suggestion was possible. Could Cathy have hated Pamela so much that she would have invited her to perform at her lodge for the sole purpose of murdering her? Anything was possible, but why? Why would Cathy do such a thing?

"What's her motive?" Joyce asked. "Why would Cathy or Patrick want Pamela dead?"

"Jealousy?" Sloan said.

"Revenge?" Freddy added.

"Boredom?" Helen said.

"Helen, be serious," Alberta sighed.

"I am! There's nothing online about Cathy's post-Olympics life so her day-to-day existence was nothing compared to the celebrity status Pamela attained," Helen rationalized. "Didn't you say she did a lot of tours and even some TV specials?"

"Yes, she did," Jinx confirmed.

"So maybe after a lifetime of being bored and seeing Pamela get all the notoriety that Cathy thought she should have had, she decided to shake things up a bit and kill her former rival," Helen theorized.

"That's interesting, Helen," Joyce began. "But it really is a bit of a stretch."

"I don't know about that," Alberta said.

"You think Aunt Helen might be right?"

"I think the combination of being jealous, wanting revenge, and living a boring life could be deadly," Alberta explained. "And remember what Pamela said herself."

"What was that, Gram?"

"That figure skating is a cutthroat sport and little girls would kill to be in the top spot," Alberta said.

"You think one little girl killed because she never got to the top and Pamela did?" Sloan asked.

Alberta took a deep breath and answered, "If that's what happened, that little girl is Cathy."

CHAPTER 18

La maggior' sventura o venutra dell'uomo è la moglie.

Alberta was standing on a sheet of ice and could see nothing else in any direction. She looked all around her and there was nothing but glistening ice as far as the eye could see. When she turned to the left something new came into view and she saw Pamela standing in the distance dressed in a gorgeous black-sequined sleeveless jumpsuit that hugged every inch of her toned body. On her feet were black figure skates whose blades also seemed to be adorned with sequins because they shimmered in the light and made it appear as if Pamela was standing an inch off the ice on a pillow of jewels.

Alberta heard a loud scratching sound and turned to the right and saw Cathy wearing a similar outfit, but hers was in blood red. She also noticed that Cathy didn't look nearly as good in her outfit, and Alberta tossed in her sleep annoyed with herself that even in her dreams she was body shaming another woman. Her subconscious made a mental note to deal with this critical flaw of being overly critical when Alberta was fully awake, but now she had to deal with being in the middle of a potentially deadly confrontation.

At the same time Pamela and Cathy began to skate counterclockwise around Alberta, who was afraid to move because (a) she wasn't wearing skates, and (b) she had no idea where she would go since the ice seemed to continue beyond the horizon of her dream. There was a very good chance that she would fall off the edge and wind up somewhere even worse. Without knowing the world outside of the ice, Alberta decided to stand still. The other two women, however, refused to stop moving.

Round and round Pamela and Cathy skated, and while they looked assured and glided easily over the ice, Alberta started to feel dizzy just by watching them. When they started to yell, Alberta felt like she was in an echo chamber and thought she might collapse under the weight of the vibrations.

"You stole everything from me!" Cathy screamed.

"I worked for everything I ever had!" Pamela screamed back. "You chose not to make anything of your life. You gave up!"

Cathy stumbled, lurched forward, and almost fell on her stomach, but quickly regained her balance, stretched out her right leg to her side, and turned so she was now skating backward.

"I was pushed aside!" Cathy yelled. "To make way for you!"

"Because there's only room for one person at the top! And that person was me!"

Pamela's cry was thunderous and it made Alberta cover her ears with her hands and brought Cathy to her knees. Cathy leaned her right hand into the ice and picked up her left leg so her skate blade was on the surface of the ice and tried to push herself into a standing position, but Pamela screamed again and her voice, amplified and filled with derision, knocked Cathy down yet again.

"You didn't deserve to be a champion! Because you didn't have what it takes!"

Pamela ignored Alberta and started to skate faster and faster around Cathy, who was desperately trying to pick herself up from the ice but was unable to get both of her skates on the ice at the same time. She was being beaten down by Pamela's voice.

"You're a loser! You always have been and everybody knew it!" Pamela shouted.

Alberta felt a shiver of memory ride up her spine and slap her across the face. The words and the tone of voice were the same, only the speaker was different. Alberta no longer heard Pamela yelling, but Sammy, her dead husband. He had been just as loud, intimidating, and could at times be as hateful as Pamela so Alberta knew exactly how Cathy felt because she had felt that way so many times over the length of her marriage.

"You're pathetic! Dimitri knew it, Patrick knows it, even you know it!" Pamela continued. "That's why you gave up! That's why you crawled away from the Olympics to go live under a rock where you belong so you wouldn't have to embarrass yourself in front of millions of eyes ever again! You deserve everything you got!"

"And so do you!" Cathy's voice howled and the venom that filled her words seemed to linger in the air and make it difficult to breathe. She raised her hand and before Pamela could understand what was happening and defend herself, Cathy slashed Pamela's wrists with the blade of her skate once, twice, three times until the blood was pouring out of Pamela's wrists like crimson rain. Pamela opened her mouth to scream, but no sound emerged. She placed one hand over one wrist, but it did nothing to stop the flow of the blood. Finally, she looked at Cathy, who despite being drenched in Pamela's blood, was smiling maniacally, thrilled with her accomplishment.

Pamela wobbled backward and started to spin, spraying the ice with her blood, staining it and creating curlicues and random designs on the surface. Alberta watched in horror as Pamela fell to the ice, sliding a bit, and then remained motionless as the blood, still alive and filled with purpose, raced out of her body in search of another host that was still alive. But what really terrified Alberta was Cathy's reaction to Pamela's death. Instead of being in shock over what she had done, she looked peaceful, as if she finally got what she had dreamed about for years. It was uncomfortably similar to the way Alberta looked when she buried her husband.

Gasping for breath, Alberta sat up in bed, and for a few seconds the faces of Cathy, Pamela, and Sammy swirled together in some eerie montage of life and death. Only when she closed her eyes and felt Lola, who had jumped on the bed when Alberta awoke, rubbing her body next to hers, did she begin to feel her heart slow down and her breathing become normal.

"I morti non rimangono sepolti," Alberta whispered in Lola's ear.

The cat responded by pressing her side into Alberta's arm hoping to convince her to engage in some middle-of-the-night cuddling. Jinx just wanted an explanation.

"What did you say, Gram?"

"I'm sorry, lovey," Alberta said. "I didn't mean to wake you."

"That's okay, I was having a bad dream," Jinx revealed. "What's that you said? Did someone else die?"

"No, lovey, I said, 'the dead don't stay buried.' "

Still drowsy and not understanding the situation, Jinx pressed on. "So did someone rise from the dead?"

"Kind of," Alberta said with a dry laugh.

"Grandma, you got some 'splaining to do."

Alberta described her dream and how her sleeping mind rationalized why Cathy would have killed Pamela. She deliberately left out the part that included Sammy and how Alberta wasn't as torn up and devastated by his death as a widow should be or as she had led the rest of her family to believe. Some family memories were better off unshared.

What Alberta did share with Jinx was enough to make her granddaughter want to put off returning to sleep for a little while. "I'm hungry."

"My dream made you hungry?" Alberta replied, never guessing that would be Jinx's reply.

"First of all, your dream was a nightmare, and second of all, we skipped dinner so of course I'm hungry."

With all the commotion they had skipped a real dinner and only nibbled on some bread and cheese, which were delicious, but hardly satisfying. Triggered by the realization, she heard her stomach rumble and was ready to join Jinx on a hunt for some food. The two women quickly put on their bathrobes and slippers and were about to leave the room when Lola started to purr loudly.

"I think my namesake could do with a midnight snack too," Jinx said.

Alberta peered down at her cat and placed her hands on her hips in mock authority. "Gina Lollobrigida, are you hungry?"

In response Lola purred even louder and circled Alberta's legs, moving in and out between her feet, until Alberta picked her up off the floor. "Well, let's see what we can find in the kitchen. Maybe there's a can of tuna fish with your name on it."

They walked down the hall in silence and padded down the steps as quietly as possible partially so they wouldn't wake anyone else up, but also because ever since they had formed the Ferrara Family Detective Agency, unofficially of course, they had learned that it's always best to move about stealthily and, more often than not, silence is golden. Luckily not everyone adhered to that golden rule.

Just as they got to the middle of the main room, they heard voices coming from the front desk area. They didn't see anyone, but instinctively, Alberta and Jinx tiptoed to the left and entered the kitchen. Surprisingly they could hear the voices even clearer. It sounded like two men were arguing. They walked toward the voices and were drawn to the back of the kitchen where there was a door. Jinx knew from when she and Freddy were snooping around in Cathy's office that the door opened into a small corridor, the left leading to Cathy's office, the right leading to the front desk. It didn't matter exactly where the men were, all that mattered was that if they pressed their ears against the door, Alberta and Jinx could hear every word they spoke.

"I can't believe you would say something like that," Patrick said, his voice full of dismay. "Dee was like family."

"He wasn't *sem'ya*, he was *d'yavol*," Max replied, disgust being the primary emotion coating his words.

The women pressed their ears closer to the door so they could hear the conversation better.

"Dee was hardly the devil, Max, and you know that," Patrick replied.

"You're going to stand there and tell me you approve of what he did?" Max asked.

They could actually hear Patrick breathing heavily for several seconds before he spoke, whatever he was thinking was making it difficult for him to corral his emotions.

"He was opportunistic, a liar, manipulative, but all coaches back then were like that," Patrick explained. "You of all people should know that."

"Why? Because I'm the same way?"

"Stop twisting my words!" Patrick cried.

"Stop making him out to be something he wasn't!" Max shouted. "He destroyed everything and everyone he touched."

"Max, that was a long time ago," Patrick stated. "You should've gone to the funeral."

"Why? So he could make an even bigger fool out of me?"

"It's called respect," Patrick said, his voice now cold and final. "Everyone noticed you weren't there. Cathy, Galina, and even Pam."

Max chuckled before he replied, "Three women, each one more stupid than the other."

They expected to hear Patrick at least defend his sister's name, but instead heard a door close and footsteps walking in the opposite direction. A few seconds later they heard another door open and close and more footsteps walking in the same direction. Even though they assumed Patrick and Max had gone back to their rooms, Alberta and Jinx crouched down behind a long metal prep table until they felt that the coast was clear.

"So now we have proof that they all know each other," Jinx said.

"This grand reopening was more like a reunion with everyone invited except Dimitri," Alberta said.

"And this Galina, whoever she is," Jinx added.

Lola purred and Alberta pressed her closer to her chest whispering into her ear for her to shush. She rummaged through a few cabinets until she found a can of tuna fish as Jinx opened some drawers in search of a can opener. Retrieving one, the women were about to head back to their room hoping not to meet anyone else along the way. Lola had other wishes.

Just as they were about to leave the kitchen, Lola squirmed in Alberta's arms and tried to paw at the tuna fish can. Alberta lurched forward and slammed her hand down on the kitchen counter before she could regain her balance, reminding her of how Cathy looked in her dream.

"You are such a bad girl," Alberta said to Lola. "You almost made Mama fall."

Jinx bent down to pick up some papers that had fallen onto the floor, and when she was arranging them into the neat pile they were in prior to being disrupted, she found one sheet of paper that held particular interest.

"Gram, I think Lola helped us find another clue."

Inside their room, Alberta quickly opened the can of tuna fish and placed it into a bowl, then set it on the floor so a waiting Lola could stop licking her lips and start eating. Once Lola was satisfied, it was time for Alberta to satisfy her own curiosity.

"What are you talking about, lovey? What clue?"

Jinx held up the piece of paper she took from the kitchen. "What does that say?"

"Two pounds of 98 percent lean chopped meat," Alberta recited.

"Above the recipe!"

"Galina," Alberta said. "Ah, *Madon*! It's Patrick's Galina!"

"Exactly!" Jinx cried. "Patrick mentioned she was at Dimitri's funeral, and the number written underneath Galina's name is a phone number."

"No it isn't," Alberta corrected. "There are too many numbers."

"It's an international phone number," Jinx clarified. "The 011 is what you need to connect to an international line, then the next number is the country code, in this case it's 7, which is for Russia."

"I know Galina sounds like a Russian name," Alberta said. "But how are you so sure the phone number is Russian?"

"A few months ago I was doing research for an article about the origins of Santa Claus and the different ways he's viewed throughout the world, so I called a bunch of international schools to talk to kids," Jinx explained. "I had a hard time getting through to the school in Moscow so I had to call repeatedly, and I always had to dial 011-7, followed by the actual phone number to get a call to go through. FYI, Russian kids are no different than American ones—they all love Santa."

"You really have a very exciting job," Alberta gushed.

"Thanks, Gram, I do love it," Jinx admitted. "But

I'm desperate to write about important things and not just the history of some imaginary character."

Alberta raised her eyebrows and forced herself not to point her finger at Jinx, but said, "That imaginary character has brought almost a century of joy and hope to children everywhere, don't underestimate the importance of that."

Smiling sheepishly, Jinx replied, "That's why I love you, Gram, you're always looking on the bright side of things."

Alberta cracked up laughing, "Oh, lovey, if you only knew me a couple of years ago, you would not accuse me of being a Pollyanna." She plopped onto her bed and said, "Now enough chitchat, let's call Russia."

Jinx jumped on the bed and sat next to Alberta. She took out her cell phone and dialed the number from the piece of paper. After a few agonizing moments of silence, they finally heard the call ringing.

Alberta shook her head slowly marveling at the fact that she was trapped in a snowed-in mountain lodge in Pennsylvania sitting on a bed next to her granddaughter as they waited for some woman named Galina who lived halfway across the world pick up a phone so they could ask her some questions. Which is when it dawned on Alberta that she had no idea what questions to ask.

"What are we going to say if she picks up?"

Jinx paused to contemplate Alberta's question. "I have no idea."

"How can you not have any idea? You don't just call Russia without any idea of what you're going to say!"

"I'm sure something will come to me," Jinx said. "I talk to strangers every day for work."

"You really are like your mother, Jinx, you love to fly by the seat of your pants."

Both women were so startled by Alberta's mention

of Jinx's mother that it took the woman on the other end of the phone three tries to get their attention.

"*Privet!*"

"That must mean 'hello' or 'who the hell is this,'" Alberta said, covering the phone with her hand so she couldn't be overheard by the Russian on the other end of the line.

Jinx hoped it was the former, picked up the phone, shrugged her shoulders, and replied, "Hello. My name is Gina Maldonado and I'm calling from the United States."

"Oh hello, yes, I speak English," the woman replied, her Russian accent still thick.

"Is this Galina?"

"Yes, this is Galina Vasilievsky, why do you want to know?"

Once again Alberta covered the phone so Galina couldn't hear her speaking and whispered, "That's Dimitri's last name, she must be his wife."

Agreeing with Alberta, Jinx continued. "I'm writing an article on your husband, Dimitri, and about the impact he had in the world of figure skating. I was hoping I could ask you a few questions."

There was a pause on the other end of the line and Jinx feared Galina had hung up, but when she replied, sniffling and her voice softer and resigned, it was obvious that she was fighting back tears.

"His death was a great loss to the skating community and to his family," Galina said. "I miss him every day."

"I'm so sorry for your loss," Jinx said. A wave of guilt washed over her and she was a bit ashamed that she was pumping a recently widowed woman for information. "If this isn't a good time I can call back."

"It's never good time to talk about Dimitri, but it's always good time to talk about him, if you know what I mean," Galina said.

Despite her young age and status as a single woman, Jinx understood loss. "I do understand."

"What do you want to know?" Galina asked.

"How did Dimitri come to coach Pamela Gregory?"

"Sandy, Pamela's first coach, brought her to Dimitri because he had done all he could. Pamela had outgrown her coaching and needed someone who could shape her into a champion," Galina explained. "That's what my Dimitri did."

"And Pamela never had another coach once she began to work with Dimitri?" Jinx inquired.

"No, there was no one better than Dimitri," Galina replied, without a hint of ego in her voice, just fact. And then some doubt. "Well, that's not true."

"There was a better coach?" Jinx asked.

"No, Dimitri was best," Galina replied. "But he had Simi, his assistant, Simi Morozov."

Jinx looked at Alberta, her forehead furrowed, and hoped that her grandmother recognized the name Simi, but Alberta shook her head and was no help.

"So Simi worked with Pamela too?" Jinx queried.

"Yes, but Simi wanted to . . . how do you say? He wanted to do more than *just work* with Pamela," Galina said.

"Was Simi interested in her? You know, socially?" Jinx asked.

"Do you mean was Simi in love with Pamela?" Galina asked rhetorically. "Yes."

Jinx and Alberta looked at each other, twin sets of eyebrows raised as they completely understood Galina's subtext.

"Did Pamela return his feelings?" Jinx asked.

"Oh no, she was baby," Galina said. "And she was focused, nothing else mattered except Olympic gold."

"Simi's feelings didn't get in the way of him being one of her coaches?"

"No, he coached some other skaters, too, a few pairs teams, but Pamela was his primary student," Galina said.

"He and Dimitri must have been close," Jinx suggested.

Galina muttered something in Russian that Jinx didn't understand, but then she continued in English. "He was like brother to Dimitri, but after the . . . how do you say? Oh yes, after the *incident* at the Olympics things changed and their relationship was never the same."

Once again Jinx and Alberta looked at each other hoping the other one had any insight about the incident, but they were both clueless. Jinx adopted a tried and true reporting technique and remained quiet, which brought her the desired outcome; Galina kept talking.

"I know Dimitri reached out to Simi after everything died down, but Simi was уперты . . . stubborn . . . and the damage was done. He pushed Dimitri away even after Simi's daughter was born," Galina said. "*Poslednyaya kaplya, kotoraya perepolnila chashu.*"

"Come again," Jinx said, completely lost by the flurry of Russian words.

"Sorry, it's a Russian phrase, it means 'the last drop that filled the cup,'" Galina translated. "I think in America it's 'the straw that broke the camel's back.'"

"Of course," Jinx said. "I'm Italian and I'm trying to learn the language, we say *La goccia che ha fatto traboccare il vaso.*"

"We are all the same," Galina said, laughing a little. "I wish I knew what happened between Dimitri and Simi, they were so close, but husbands, they have secrets and he never told me."

When Alberta heard Galina's comment, she forced her face to remain a mask so she wouldn't give any emotion away and let Jinx know that she understood Galina completely and experienced the same relationship with her husband. The women, however, had different points of view when it came to how their husbands died.

"I've heard reports that Dimitri didn't die of natural causes," Jinx said as gingerly as possible.

"Враньё!" Galina exclaimed. "Lies! One moment he was eating soup on a cruise and the next he had heart attack."

"And you're sure that's how he died?"

"Absolutely! The doctors don't know a thing, neither does my daughter, she disagrees, she thinks there was . . . how do you say? Foul play, but she's as stupid as his doctors, it was his heart," Galina confirmed. "Dimitri was good man, no one would want to hurt him, and I won't hear of anything that says otherwise."

Galina didn't want to hear anything else at all and to prove it she ended the phone call.

Jinx stared at her phone for a few seconds before saying, "Well, that was illuminating."

"*La maggior' sventura o venutra dell'uomo è la moglie,*" Alberta sighed.

"I feel like I'm still speaking with Galina."

"Sorry, an old saying. A man's best fortune or his worst is a wife."

"Why would you say Galina is Dimitri's worst fortune?"

"If Dimitri was murdered like we think he was, he

had a secret that someone killed him over," Alberta started. "That means Galina didn't know her husband at all."

"And the only thing we learned is that Dimitri royally ticked off someone named Simi," Jinx summated. "We just have no idea who Simi is."

Before they could contemplate further on the subject there was a knock at the door. Cautiously Alberta opened the door and was relieved when she saw that it was Helen and Joyce. She grew anxious when Helen spoke.

"Something strange is going on outside."

In silence Alberta and Jinx followed Helen and Joyce downstairs and out into the back of the lodge. For a moment the only sound was the howling wind and their own shivering until they heard banging.

"You hear that?" Helen asked. "It woke me up."

They heard the noise again and they all turned in the same direction. "It sounds like it's coming from the shed over there."

The third time they heard the banging sound they were convinced it was coming from the shed, and huddled together they trudged in their slippers and robes to investigate. They held on to each other as they rounded the skating rink, holding each other up so no one would fall, and just as they were standing in front of the shed the doors burst open.

The four women held each other even tighter and stood dumbfounded at the sight of the Zamboni machine breaking through the doors and barreling right for them.

"Run!" Alberta screamed as she took her own advice and ran as fast as she could. She heard Jinx, Helen, and Joyce all behind her, but their screams were being muffled by the wind and the Zamboni motor.

Alberta thought the safest place to go would be someplace where the Zamboni couldn't get, which was in the ice rink, so she grabbed onto the side of the rink and hoisted herself over onto the ice. The rest of the women followed suit and they held on to each other as they slipped and slid across the ice to get to the safety of the other side. Unfortunately, they underestimated the power of the Zamboni.

Just as they were in the center of the rink they heard an even louder sound, this time a crash, and turned around to see that the Zamboni had broken through the side railing and was now gliding on the ice straight for them.

"We're gonna get run over!" Alberta screamed.

"Who's driving that thing?" Helen cried.

"Stop!" Jinx yelled. "You're gonna kill us!"

As the Zamboni got closer they saw that a man was sitting in the front seat, his hands on the wheel, but his body was slumped to the side. They all kept screaming, but the driver couldn't hear them because it looked like someone had already killed Patrick.

CHAPTER 19

Solo una stella può brillare di più.

"Oh my God, he's dead!"

Jinx's scream reverberated up into the pine trees, across Lake Ariel, and inside Icicle Lodge. Lights went on, windows were opened, and voices started shouting. None, however, were louder than the ladies as they were scrambling on the ice to get out of the Zamboni's path.

Helen was just about to make it to the opposite side of the rink when she fell onto her side and slid. At the same time, Patrick's body shifted and he slumped forward onto the steering wheel making the Zamboni turn to the right and exactly where Helen was lying on the ice.

"Helen!"

Alberta tried to run toward her sister, but realized she would reach her much quicker if she just slid so she deliberately fell on her backside and used the momentum to crash into Helen, pushing them both out of the way of the Zamboni that swerved in the opposite direction a few inches away from clipping Alberta's foot.

Still on the ice, Alberta and Helen saw two legs move quickly past them, work boots pressing down onto the ice firmly and securely as if they were walking through a forest. They looked up and saw Max climb onto the footboard on the driver's side of the Zamboni, open the door, and grab hold of the steering wheel. Next, he pushed Patrick's body out of the way and sat in the driver's seat manipulating gears and levers until the Zamboni came to a complete stop.

Alberta and Helen simultaneously made the sign of the cross and reached for each other's hand. They didn't need to say a word, they only needed to hold on to one another. Jinx and Joyce felt the same way. Together, they slowly walked over to Alberta and Helen, helped them stand up, made sure they weren't injured, and exchanged hugs. They only separated when they heard a commotion behind them.

"What is going on around here?" Stephanie had a point, unfortunately, no one had a logical answer. Or at least an answer that anyone wanted to hear.

"It looks like someone killed Patrick," Alberta said to the crowd.

Gasps and shocked cries rose up in a tidal wave of emotion. Freddy and Sloan hopped over the side of the rink and gave their girlfriends a quick, reassuring hug before answering Max's calls for help. They bounded carefully to where the Zamboni had stopped, and as Max lowered Patrick's body down, Freddy and Sloan grabbed him and gently placed him onto the ice.

As Charlie and Stephanie helped the women climb over the side of the rink, another woman made a mad dash to get onto the ice and next to her brother's body.

"Patrick, no!" Cathy screamed as she knelt down

next to Patrick's seemingly lifeless body. She shrieked again to announce, "He's alive!"

"What?" Max cried, jumping out of the Zamboni.

"He's still breathing," Cathy assured. "We have to get him to a hospital."

"Cathy we can't do that," Max said, his voice calm, but firm. "The roads are too dangerous."

"We can't just leave him here! He needs help."

"Let's take him to his room and then we'll see if we can get an ambulance to come here," Sloan suggested.

Cathy, couldn't answer, she merely wiped away her tears and nodded.

"Max, can you lift his shoulders if Freddy and I each take one leg?" Sloan asked. "You seem to be a lot surer of yourself on the ice."

"Yes," Max replied. "We lift on my count of three."

Slowly, the men walked on the ice holding Patrick's body, and everyone held their breath that they wouldn't fall and worsen Patrick's condition. When they got to the side of the rink, Max instructed Charlie to come over and help them so they could lift Patrick onto safer ground.

Charlie held on to the leg Freddy had been holding as he climbed over the side. Once on snowy ground instead of ice, Freddy grabbed Patrick's other leg and then Sloan straddled the side of the rink. They moved farther away from the rink until Max was pressing against the side and Sloan took the weight of Patrick's shoulders as Max expertly grabbed the railing and flung his body over. In an instant he was back underneath Patrick's body holding him by the shoulders. They quickly went into the lodge with the women behind them.

Cathy watched the men carry her brother into the lodge and seemed lost. She looked like she couldn't

comprehend what was happening and instead of joining them, she stayed behind. Alberta and Joyce were
the last to enter the lodge and as they were about to
enter they saw Cathy still next to the rink, unable to
move. They ran to her and stood on either side, each
grabbing an arm.

"We'll stay here as long as we need to, Cathy," Joyce
said.

"But I think your brother would rather you be by his
side," Alberta added.

Startled into movement, Cathy turned to face Alberta and looked like the little girl Patrick must have
grown up with. "You know?"

Alberta nodded and she felt Cathy's entire body
relax. It really did feel good to disclose a long-kept secret.

Joyce patted Alberta's hand and the women tugged
on Cathy's arms. It was time they got inside or else
they'd be frozen and they'd all have to be carted into
the lodge just like Patrick.

Once inside, they found the main room empty.
Cathy stood immobile and squeezed Alberta's and
Joyce's hands as if hoping to siphon some of their energy to get her moving. That didn't work, but Stephanie did.

"Patrick opened his eyes!"

Without saying a word, Cathy let go of their hands
and raced down the hall after Stephanie who disappeared into Patrick's room. Alberta and Joyce quickly
followed, brushing off all the snow from their bathrobes and hair.

"I don't know about you, Berta, but I'm going to
need a vacation from this vacation."

"If we make it out of here alive, we're starting to
drop like flies around here," Alberta said. "I'm still ter-

rified something bad has happened to Vinny. If he doesn't show up soon I'm going to have to call the police station. We can't wait much longer."

"Agreed," Joyce said. "But let's focus on one crisis at a time."

As worried as Alberta was about their survival in what was fast becoming a very dangerous place to be, she was thrilled to see Patrick's eyes wide open when she walked into his room. Cathy was kneeling by his bedside holding his hand, and Max was kneeling on the other side.

In the corner of the room that faced the bed, Helen was sitting in a chair silently saying the rosary with Jinx, Freddy, and Sloan flanking her on either side. Charlie was on the opposite side of the room with Stephanie while Alberta and Joyce were standing in the doorway. The room was crowded, but all Alberta could think was that one of these people was a murderer. And if Patrick didn't keep his eyes open, there might be another victim to add to the list. All of those thoughts, however, became unimportant when Patrick started to speak.

"Cathy," he whispered.

"I'm right here."

"She . . ."

"What, Patrick," Cathy pleaded. "What are you trying to say? Who did this to you?"

Patrick shook his head slightly and repeated, "She . . ."

"Who, Patrick? Who are you talking about?" Cathy begged. "Pamela?"

Instead of answering Cathy's question, Patrick closed his eyes.

"No!" Cathy shrieked. "Wake up! Patrick, don't you dare leave me!"

Cathy grabbed Patrick by the shoulders and shook

him in an attempt to revive his now limp body. Alberta and Joyce raced to Cathy's side and pulled her away fearful that her impassioned, but physical, pleas would do more harm than good.

Helen got up and picked up Patrick's arm by the wrist to check for a pulse, she also put her hand inside his shirt to feel his heartbeat. Then, she lifted up his eyelids to examine how they reacted to the light.

"He's not dead," she pronounced.

"Thank God!" Cathy gasped.

"I think he might be in a coma," Helen said. "I'm not certain, but he's breathing and his pulse rate is slow, but normal."

Jinx stood next to Helen and put her arm around her shoulder. "You really do know everything, Aunt Helen."

"Keep it a secret," she replied. "I don't want it to get around."

"Speaking of secrets, it looks like there's no longer any doubt that you two are brother and sister," Charlie said, his words slurring making it no secret that he'd been drinking. "And if anyone is still in the dark, I'm talking about Cathy and Patrick O'Dell sib . . . sibyls . . . siblings!"

Still kneeling next to the bed, holding Patrick's hand, Cathy replied, "We didn't mean to lie to everyone, we just didn't want to spoil the reopening."

"Too late for that," Charlie quipped.

When he saw that no one appreciated his attempt at humor, he shrugged his shoulders and turned his hands over, palms up, in the universal sign that says, "Yup, I'm an idiot."

"How could knowing you and Patrick were brother and sister ruin the reopening?" Freddy asked.

Shaking her head, Cathy stood up, never letting go

of Patrick's hand. "Because of our baggage. We're not just siblings, we were partners, U.S. national bronze medalists in pairs figure skating." She smiled wistfully and looked at Patrick. "Isn't that right, brother? Whoop-de-doo."

"I think what you achieved was pretty amazing, if you ask me," Jinx said.

"That's because you've never been a skater," Cathy scoffed. "Our career or whatever you want to call it was over a long time ago. It's ancient history and it didn't end well. Pamela was the star, not us."

"Is that what Dimitri thought?"

Cathy snapped her head to look at Alberta. "How do you know about Dimitri?"

Ignoring Cathy's question, Alberta responded with another. "He was your coach, wasn't he?"

Sitting back down on the bed, Cathy shot a quick glance at Max. Alberta wasn't sure if she was trying to be subtle, but it didn't matter, she already knew Max knew about Dimitri and their past relationship on and probably off the ice.

"For a while he was until the Olympics, and then everything changed," Cathy conveyed. "Like I said, Pamela was the star."

"Solo una stella può brillare di più," Helen said.

Joyce translated for the confused faces around the room, "Only one star can shine brightest."

"And that star was most definitely Pamela Gregory," Cathy said. "But I'm done talking about the past and about Pamela and things that never were. We need to focus on my brother. I really think we should try to get him to a hospital."

"No," Max declared. "I called the hospital and the roads are blocked. They're going to send an ambulance the moment the weather clears up. We have to keep him stable and comfortable in here until then."

"But that might be too late," Cathy said, her voice quivering.

"Would you like me to ask Father Sal to perform last rites?" Helen asked.

"No!" Cathy screamed. "You keep that sick man away from my brother. He'll only make things worse."

"And how exactly can things get any worse around here?" Charlie blurted out. "I mean, come on! First Pamela is murdered, then Vinny disappears, and now Patrick's in a coma. It's like we're in some crazy remake of *And Then There Were None*! Seriously, who's gonna be next?"

No one responded to Charlie's drunken outburst because no one could deny that what he said was the truth. They were stranded at a remote mountain lodge with no way of leaving, and one by one they were being knocked off. They all looked around the room wondering who was going to be the next person to surrender to harm's way and become the fourth victim. And scarier than that, who was the person doing the harm?

"Somebody in this room is behind all of this mayhem," Charlie said. "And, you know sumpthin'? I'm getting a little sick and tired of it."

"Okay, that's enough, Charlie," Sloan said. "We're all dealing with a lot of stress."

"This isn't stress!" Charlie yelled. "This is insanity! Let's not forget that one of you people is a murderer!"

"One of us?" Freddy cried. "You're as much of a suspect as the rest of us."

"I'm a photographer, not a killer."

"Dude! You suck at photography!" Freddy shouted. "I doubt you're even a real photographer, and you probably faked your way in to get close enough to Pamela to kill her."

"Like your dumb girlfriend is any better at being a reporter?" Charlie shouted. "She's got the scoop of the year and she hasn't written one word about it."

"That's because Vinny made us promise we wouldn't leak any info to the press or the outside world," Alberta reminded him. "And my granddaughter knows when to play by the rules."

"That's not entirely true, Gram."

"What are you talking about, lovey?"

"I'm sorry, I couldn't wait any longer, not with Vinny missing along with Pamela being murdered," Jinx explained. "I submitted an article to Wyck yesterday and asked him to wait twenty-four hours to publish it in case Vinny shows up and can explain his absence. But if Wyck doesn't hear from me, he's going to publish the article."

"So much for your precious granddaughter playing by the rules," Charlie spat. "She's like every woman I've ever met! Selfish, no good, and out for herself!"

"You watch your mouth!" Freddy lunged at Charlie from across the room, and it took Max and Sloan to pull him back so there wasn't a brawl at Patrick's bedside.

"You say another word about my girlfriend and I'll make you pay!"

"Is that what happened to Vinny and Patrick?" Charlie asked, finding courage now that Freddy was being held back by the two men. "Did they say something mean about your girlfriend that you didn't like?"

Charlie's courage quickly faded when Freddy, enraged, broke free from Max and Sloan's grasp and attacked him. While Freddy held Charlie by the throat with his right hand, his first punch landed square against Charlie's jaw, and his second was aimed right at his stomach. Stephanie tried to scurry out of the way but didn't make it in time, and Charlie fell to the floor on top of her. He grabbed at Stephanie's sweater, pulling so hard that he ripped it at the seam. Alberta came to her aid and pulled her away from Charlie so more of her outfit wouldn't get ruined, while Jinx pulled on her boyfriend's arm.

"Freddy, stop!" Jinx cried. "This is really sweet and all, but knock it off!"

Words, no matter how forceful, weren't going to stop Freddy from pummeling Charlie, who despite his mouthy bravado was no match for the younger, more physically fit, and furious Freddy. Max bent down and wrapped his arms around Freddy and lifted him off the floor. At the same time, Sloan pulled Charlie out of the way and back into the corner. Sloan stood in front of Charlie as Max continued to bear-hug Freddy until both men calmed down.

"As Alberta would say, *basta*!" Sloan cried.

"Let go of me!" Freddy shouted.

"Not until you promise not to go all Incredible Hulk again," Jinx demanded.

Breathing deeply through his nose several times, Freddy finally agreed, "Fine." Max let him go but didn't move an inch away from him, which was good because Freddy pointed a finger right at Charlie. "As long as he remembers what I said."

"Maybe if you didn't toss Vinny into Lake Ariel, he'd arrest you for assault and battery!" Charlie retorted, clearly not having learned his lesson.

Once again Freddy lunged to attack Charlie, but luckily this time Max was ready and grabbed Freddy, twirled him around, and pushed him into the open closet. The impact of Freddy crashing into Patrick's clothes made them and the hanging bar holding the items fall to the ground, upending the shelf so some of the contents fell onto Freddy.

"Freddy!" Jinx cried, running to his side.

"Now that is enough!" Alberta cried. "There's a man fighting for his life right here, in case you've forgotten."

"Um, Gram."

"We should be doing everything we can to help him recover," Alberta said. "And he isn't going to recover with all of this shouting and carrying on."

"Gram, seriously, you need to see this."

"Jinx, what are you talking about?"

She didn't have to do any talking, all she had to do was hold up something that had fallen on top of Freddy. It was the other missing skate with the letters CO written on the bottom. And now they knew who the owner of the pair of skates was.

"Cathy O'Dell," Alberta muttered. "Those skates are yours."

Frightened, Cathy looked around the room and knew that there was no way she could talk her way out of this. "Yes, the skates are mine," Cathy admitted. "But I didn't kill Pamela, someone must have stolen my skates."

"Your brother?" Jinx asked.

"No, never! Patrick isn't a killer."

"Are you?" Alberta asked.

"No! This is ridiculous!" Cathy cried. "I invited Pamela here to skate at the grand reopening and she agreed because she owed me, she owed both of us."

"Why?" Joyce asked. "Because she had a lucrative professional career and you didn't?"

Shaking her head furiously, Cathy looked at her brother and squeezed his hand harder as if she was desperately trying to get him to wake up and come to her defense.

"None of that matters," Cathy said, starting to cry. "The only thing that matters is finding out who killed Pamela and who's doing these other things before someone else gets hurt."

"According to what I'm holding in my hand the suspects are either you or your brother," Jinx declared. "So which one is it?"

"Neither one of us would have killed Pamela!" Cathy cried. "I haven't put on those skates in years, someone must have used them as the murder weapon and planted them in Patrick's closet to frame him."

"Or Patrick used one of your skates to kill Pamela and kept the other one hidden in his closet," Alberta deduced. "The most logical reason is usually the right one."

"Your theory is completely illogical!" Cathy cried. "My brother is innocent! He would never have killed Pamela!"

Alberta understood the primal urge to protect a relative so she wasn't surprised by Cathy's passionate defense of her brother's innocence. But she felt she wasn't being honest, she wasn't telling the whole truth.

"You're lying, Cathy," Alberta claimed.

"Alberta, please . . ." Cathy begged.

"How can you be so sure that Patrick didn't kill Pamela?" Alberta demanded.

"Because Patrick was in love with her!"

CHAPTER 20

Il peggior mal di cuore di tutti.

Love comes in all shapes, sizes, and configurations, Alberta knew that as well as anyone else in the room, but she was surprised to learn that there was love right under her nose that she didn't detect.

She did a quick inventory of all the times she was in Patrick and Pamela's company and couldn't remember ever getting the feeling that there was a physical or emotional attraction between the two or that either of them was concealing their true feelings from the rest of the group. Cathy's revelation was a bombshell.

"Is that why you invited Pamela back?" Alberta asked. "To stage a more intimate reunion between her and Patrick?"

"No," Cathy replied softly. "Patrick may have loved Pamela, but the feeling was definitely not mutual."

"Il peggior mal di cuore di tutti," Alberta said. "Unrequited love is the worst heartache of all."

"I wouldn't be so sure of that, Cathy."

Stephanie's remark, while provocative, was logical. Cathy knew the Pamela of the past, but Stephanie had a better handle on the Pamela of the present or at least the pre-deceased present. Even though Stephanie and Pamela had a cantankerous relationship and Stephanie was more of a servant, she was privy to Pamela's schedule if not her innermost thoughts. She should know more about Pamela's feelings toward Patrick than Cathy would. Jinx was thinking the same thing.

"Why would you say that, Stephanie?" Jinx asked. "Did Pamela confide in you?"

Now that she was under a spotlight, Stephanie's confidence waned. But short of fleeing from the room, there was no way to avoid answering the question.

"No, Pamela didn't do girl talk," Stephanie said. "It's just that whenever she talked about the reopening of Icicle Lodge she always included Patrick's name, dropped it into the conversation, and often instructed me to speak with him directly instead of Cathy."

Laughter filled the room, which was unsettling because the focal point of the room was a man in a presumed coma, but it was Cathy's lodge so she could do whatever she wanted. The way Max was looking at Cathy, however, it was clear that he didn't appreciate her sense of humor.

"That is just like her!" Cathy howled. "She didn't love Patrick, but she loved being the center of his universe, anyone's universe for that matter, so she strung him along."

"I never saw any evidence of that," Stephanie protested. "But like you all witnessed firsthand, she barely treated me like a human being so what do I know?"

Alberta cast a glance over at where Jinx was standing, and as hoped Jinx was staring back at her. It was the first time they heard Stephanie speak ill of the dead.

"Did you resent Pamela for treating you disrespectfully?" Alberta asked.

Tossing her hair to the side, she blew off the comment. "I knew what I was getting into before I signed up for the gig," she replied. "Learning from Pamela was worth every insult."

"You must think very little of yourself, young lady, to believe that," Helen said.

Stephanie turned to face Helen and her countenance changed so drastically that by the time she was looking at Helen it appeared that she was facing down her greatest foe.

"With all due respect, *sister*," Stephanie hissed. "You know nothing about me so don't assume that you do."

Alberta knew that during her many decades' tenure as a nun, Helen had faced more formidable opponents and wasn't worried that she would be upset by Stephanie's vitriol. On the contrary, Alberta was worried Helen would continue to push Stephanie, either off the ledge or to lash out with even more fury. True to form, Helen surprised her sister once again.

"I apologize, I was merely making an observation," Helen said. "But if you ever need to talk, I'm a really good listener."

"I've got nothing to confess or to share," Stephanie informed. "So I don't need some former *nun* to listen to my sins!"

"You're nastier than your dead boss!" Jinx screamed.

"I take that as a compliment," Stephanie replied.

"Ah, *Madon!*" Jinx cried.

"What?" Stephanie looked at Jinx like she was speaking a foreign language, which she was.

"*Madon!*" Jinx repeated. "Do not tell me you never heard of that word?"

Waving her hand in the air in complete disgust, Stephanie ignored Jinx and continued to defend her aforementioned dead boss. "All I know is that I never saw any evidence that Pamela led Patrick on. Maybe it's just one more example of Cathy being jealous of Pamela."

"Jealous?" Cathy cried. "Of that egotistical, narcissistic, self-centered . . . don't insult me!"

"I'm telling the truth," Stephanie retorted. "Which is in pretty short supply around here."

"You want the truth?" Cathy howled. She was so enraged that she let go of her brother's hand, letting it fall limply at his side, and walked right up to Stephanie, using her finger as an exclamation point aimed at her face.

"Pamela Gregory was ruthless and never loved anyone but herself. She didn't have any friends on or off the ice because she didn't know *how* to be someone's friend," Cathy railed. "The only thing Pamela understood was doing whatever she had to do to be the best figure skater she could possibly be. That's it! I knew it and Patrick knew it, but despite that he was in love with her and pursued her for years. Pamela would dangle the carrot of her affection and then snatch it away whenever Patrick got too close."

Shrinking from Cathy's verbal attacks, Stephanie called upon all her strength not to cower completely in her presence. "I never saw any of that!" Stephanie asserted.

"Because she didn't want anyone to know! That was her game plan," Cathy said. "Keep everyone in the dark so she could fool everyone. Let Patrick think that he had a shot and then toss him aside. She did it to countless other men all her life."

"Would you agree with that, Max?" Alberta asked.

Shocked, Max didn't have a quick reply, but just shook his head from side to side.

"What would Max know?" Cathy said. "He's a man,

they were all hoodwinked by Pamela's charm and deception, even Dimitri. He never saw her for the conniving witch she was."

"Patrick's love for Pamela does explain one thing," Alberta said.

"What?" Cathy replied.

"I overheard him refer to Pamela as Pam," Alberta explained. "No one else ever called her that."

"Except the dead woman herself," Helen corrected.

"When?" Alberta asked.

"In the note she left behind," Helen replied. "She signed it 'Pam.'"

"You know something? You're right," Alberta said. "Maybe the two of them were closer than anyone thought."

"That's ridiculous," Cathy protested.

"Not really, maybe Patrick had better vision than you give him credit for," Jinx suggested. "He couldn't take the rejection any longer and killed her."

"What are you talking about?" Cathy asked.

"I think you know, you just don't want to say it out loud," Jinx said.

"I don't know what you're insinuating, but my brother loved Pamela for years, decades!" Cathy cried. "And Pamela just strung him along."

"Which might be why he killed her," Alberta said calmly.

"Don't you people listen?" Cathy yelled. "I told you he could never kill her, he was in love with her."

"But Pamela wasn't in love with him," Jinx said.

"Or he killed her so no one else would ever have her," Alberta finished.

Cathy looked stunned by the accusation and Alberta and Jinx could tell that she would never have thought of either scenario on her own. It was beyond comprehension that her brother would kill someone out of jealousy or spite or some insane rationalization that with Pamela out of the picture he could rest easy knowing that she would never be with someone else.

Slowly the acceptance came to her, rising like a balloon, unable to stop itself, and it seemed to fill her up with too much air so she couldn't breathe. Cathy started to hyperventilate and Sloan was the first one to reach her before she fainted. He grabbed her in his arms as she was about to fall to the floor.

"Freddy, help me," Sloan commanded and Freddy rushed to grab Cathy on the other side.

"You should bring her out to the main room and get her some water," Alberta instructed.

"Try something stronger," Helen suggested. "Whiskey usually works in situations like this."

"C'mon, ladies," Joyce said. "Help me find some in the kitchen."

Helen and Jinx followed Joyce out of the room, and Alberta made it look as if she was going to follow, but at the last moment she stepped to the side to let Freddy and Sloan walk Cathy out.

After they left, it was only Alberta, Stephanie, and Max in the room. Alberta wanted them to leave her alone with Patrick, but she didn't want to be obvious about it. She was just about to suggest they take a break and she'd sit with Patrick when Max beat her to it.

"Stephanie, come help me," Max said. "I want to get some things to make Patrick more comfortable."

Before Stephanie could nod in agreement or protest, Max was by her side leading her out of the room. "Will you stay and watch Patrick until I get back?"

"Of course," Alberta agreed. "Take your time."

When Alberta knew that she was alone with Patrick and the only sound filling the room was the even flow and ebb of his breathing, she sat in the chair next to his bed and was finally able to reach under the bed to pick up the piece of jewelry that had caught her eye earlier. It was a perfect clue, an ID bracelet with a name written on it.

"Don't worry, Patrick," Alberta said, whispering in Patrick's ear. "I know who did this to you and who killed Pamela."

Alberta wasn't sure if Patrick understood her, but his eyes flickered. They didn't fully open, but she took it as a sign that he gave her his approval to step up her investigation.

"*Facile* . . . don't get yourself excited," she said. "Alberta and the rest of the Ferrara family will take care of everything."

CHAPTER 21

Se non è zuppa, è pan bagnato.

The others may not have known it, but Alberta knew that the night's dinner was the beginning of the end.

She hadn't shared this with anyone else including Jinx because she wanted the element of surprise to be on her side. What was originally intended to be a week-long vacation, a celebration for the grand reopening of Icicle Lodge, and a fun getaway had turned into a nightmare, unequivocally, one dead, one missing, and one on the brink of falling into a coma if he wasn't there already. Alberta had taken some bad trips in her lifetime, but this one most assuredly took the blue ribbon for worst trip ever.

And for one person in particular seated around the table, it was about to get even worse.

Sloan was seated on Alberta's left, with Stephanie and then Charlie on her right. On the opposite side of the rectangular wooden table was Freddy, Jinx, Joyce, and Cathy. Max was working in the kitchen, Father Sal, who was still suffering from a respiratory cold, was resting in his room, and Helen was watching Patrick.

The players were all in their places and now Alberta was waiting for the perfect time to start playing her scene, for which she alone knew all the lines. The rest of them thought they were simply gathering one final time before making the difficult journey home. Cathy had announced that no matter what the roads looked like and no matter what the weather conditions were, she was leaving in the morning and bringing her brother to the nearest hospital. They all planned on doing the same thing with Max staying behind to wait for the police to retrieve Pamela's body.

Alberta was terrified that something irreversible had happened to Vinny, even though she couldn't bear to say the word "murdered" even in the silence of her own thoughts, but she knew that he would want her to continue their investigation and see it through to its inevitable conclusion. That was the last thing he had said to her, giving them all free rein to investigate and solve Pamela's murder, and that's exactly what she intended to do. But first, they had to survive dinner.

Instead of the usual lavish fare Max produced from his kitchen, tonight's spread was more unconventional and eclectic. The remains of Entenmann's cakes they had brought with them were strewn about the table surrounded by a few bottles of flavored vodka. There were plates of cold cuts and chunks of cheese, two large bowls filled with salad, even some shrimp arranged in a circle on a platter with a jar of cocktail sauce in the middle. The place settings didn't match, one plate was white with the Icicle Lodge logo in the center and others had a snowflake design. The plate in front of Charlie even depicted well-known tourist sites in London. After all the tragedy and upheaval there was no reason for Max or anyone to stand on ceremony and force the dinner to be a formal affair.

In front of everyone's plate were soup bowls. Some matched, others didn't, but all were empty waiting for Max to fill them with whatever concoction he had whipped up. Until that course was served, Alberta thought it was the perfect time to start Act 1. Unfortunately, Jinx had other ideas.

"Stephanie, would you mind telling me why you're a liar?"

"Dude!" Freddy cried. "That's kind of rude."

"And not accurate," Stephanie said, biting into a piece of Entenmann's crumb cake. "I haven't lied about anything."

"Really?" Jinx replied. "So then you're one hundred percent Italian?"

"No, not one hundred percent," Stephanie said, biting off an even larger piece of cake.

"What percentage are you?" Jinx pressed. "Fifty? Thirty? Zero? Because you're about as Italian as I'm Filipino."

"My last name is Rangusso," Stephanie said. "That's about as Italian as you can get."

"I doubt that's your last name, but even if it is, you still aren't Italian," Jinx protested.

"I don't know where my girlfriend's going with this," Freddy admitted. "But I've learned that if she's convinced about something, it's usually right."

Alberta smiled at Freddy's unabashed support of Jinx as well as the fact that Jinx was completely right. She was eager to join in the conversation but thought it best to let Jinx go it alone. Alberta had already waited a few hours to reveal what she knew, she could wait a little longer.

"Then you're as stupid as your girlfriend, Freddy," Stephanie replied, her tone of voice edgier than before. "Because she's wrong, my entire family is Italian."

"I don't know if it can be proved," Joyce added. "But I agree with Jinx. I think you're about as Italian as I am."

"Aunt Joyce, you're way more Italian than this one," Jinx interrupted. "Stephanie never heard of mozzarella being called mutz, and she dyes her hair black. What are you . . . blonde?"

Self-consciously, Stephanie ran her fingers through her hair before replying, "I don't dye my hair."

"Stephanie, you may want to choose your battles wisely and only protest if you can actually win," Sloan advised.

"What are you talking about?" Stephanie asked.

"We found your hair dye!" Jinx cried. "It's the same kind my grandmother uses. Sorry! I didn't mean to out you, Gram."

"Please," Alberta said. "No woman my age has hair this black."

"My father was Italian but left when I was very young and my mother raised me," Stephanie explained.

"And I'm guessing your mother wasn't Italian?" Charlie asked.

"No she wasn't."

"What nationality is your mother?" Jinx asked.

"What does it matter?" Stephanie cried. "I don't have to tell you anything!"

"Is there a problem out here?" Max stood at the head of the table holding a tureen of soup against his hip and a ladle in his other hand. "Because I'm about to serve the soup," he declared.

"That sounds wonderful, Max, thank you," Cathy said. "We could all use some home cooking right now to tide us over until the morning."

Max started doling the soup into everyone's bowls, and the atmosphere around the table quieted down a bit until Jinx, true to character, couldn't overcome her inquisitiveness or her impatience and continued to pursue her earlier line of attack.

"Was your mother French?"

"Oh, *Madon!*" Stephanie cried, her pronunciation of the word much different than it's ever been spoken before.

"You see!" Jinx yelled. "You don't even say *Madon* like a real Italian!"

"Also too," Joyce added. "Stephanie didn't even know that *Madon* was a word until a little while ago."

It was unclear if Stephanie responded out of fear or anger or a combination of the two. Her scream, nonetheless, was loud and unexpected.

"I know that you people think you're some kind of amateur detective team, and that's fine if it makes you feel better about yourselves," Stephanie said. "But do not try to investigate me."

"Then answer the question," Jinx demanded. "Where's your mother from?"

"All over!" Stephanie cried. "She's a European mutt and we traveled all over the world, if you must know."

Alberta had learned that opportunity could be a frugal visitor so when it arrived, you had to strike. And that's just what she did.

"Speaking of travel," Alberta said. "Have you ever been on a cruise?"

"Me?" Stephanie asked.

"No," Alberta corrected. "Max."

Max hesitated before filling up Alberta's bowl with lentil soup. It was enough of a pause, however, for the others to notice and for Alberta to know that her instinct was indeed correct.

"So have you, Max?" Alberta repeated. "Been on a cruise."

"That's an odd question," Max replied. "Why do you ask?"

"Since this vacation has turned out to be not nearly as restful as we initially hoped, I was thinking of taking my family on a cruise," Alberta lied. "But I'm not sure about it. You hear so many terrible stories."

"People are always getting sick from rampant viruses on a cruise," Sloan said.

"Or falling overboard accidentally," Freddy added and then smiled impishly at Jinx. "Especially, you know, if they go for their honeymoon."

"So, I was wondering if you have any experience being on a cruise," Alberta said.

"Berta, you never mentioned a cruise before," Joyce said.

"I was keeping it a secret, but when Stephanie mentioned travel it popped into my head," Alberta explained. "So, Max, you still haven't answered me, have you ever been on a cruise?"

Again, Max paused, but this time he didn't try to hide it. Whatever he was thinking he kept his expression blank so no one could tell if he was seething at Alberta's question or contemplating why she asked.

"Do you need me to repeat the question again?" Alberta asked.

Freddy leaned to his right and whispered to Jinx, "Any idea where your grandmother's going with this?"

"I most certainly do," Jinx whispered back. "I can't believe I didn't notice it sooner."

"Do you want to fill me in?" Joyce asked, leaning to her left and whispering in Jinx's ear. "Because I'm completely lost."

"Keep listening, Aunt Joyce, Gram will explain it all."

"No, I don't like the water," Max replied, retreating to the kitchen.

"That makes sense," Alberta said, swirling her spoon in her soup. "I guess you much prefer the ice."

"Looks like you don't prefer your soup, Alberta," Cathy said, trying to steer the conversation onto safe territory.

"It looks good, but it smells sour," Alberta said. "I think I'll pass."

Jinx and Joyce smelled their own soup and it smelled delicious. They watched Freddy and Sloan do the same thing and could tell from their faces that their soup had the same intoxicating smell. Either something was wrong with Alberta's olfactory senses or she was trying to tell them something. But what that something was no one could tell.

"That's ridiculous!" Stephanie cried. "My soup is delicious and it smells fine."

"I agree," Cathy said. "I have suffered enough humiliation this week and I refuse to add to it any thought that Max can't cook or that I would serve my guests sour soup."

With that, Cathy got up, spoon in hand, and walked around the table to where Alberta was sitting. "I may only be Italian by marriage, but I know the number one rule in an Italian household."

"What's that?" Jinx asked.

"We all eat from each other's plates," Cathy said. "Or bowls."

With an exaggerated flourish, Cathy dipped her spoon into Alberta's bowl, and raised the spoon to her lips. Jinx watched Alberta's face fill with fear, and just as Alberta reached up to grab the spoon out of Cathy's hand, Max raced to the table and did the deed for her.

"No!" Max cried, knocking the spoon to the floor.

"Max!" Cathy cried. "What did you do that for?"

Speechless, Max stood in front of Cathy, his face red and his chest rising and falling.

"Max! Answer me!" Cathy demanded.

"Maybe he'd answer if you called him Simi?" Alberta suggested. "Or how about Maksim? Which is your real name after all."

As the other guests began to murmur and ask each other what was going on, Max finally regained control of his voice. "My name is Max Morrow."

"Which is an Americanized version of your real name, Maksim Morozov," Alberta insisted. "Simi for short."

"That's brilliant, Gram!" Jinx cried. "But it stinks too."

"Why does it stink, lovey?"

"Because I should've figured that out," Jinx whined. "I'm the poster child for nicknames. I mean, seriously, who has a better nickname than I do?"

"No one I know, lovey," Alberta agreed. "Now, Simi, are you ready to confess?"

Suddenly Max's hulking stature deflated and he looked like a little boy caught stealing by his mother. "How? How do you know that?"

Alberta smiled. She wasn't happy about what she had to say next, but she was happy that she could still speak.

"Never underestimate an old lady, Simi," Alberta declared. "I know your true identity just like I know you were going to poison me because you know that I found out you're the killer."

"That's crazy!" Cathy cried.

"Se non è zuppa, è pan bagnato," Alberta replied.

"Stop talking in tongue and speak English!" Stephanie yelled.

"I think she said if it's not soup, it's wet bread," Joyce translated.

"Very good, Joyce," Alberta praised. "You haven't lost your Italian at all."

"Maybe not," Joyce said. "But what in the world does it mean?"

"Six of one, half dozen of the other," Alberta explained. "Max was going to kill me with poisoned soup in the same way that he killed Dimitri."

CHAPTER 22

Cotto a puntino.

Jinx was as shocked by Alberta's accusation as the rest of the people around the table, but she felt even more blindsided because she had expected her grandmother to confide in her before she made such an announcement. But knowing her grandmother the way she did, Jinx knew that Alberta had more than likely remained silent to protect Jinx and keep her in the dark so she didn't act impetuously and get herself into danger.

Reluctantly, Jinx had to admit that she could sometimes, well oftentimes, act first and think later. And when dealing with murderers it was always best to do some thinking and have an exit strategy before tossing out an accusation. Otherwise she could unwittingly put her life in danger as well. Which, come to think of it, was exactly what Alberta had done since she was accusing Max of homicide while they were stranded and snowbound at a remote mountain lodge. Like grandmother, like granddaughter, Jinx thought.

Looking around the table, Jinx could see that while Joyce, Sloan, and Freddy were surprised by Alberta's announcement, there wasn't a flicker of doubt in their eyes—they believed Alberta was telling the truth. It was a testament to her grandmother's growing confidence that when she spoke, people listened. She couldn't be prouder of her at that moment. Or more scared.

Max hadn't said a word in his defense yet, but he was seething. Cathy was equally furious, but unlike Max, she refused to remain silent.

"That is absurd!" Cathy shouted. "Max would never do such a thing."

Alberta merely smiled, visibly unconcerned by Cathy's outburst. "How can you be so sure about that?"

"Because I've known Max almost my entire life," Cathy replied. "I know the man and I know what he's capable of, and Max is not capable of murder."

"Max might not be," Alberta said. "But murder is definitely in Simi's wheelhouse."

"I still can't believe that you're Maksim Morozov!" Charlie interrupted. "I haven't heard that name in decades."

"Neither did Dimitri," Alberta said. "Until he sat down for dinner that fateful night on the cruise and had his last meal."

"Alberta, I know that you believe what you're saying, but it isn't true," Cathy protested. "Max didn't poison Dimitri. He died of a heart attack, it's that simple."

"There's nothing simple about this whole affair, Cathy," Alberta replied. "Just ask Stephanie."

"Oh my God!" Stephanie cried. "You people are insane! Why are you so obsessed with me?"

"Because you're so obsessed with Pamela and everything to do with her!" Alberta shouted.

"I was her assistant, not her stalker!"

"You were both and you were stalking her long before you started working for her," Alberta said. "Isn't that right?"

"I don't have to take any more of this." Stephanie got up from the table, but before she was near the doorway, Jinx and Freddy ran over and blocked her from leaving.

"Are you going to keep me a prisoner in this room?" Stephanie asked.

"No, we're just not going to let you out of our sight," Freddy replied.

"I didn't know you cared, Freddy," Stephanie replied sexily. "You might want to put a leash on this one, Jinx. He might not be so into you as you think."

"Your chances of stealing my boyfriend are about as good as you getting away with whatever crime you're concealing," Jinx stated. *"Negativo!"*

"Berta?" Joyce asked. "Has Stephanie actually committed a crime?"

Alberta smiled a bit maliciously and said, "Why don't we start at the beginning when both Max and Stephanie were on the cruise together."

"What?" Stephanie cried.

"Is that true?" Cathy asked looking directly at Max and not at Stephanie. His silence told her and everyone else what the answer was.

"Cathy, you may not have known that there was poison in my soup, probably the same poison that was in Dimitri's," Alberta started. "But I guarantee that Stephanie knew it."

"You think the two of them were in cahoots from the beginning?" Sloan asked.

Tilting her head from side to side, Alberta replied, "I'm not sure if it was coincidence or prearranged, but I do know that they were both on the same cruise together."

"How in the world could you know that?" Charlie asked. "What are you, psychic?"

"No! She's smart, you idiot!" Jinx yelled, slapping Charlie on the shoulder. "Now pay attention to my grandma and you might learn something. Go ahead, Gram, the floor is yours."

"Thank you, lovey," Alberta said smiling.

She got up from the table and to her surprise her legs weren't shaking. She had been in this position before, at the point of disclosing the motive and specifics about an unsolved murder, but there was something different this time. Maybe it was because there was truly no escape from Icicle Lodge and no one was going to be able to run away or, and she hoped this was the real reason, she was stronger than she was before. She trusted herself and she knew that she was right, not by instinct alone, but good old-fashioned detective work.

"I recognized Max from the photo Jinx found in your office," Alberta said.

"You were in my office?" Cathy said, visibly stunned.

"Yup. And we saw your really extensive montage of Pamela's career," Freddy said. "Dude, it was like some totally inappropriate piece of art or something you'd see on those real-life murder stories on cable. Definitely not something I'm going to be able to get out of my head anytime soon."

"That's private property!" Cathy shouted. "I could have you arrested."

"We might be able to say the same thing about you," Jinx retorted. "Carry on, Gram."

"Even though Max was wearing a toupee and had facial hair in the photo, there was one feature that could not be hidden," Alberta said. "His eyes."

Everyone turned to look at Max and scrutinize his

eyes. Suddenly they all saw what Alberta had seen days before.

"Eyes that beautiful and painful are hard to hide," Alberta explained. "He was wearing a shirt and tie, but crumpled in his left hand, obscured by Dimitri's wife, Galina, who was sitting at the table in front of him, was a white cloth or more precisely a chef's apron. It wasn't hard for me to connect the dots after that."

"That's excellent detective work, Berta," Sloan said, his voice filled with admiration. Which was quickly followed by caution. "But where does Stephanie fit in?"

"Pamela mentioned that Stephanie liked to control things and referred to her as Julie McCoy, the cruise director from *The Love Boat*," Alberta conveyed. "At first I thought it was just a joke, but once we found the photo of Dimitri on the cruise ship, I realized she could have been making a literal reference."

"That's the clue you're talking about?" Stephanie asked, sounding not nearly as impressed as Sloan.

"I also recognized the tattoo."

Involuntarily, Stephanie pulled on her sweater to cover the exposed flesh near her left shoulder.

"She's got a tattoo?" Jinx asked.

"The same one as the blonde in the photo," Alberta started. "When Charlie fell on top of Stephanie earlier in Patrick's room, her shirt got pulled down and I saw it. They're identical."

"A lot of people have tattoos," Stephanie said in her defense.

"Add to it the fact that your real hair color is most assuredly blonde and we've found the cruise director of Dimitri's fatal trip," Alberta declared.

"You can never prove it," Stephanie spat.

"We can if Max tells the truth," Alberta said. "Max,

did you get coloring tips from Stephanie before you decided to dye your hair blonde?"

Finally Max could no longer listen or avoid speaking. When his voice was finally heard it was remarkably softer than anyone expected.

"I wasn't working with her," Max said. "The moment she arrived on the ship, I told her to leave, but she wouldn't listen."

And just like that Stephanie got chattier too. "Because I had a goal in mind, that's why!"

Surprised by Stephanie's outburst, Alberta had to think quickly and decide if she wanted Stephanie to continue talking or if she wanted to take over the reins as cruise director herself and control the situation. Alberta chose the latter.

"You'll have your turn, Steph, but for now I want to focus on Maksim," Alberta announced. "Tell us, Simi, what did Dimitri do to you to make you want to murder him?"

When Max opened his mouth, Jinx clutched Freddy's arm as if she needed to brace herself and assure her footing to hear the explosive confession. But after taking a sharp intake of breath, Max's lips closed tight and all that could be heard was the sound of the wind howling against the large panel of windows. It was a sound that soon had a rival.

The primeval cry that erupted out of Max's throat was both frightening and heartbreaking. Pain, passion, pity were all splattered throughout the room as Max grabbed the sides of his head and bent forward with such speed that it looked like he was going to bash his forehead into his knees. Still bent at the waist, his head dangling forward, he screamed again, this time his cry was a bit more muffled, but still deeply felt by all those in the room.

"Don't say anything, Max," Cathy ordered.

Standing up straight, Max looked at Cathy, his eyes aching, his cheeks stained with tears. "I can't keep quiet any longer," he confessed.

"Max, please, don't say another word," Cathy pleaded. "Remember he did this to all of us."

"No, you're the one who suffered the most," Max replied. "It was supposed to be a celebration, it was supposed to be the best time of our lives."

"What was, Max?" Alberta asked as unobtrusively as possible.

"The Olympics," Max answered. "It was supposed to be the beginning of our future, but that never happened because of Dimitri."

"Max, shut up!" Cathy declared.

"I don't understand you, Cathy," Max said. "Your life changed forever that day, you're the one who got sick."

"Ah, *Madon*! That's it!"

Jinx desperately wished she knew what her grandmother meant, but she had no idea. She was trying to follow the trail of logic, but kept getting lost. Max was actually Maksim "Simi" Morozov, Dimitri Vasilievsky's assistant coach. Something happened at the Olympics that destroyed Cathy's and most likely Patrick's lives while Pamela won gold and became an international figure-skating sensation. As a result of those events, Max was forced out of coaching and became a cook and wound up years later on a cruise ship as a chef who served poisoned soup to his former boss and killed him. For some other unknown reason Stephanie was on the same cruise, which meant she was either connected to Dimitri or Max or possibly both. And despite knowing all of that, Jinx was still having trouble understanding how her grandmother could make sense of Max's last comment about Cathy getting sick.

"That's it!" Alberta repeated. "Cathy had to withdraw from the Olympics because she had the flu."

"How did you know that?" Cathy asked, completely shocked. "No one knew that, we didn't tell any of the reporters and we lied to the officials, we said that I reinjured my back."

"Why would you lie about such a thing?" Alberta asked.

"Because Dimitri didn't want anyone to think that Pamela could have caught our illness," Cathy replied. "She needed to be protected at all costs."

"Because no one else mattered except Pamela," Max added.

"Pamela didn't want to become another Caryn Kadavy," Charlie announced.

"Who?" Sloan asked.

"U.S. bronze medalist, was in sixth place after the short program at the Olympics, then withdrew because she got the flu," Charlie explained. "It's the definition of 'totally sucks to be her.' "

"That's true, but seriously, Alberta, how did you know that happened to me too?" Cathy asked.

"You and Patrick are both obsessed with flu shots and each claimed the flu could ruin your life, Patrick even slipped and said it could ruin your career," Alberta explained. "I would say withdrawing from the Olympics could qualify as having your career ruined in one fell swoop."

"It's definitely a tragedy to have to withdraw from the Olympics," Sloan said. "But enough of a tragedy to kill someone over it?"

"Yes!" Max bellowed. "Dimitri knew that the flu was

going around, but he refused to let any of his students get a flu shot because he was worried it would show up on a random doping test and they would be banned from skating. He was old school, behind-the-red-curtain Russian and trusted no one. He was so paranoid he didn't even protect himself and get the vaccine."

"This is ancient history, Max," Cathy reminded him.

"No, it's *our history* and it's the reason she became a star and we were left behind," Max explained. "Dimitri grew up in the old system where the West always tried to find ways to ruin Russia, and he didn't want to give those *Yankee bastards* as he liked to call them any more ammunition."

"So what happened?" Sloan asked. "Did Cathy get sick with the flu?"

"Yes, thanks to Dimitri," Max said.

"He had the flu and passed it on to everyone?" Alberta asked.

"Not everyone," Max said. "Only Cathy."

Max explained that when Dimitri felt like he was coming down with the flu, he made Pamela skate outside of the Olympic grounds by herself. Everyone thought it strange, but they chalked it up to Pamela's growing status as a prima donna on and off the ice. While Pamela was away in a no-flu zone, Dimitri worked with Cathy and Patrick and gave them his undivided attention, and he gave Cathy the flu. After she and her brother skated their short program and came in a surprising eighth place, Cathy got violently ill. Although she wanted to skate through the pain, she could hardly lift her head off her bed let alone dazzle them on the ice.

"Which explains the note that Pamela left in her room," Jinx said. "Pamela's apology was to Cathy for standing behind Dimitri and not stopping him from infecting her alleged best friend."

"That deliberate betrayal ruined your career, yours and Patrick's," Max started. "And you never got over the shame and the emotional trauma of having to withdraw from the Olympics when you were only four minutes away from completing something very few others in the world have been able to do."

"So you killed Dimitri to avenge Cathy having to withdraw from the Olympics?" Alberta asked.

"No, I killed Dimitri because he sabotaged my career," Max said plainly. "And then he destroyed it with his comments and insinuations and lies! I couldn't get hired anywhere, which is why I became a chef. It was the only thing I could do to feed my family."

"And it's how you wound up on the cruise where you met Dimitri and Stephanie," Alberta said.

"It was all by coincidence," Max replied. "But the second I saw Dimitri walk into the ballroom on the boat, I knew that the perfect opportunity had fallen into my lap. I dyed my hair so he wouldn't recognize me, and then I took advantage of what fate had brought to my front door."

"*Cotto a puntino*," Alberta said. "And it surely was a meal cooked to perfection."

"I'm not proud of what I've done," Max declared. "But I had to do it. I wouldn't have been able to live with myself if I didn't get revenge for all of us, you, me, and Patrick."

"Oh, Max," Cathy pleaded. "We didn't need you to avenge us."

Max laughed maniacally and slammed his fist down on the table. "Don't be like her, Cathy! Don't be an ingrate. I did what I had to do to protect us."

"Which is exactly what you did for Max, isn't that right, Cathy?" Alberta asked.

"What are you talking about?"

"Maybe you didn't have proof, but you knew in your heart that Max killed Dimitri, and you also knew that he blamed Pamela for her role in the destruction of your career," Alberta explained. "And yet you still invited Pamela here to skate in the grand reopening ceremony."

"I thought it might bring us all together," Cathy said weakly. "Help us heal."

"Or maybe you thought it would be the perfect way for Max to kill two birds with one stone," Alberta revealed. "Seems to me that you set Pamela's death into motion, and it really does pain me to say this, but you're just as guilty of murder as Max is."

CHAPTER 23

La vendetta è meglio servita fredda.

"**Y**ou don't know anything about me," Cathy seethed. "If you did, you'd know how wrong you are."

Cathy's words sounded frighteningly similar to one of the last things Alberta's daughter, Lisa Marie, had said to her. Instantly, Alberta was taken back to the past, to a time before she moved to Tranquility, when her husband was alive and her daughter was living nearby with her family, and she felt her heart break. *If only I did something different,* Alberta thought. *If only I said something less hurtful maybe Lisa Marie would never have moved away and given up.*

The past couldn't be changed no matter how many hours were spent wishing it could be, no matter how many rosaries were said or how many prayers were made to God, the Blessed Mother, and all the angels and saints. Everything that has already happened remains the same, and the only thing that can be changed is the future. And Alberta was determined to say and do the right thing to uncover the truth and make sure that Pamela's murderer was handed over to the police.

Alberta was sometimes surprised at how strongly she felt when it came to solving a crime, but thanks to Jinx she had been given a purpose and it made her feel good. Because in a life and death situation, there are usually two sides—evil and good—and Alberta was proud to be on the side of good. Even if being on that side often brought with it more names in the enemies column.

"I thought you were my friend, Alberta," Cathy said.

That was a bit of an overstatement. Alberta and Cathy had certainly developed a relationship that given some time could have developed into a friendship, but at the present moment they weren't friends. There was also the matter of some secret piece of information Cathy wanted to share with Alberta. Nothing had yet been revealed or hinted as to the subject matter Cathy wanted to discuss with Alberta other than the fact that the conversation was to be private and kept getting interrupted. After the combative dialogue they were currently having, it wasn't clear if that conversation would ever take place.

"You shouldn't take this personally, Cathy," Alberta said, "I'm only trying to get to the truth."

"This is almost as riveting as the Battle of the Carmens in '88," Charlie commented.

"The what?" Sloan asked.

"At the Calgary Olympics, Katarina Witt and Debi Thomas both skated to music from the opera *Carmen* in their long programs," Charlie explained. "Katarina won and became the second woman in history to win back-to-back gold medals. No one else has done it since."

"That's fascinating, but Vinny told us not to mention that German skater's name," Freddy remarked.

"He told us not to say Katarina's name *in front of Pamela*!" Charlie screamed. "Pamela's dead! She's beyond upset."

"Will you two quit it?" Jinx shouted. "We're trying to solve this murder and you're not helping."

"Sorry, Jinx," Freddy said. "He just pushes my buttons."

"Like Alberta's pushing mine," Cathy said.

"With all the lies you and your ice posse here have been spewing, it's hard to untangle the web," Jinx added. "I mean, you've all been lying since the first day we got here."

"I'd like everyone to know that I haven't lied," Charlie interjected.

Freddy scowled at the man. "Dude, you seriously need to shut up and let the ladies talk."

Charlie scowled at Freddy, but since he was still nursing the shiner Freddy gave him with a bag of ice, he did as he was told and didn't risk another altercation.

"Thank you, Freddy," Alberta said.

Freddy beamed with pride at the acknowledgment and despite the seriousness of the situation, Jinx couldn't hide her own smile as she was delighted that two of her favorite people got along so well. But then one of her favorite people had to remind her that they weren't here to smile or laugh or get closer to each other, they were only here to get closer to the truth of who killed Pamela Gregory. And Alberta was inching toward that goal every time she spoke.

"You can't deny what you've done, Cathy," Alberta stated.

"I didn't kill anyone!" she protested.

"But you didn't do anything once you knew that someone was killed," Alberta continued.

"Alberta! How many times do I have to say it, I don't know who killed Pamela!" Cathy shrieked.

"I'm not talking about Pamela, I'm talking about Dimitri," Alberta corrected. "You knew what Max did and yet you kept quiet about it. Not only that, but you willingly set the stage for another murder."

Cathy began to pace the room and if the weather outside wasn't still blizzard-like conditions, someone would've have barred the door for fear that she would run outside and into the woods. But there was nowhere for Cathy to hide, and by the frantic way she kept shaking her arms at her sides and then running her hands through her hair, it was clear she understood that not only was she being accused of participating in a murder, she also had nowhere to run. There was no salvation except for the truth.

She turned to face Alberta and the others, and finally her body stopped moving. She stood still and breathed deeply. Slowly, her features relaxed and her shoulders lowered, her arms stopped shaking and she temporarily bowed her head as if she needed to avoid eye contact for a few moments while she found the courage and the words to continue. When she found what she wanted to say, she adopted Alberta's tactic and lobbed an accusation at her inquisitor.

"What would you have done if you suspected someone in your family of committing murder but couldn't prove it?" Cathy asked. Her voice was soft, but her words were explosive. "Would you turn them in to the police without sufficient proof and risk destroying their life? Or would you believe in their innocence and hope and pray every night and day that your baseless intuition was wrong?"

Alberta looked over at Jinx and Joyce and smiled wistfully. Cathy was using the family card. She may not have known Alberta for very long, but she knew her well and she knew that Alberta would answer the question in only one way.

"That's exactly what I would do," Alberta admitted. "But that's not to say it isn't wrong."

"See! You're just like me," Cathy said. "So stop persecuting me."

"She isn't persecuting you, Cathy, she's asking questions," Sloan said in Alberta's defense. "And you continue to avoid answering. Why did you bring Pamela here if you suspected that Max killed Dimitri, given your past history?"

"I told you! I thought it would finally bring us all together," Cathy clarified. "I knew it was risky, but for God's sake, I needed to make this lodge a success and Pamela owed me that much!"

"And she knew it," Max said. "That's why she accepted. Pamela knew that she needed to make up for her past sins."

"She was just a kid when it happened, Max," Cathy said, shaking her head in sympathy with her fallen friend. "Pamela wasn't able to fight back against Dimitri and neither were we. He was too powerful."

"Sounds like Dimitri was more than just a coach to all of you," Joyce remarked.

"He was like a father," Cathy said. "So when he betrayed me by not only choosing Pamela over me and Patrick, but deliberately putting me in harm's way while protecting Pamela, it took me years to come to terms with that. Could you imagine your father acting in such a way?"

"I could," Charlie confessed. "My old man was a *figlio di*—"

"Language, Charlie," Alberta interrupted before he could finish.

"Sorry," Charlie said, duly chastised. "Daddy was an SOB."

Thankfully none of the others could imagine their fathers causing them such pain, even though Alberta and Helen's father, Frank, could be—as their mother would often say—as strict as a Lutheran.

"You may find this hard to believe, but I never blamed Pamela," Cathy shared. "She was a kid at the Olympics. She was focused on winning gold and that's all she thought about. I'm not entirely sure she knew that Patrick and I withdrew until the closing ceremonies when we weren't there. That's the life of a figure skater, the only thing that matters is what happens on the ice, everything else is unimportant, irrelevant."

"But what about when the Olympics were over?" Jinx asked. "What about afterward when Pamela shot to stardom and you and Patrick were tossed to the side?"

Cathy turned away and stared blankly at the window most assuredly looking into her mind's eye and seeing the past. She smiled at some random memory and clasped her arms around her shoulders. When she spoke she didn't look at anyone as if she was addressing the Pamela she knew from so many years ago.

"She did what she had to do in order to survive," Cathy said. "The life span of a figure skater to make it big and recoup all the money that she and her family invested into her career is not very long. Pamela couldn't waste time worrying about why we left the sport. She had to focus on making as much money as possible to repay her parents and sock enough away because at some point thanks to age or injury a skater wakes up one day and can't skate anymore. Or at least not skate well enough to compete or perform in a show, and what then?"

"You open up a lodge and hope your former teammate will help make it a success," Alberta said.

"Exactly," Cathy replied. "And Pamela, despite everything, despite knowing there were still hard feelings, despite knowing that Patrick was still in love with her, despite blaming herself for not doing something to help us, she agreed. And how was she repaid? By getting murdered."

"Don't forget Patrick," Alberta added.

"How could I forget my brother?" Cathy asked disgustedly. "He's in the other room right now fighting for his life."

"And how did he get there?" Joyce asked. "Pamela surely didn't do it."

"But once again she was the reason for it," Sloan added.

Lines appeared on Cathy's forehead as she scrunched up her face and threw her hands in the air. "You people don't talk in straight lines, do you know that? I can never understand what you're talking about!"

"That's because you're too afraid to listen," Freddy said.

"Afraid? What am I afraid of?" Cathy asked.

"That Max struck again," Alberta announced. "Both times because of Pamela."

"I'm starting to get offended by every untruth that slithers out of your mouth, Alberta." Max's voice was as cold as the ice that Pamela died on. "You seem to have quite a lot to say even though you can't prove any of it is true."

"I've already proven that you were on the cruise with Dimitri," Alberta stated.

"Based on the eyes of some man in a newspaper photo," Max countered.

"And I've proved that your name isn't Max Morrow, but Maksim Morozov."

"So I changed my name to sound more American and how do you say? Assimilate."

"And thanks to Dimitri's widow, Galina, I also know a little bit about Simi that I don't think the rest of our group has figured out yet," Alberta teased.

"Gram, I'm the one who spoke with Galina," Jinx said, astonishment filling her voice. "How did you pick up on clues that I didn't even know existed?"

"Maybe you're not as smart as the old lady?" Stephanie suggested. "Or you're just stupid."

"Lovey, I've told you before, sometimes you have to listen with your heart and not your ears," Alberta said. "If you did, you might have heard Galina divulge Simi's secret."

"I don't have any secrets!" Max bellowed.

"So you're willing to admit that you were also in love with Pamela?" Alberta asked.

"What?" Cathy shouted.

"Galina said that Simi wanted more from Pamela than just being one of her coaches," Alberta explained. "But it wasn't meant to be. Based on how you acted when she was here, like a frightened, lovelorn puppy, I'm guessing you still love her and didn't like hearing that Patrick and she were having an affair."

"That's ridiculous!" Stephanie shouted. "I told you

before there were no clues that Pamela and Patrick were sleeping with each other."

"Then how did this get in Patrick's bedroom?"

Everyone saw the piece of gold jewelry Alberta was holding up, but no one knew exactly how it confirmed Patrick and Pamela were having an affair.

"Gram, could you maybe explain how that bracelet is a clue?"

"Because it's an ID bracelet with the name Pamela etched on it that I found under Patrick's bed," Alberta explained. "Proof that Patrick and Pamela were sleeping together. Isn't that right, Max?"

"Max, is this true?" Cathy asked.

"And how did it make you feel, Max?" Alberta asked. "Knowing that Patrick had the one woman you were denied."

"Don't be shy, Max," Stephanie said. "Alberta might be old, but she's not innocent, nothing you say will offend her. Tell her, in fact, tell everyone how you've been in love with Pamela your entire life."

"Come on!" Charlie shouted. "First you want us to believe you weren't on the cruise ship with Max, and now you want us to believe you know his innermost thoughts. You're like my wife, you make my head spin!"

Stephanie smiled devilishly, and more than ever appeared nothing like the awkward, insecure personal assistant she professed to be. "Let's just say that I know Max a lot better than most anyone else here."

"Shut up!"

Grasping the air with his hands, Max couldn't contain the anger and rage filling his body. He pounded his fists on the table causing it to jostle and jump an inch off the ground. His cheeks were beet red and some spittle was clinging to his lips. He was furious and for the first time since initiating the interrogation Alberta felt uneasy. She had the sneaky suspicion that very soon things were going to get out of control. But what choice did she have? She couldn't just call for a time-out. She couldn't tell everyone to go back to their rooms and sleep it off. No, there was nothing else she could do but continue down the path she had started. She did, after all, take the first step. She might as well take the next one.

"That's the real reason you killed Dimitri, isn't it, Max?" Alberta said. "Because he separated you from Pamela. He banned you from ever coaching her again and Pamela, the dutiful student, obeyed him and re-buffed every one of your advances."

"If it weren't for him we would've been together!" Max howled. "He took everything from me—my career and the only woman I ever loved! I should've killed him years ago!"

"And yet it wouldn't have changed anything when it came to Pamela," Alberta said.

"What?" Max replied, totally confused. "No, it would've changed everything."

"No, because Pamela never loved you," Alberta corrected. "She loved Patrick."

Max looked like he was about to explode. "Damn him!"

"And that's why you tried to kill him too."

Alberta looked over at Cathy after she spoke and could see that the woman was in turmoil. A man she knew almost her entire life, a man who she regarded as a family member, had tried to kill her brother. She didn't know what to do with the flurry of emotions swirling around in her head. She had no idea how to react or how to rationalize Max's actions. And so she shut down.

Cathy reached to her side and grabbed the back of one of the dining room chairs. Cautiously she sat down and allowed her body to relax. She looked at Max with perplexed eyes that begged him to contradict every word that she had just heard. But he couldn't. All he could offer was an apology.

"I'm sorry, Cathy," Max said, his voice breaking. "I didn't mean to hurt him, but I couldn't bear it. First Dimitri and then—"

"Patrick loves you like a brother, Max," Cathy said, her voice barely above a whisper. "Like I do. How could you?"

Cathy quietly cried and Max, at the other end of the table, bowed his head and his body started to quiver. They were both devastated that the truth had come out. Joyce, however, still had no idea how Alberta had come to the realization that Max was actually Russian, not to mention Dimitri's assistant coach.

"Berta, I know that you've done some pretty impressive things," Joyce said quietly as she stood next to her sister-in-law. "But how in the world did you figure out Max was Russian? Was it just because of your call with Galina?"

"Yeah, Gram, I just accepted the fact that you put two and two together," Jinx added. "But it's still adding up to thirty-seven in my head. How'd you do it?"

Without letting the rest of the group hear, Alberta quickly explained that she overheard Max saying words that she had never heard of and they were either dismissed as English words that he muttered or that weren't heard correctly. *Yept* is a common Russian exclamation, *sem'ya* means "family" and *d'yavol* means "devil." But when Alberta found the recipe for the gingerbread cookies, Max made it with a spice she had never heard of, *prynka*. It was a Russian spice very uncommon in America and not even that familiar to Russian bakers.

"It always comes down to food with you, doesn't it?" Joyce said, clearly impressed.

Jinx, on the other hand, was excited by the news.

"Wait a second," Jinx whispered so only Alberta and Joyce would hear. "I thought I heard Stephanie calling Cathy a prostitute."

"Lovey, I think Cathy's many things," Alberta declared. "But I wouldn't say prostitute was one of them."

"It isn't," Jinx confirmed. "Because *prost* doesn't mean prostitute in Russian."

"What does it mean?" Joyce asked.

"How should I know? I don't speak Russian," Jinx said. "But it sure sounds Russian and I'm convinced Stephanie is faking her Italianness no matter how many excuses she comes up with so chances are really good that our faux Italian is really a comrade."

"I think I can prove it," Alberta said.

"How?"

She smirked and told Jinx and Joyce to watch.

"*Kak vy sebya chuvstvuyete?*" Alberta said in a solid Russian accent.

"*Ya v poryadke, pochemu?*" The second after Stephanie replied she knew that Alberta had bested her and forced her to reveal her true heritage.

"You're Russian?" Jinx asked, shocked by Stephanie's words and flawless accent.

Her cover blown, Stephanie no longer had to keep up a façade. In a few seconds she transformed from the mousy assistant into a poised young woman. It was startling to watch and intimidating. There was suddenly a new person in the room that no one had ever met and no one knew how she was going to act.

"Of course I'm Russian," Stephanie replied, her

voice now tinged with an accent that previously remained dormant.

"I knew you weren't Italian!" Jinx cried. "But seriously, I didn't think you were Russian."

"I can't believe this," Max uttered. "You've been covering up your true nationality all this time?"

"I'd still be fooling all of you if it weren't for the old broad here," Stephanie said. "I have to admit, Alberta, you're old, but you're smart. How'd you figure out I'm Russian?"

"I've had my suspicions, but it all just clicked when Jinx said she overheard you say *prost*, which is the word for 'excuse me,' and I knew my suspicions were right," Alberta said.

"Since when did you learn Russian?" Joyce asked.

"I hardly know the language, just a few phrases I picked up since I've been spending more time in the research library thanks to Sloan," Alberta explained.

"I'm glad I could help," Sloan said smiling.

"What other clues were there, Mrs. Scaglione?" Freddy asked.

"The tattoo on Stephanie's shoulder is a hammer and sickle, isn't it?" Alberta asked.

"Part of my country's flag," Stephanie confirmed.

"Well, one of your country's flags," Alberta corrected. "The other one is red, white, and green, which were the colors you wore when you first arrived. I don't know if it was a deliberate costume choice, but the combination struck me as odd, and when I noticed they were the same colors as one of the Russian flags, it all added up. Stephanie Rangusso might sound like an Italian name, but there's nothing Italian about you."

Now that Stephanie's nationality had been revealed, it was time for her true identity to come out in the open as well.

"If you aren't Stephanie Rangusso, then who are you?" Cathy muttered.

Smiling in disbelief, Stephanie replied, "None of you know?"

"Hold on a second," Sloan said.

"What's wrong?" Alberta asked.

"Everyone's ignoring the most obvious question of all," Sloan said.

From the silence in the room it was obvious that no one knew what that obvious question was.

"I think you're going to have to spell it out, Sloan," Alberta announced.

"If Max met Stephanie on the cruise, which was before she reinvented herself and became Pamela's assistant, then Max must know her real identity."

"Tell us!" Jinx cried.

"Such a typical impatient American," Stephanie hissed. "Always so quick to judge and speak and act. You could learn from how the Russians do things. They take their time. They plot, they make sure that they control the situation, isn't that right, Simi?"

"You need to stop talking," Max ordered. "Right now."

"Why?" Stephanie asked. "You're afraid I'll tell the truth and it'll make you look even guiltier?"

"No one needs to know," Max pleaded.

"No more lies, Simi!" Stephanie screamed. "You knew that killing Dimitri when he least expected it, when his defenses were down and he thought his enemy had long forgotten their quarrels and had given up any thought of revenge, was the perfect time to commit murder. What's that old saying about revenge?"

"*La vendetta è meglio servita fredda,*" Alberta said.

"It's best served cold?" Sloan translated.

"Yes!" Stephanie shrieked. "Revenge is best served cold . . . like a good soup. I was right there when you served Dimitri his soup, I saw your eyes and I knew, but before I could intervene he had taken a sip. And that's all that he needed to do to finish out your plan. Right in front of Dimitri's daughter."

"Of course!" Alberta cried. "That makes perfect sense."

"It does?" Joyce asked, then corrected herself, "I mean, it does!"

"You were right all along, Jinx, I'm not Stephanie Rangusso, I'm Stefania Vasilievsky, Dimitri's daughter."

"Dimitri had a daughter?" Cathy cried.

"Papa didn't like to brag," Stephanie informed. "He had some dealings with some not-so-legitimate businessmen and so he made sure very few people knew about my mother and about me."

"I didn't suspect you were Russian, and I would never have guessed you were Dimitri's daughter," Jinx said. "I have to admit it, Stephanie, you fooled me twice."

"My name's Stefania, isn't that right, Simi?"

"Yes," Max replied guiltily.

"Well, Stefania, you're more than just the coach's daughter," Alberta declared.

"And just who do you think I am, little Mrs. Amateur Detective?" Stephanie asked.

"You're also Pamela Gregory's killer."

CHAPTER 24

Tale padre tale figlia.

Laughter filled the lodge quicker than the snow was falling outside.

All eyes were on Stephanie as she hunched over, her hands pressed onto her knees, her long, dyed-black hair covering her face so no one could tell if her laughter was genuine or rather a manufactured ploy to give her time to consider how to defend herself.

When she finally stood up, her right hand on her hip, her left brushing her hair and some tears out of her face and eyes, she did not look like someone who had just been accused of killing her boss, but more like someone who was still playing a hilarious, unexpected moment in her head.

"You have really been watching too many American TV shows," Stephanie said, her Russian accent thick and defiant. "Are you trying to be that old lady mystery writer who solved murders every episode? Or maybe you think you and your family are those angel girls who worked for Mr. Charlie."

"You can try to deflect and avoid the question,

Stephanie or Stefania or whatever your name is," Alberta said. "But the truth is you killed Pamela."

"Did anyone see me do it?" Stephanie asked the group. When silence was her answer, she continued. "Is anyone here psychic? Did Pamela reach out from the great beyond and tell you it was me?"

"She didn't have to," Alberta said, her voice stronger than it had been in quite a while. "Because we investigated, we put the clues together, and came to one solution, that Max may have killed Dimitri, but Dimitri's daughter is the one who killed Pamela."

A flash of panic washed over Stephanie's face. It didn't last long, but something about the way Alberta spoke made Stephanie question if she was going to be able to talk her way out of this. So instead of searching for the right words to convince the others that she was innocent, she challenged Alberta to explain how she was guilty.

"Tell me, Alberta," Stephanie said. "Why are you so certain that I killed Pamela when there are many other possible suspects right here in this room?"

Smiling, Alberta was delighted that Stephanie had tossed her the line so she could explain how she had come to her conclusion. Before she spoke she marveled at how all her life she had never sought the spotlight, and now, in the golden years of her life, she had become comfortable being the center of attention and even, she admitted to herself, enjoyed the glare of the light.

"It's against Max's nature to be violent," Alberta said. "He may have murdered Dimitri, but it was a passive act, an act that he didn't need to be present for, an act that required no physical contact whatsoever, which is completely the opposite of how Pamela was killed. Her murder was one of aggression, rage, even symbolism, none of that occupies Max's mind."

"That's very insightful, Berta."

Alberta didn't turn around to thank Sloan directly, she merely smiled and glanced to the side to look at him. She would thank him for his support later, but she still wasn't finished speaking to her audience.

"When we spoke with Galina, she spoke about Simi," Alberta shared. "Jinx, do you remember what she said about him?"

Jinx pondered and tried to recall everything that Galina had said, acknowledging that there were many things she didn't understand at the time. She replayed the conversation in her mind and stumbled upon the adjectives Galina used to describe Simi that Alberta was referring to.

"She said he was kind and gentle," Jinx revealed. "And that she felt sorry for him."

Beaming at her granddaughter, Alberta replied, *"Molto bene."*

"That doesn't mean anything," Stephanie said, rolling her eyes in disdain. "People crack, people change, just because my mother, who by the way is an *idiot*, thinks Max was kind and gentle when he was younger doesn't mean he stayed that way."

"I hate to agree with the enemy, but she's right," Joyce reluctantly agreed. "We all thought Stephanie was this dowdy, socially awkward personal assistant, and she's basically a Russian spy."

"What do you think this is, some James Bond movie?" Stephanie snarked.

"Maybe not, but remember what happens in all those movies, Stephanie," Sloan said. "The villain always gets caught in the end."

"And because Max and I are Russian we're the villains?" Stephanie cried.

"No, you two are the villains because you two are the only murderers in the room!"

Alberta's uncharacteristic scream shocked everyone into silence. They were all watching her and stayed transfixed when she started walking slowly toward Stephanie. Jinx moved to follow her grandmother, but Freddy grabbed her arm to stop her, and Jinx understood it was time to let her grandmother walk the tightrope on her own. Although Jinx was worried for Alberta's safety since she was dealing with a loose cannon in the likes of Stephanie, she knew that her grandmother had a bunch of loved ones right behind her as a safety net.

"If Max was going to kill Pamela, he would've poisoned her like he was going to poison me," Alberta said, taking each step slow and deliberate, the soft heels of her shoes making a muffled sound that created an unexpected tension in the room. "He wouldn't have slit her wrists and left her to die in an ice rink where she had seen her greatest triumph. Only someone much more devious and vindictive and vengeful could have done something like that. Only someone who was filled with so much hate that it flowed out of her skin like the scent of garlic after a good meal could kill Pamela in that way. And there's only one person here who fits that description."

Alberta stopped moving and was an inch in front of Stephanie who was equally immobile, her body frozen, her face a mask. Her eyes, however, were struggling to remain focused on Alberta and were darting around, twitching, and altogether betraying the steely, unaffected persona she was so valiantly trying to convey.

"And that one person is you."

Like a lemming at the edge of a cliff, like a hungry vulture hovering over a gazelle in its final moments before death, Stephanie had no other choice and so she finally told the truth.

"Yes! I killed Pamela and with that one act I proved I'm more of a man than Max will ever be!" Stephanie wailed. "He took the easy way out when he poisoned my father! He killed like the coward he's always been! You, Max, are nothing but a *trus!*"

Freddy leaned over to Sloan and whispered, "I'm guessing that means *coward* in Russian, right?"

Sloan frowned and shrugged his shoulders. "I can barely understand the conversation when it's in Italian, you think I can translate Russian too?"

"Yes, Max is a coward, always was and always will be," Stephanie sneered. "He's nothing more than a scared little boy that all I had to do when he saw me here was threaten him, tell him that I would expose him for the lying murderer he was if he ever told anyone that we had already met on the cruise ship. and instantly he kept quiet, afraid to tell a soul."

"I can't believe you went along with her, Max," Cathy proclaimed. "Letting her fool all of us just to protect yourself."

Cathy looked at Max, but he could only hold her gaze for a moment before directing his eyes toward the floor.

"What choice did he have," Stephanie asked. "He knew I was on the cruise, he didn't know I was Dimitri's daughter—like I said, my father had enemies so we didn't advertise to the world that we were family. But Max did know I was the one person who was convinced he poisoned my father. So when we met here, I told him I would keep his secret if he kept mine."

"So many lies, Max," Cathy said in shock. "So many unnecessary lies."

"Necessity is the twisted mother of lying," Stephanie said. "Without lies we would all have to face the truth, and who here is capable of doing that?"

"You'd be surprised, Stephanie," Alberta asserted.

"Why don't you tell us your truth?" Jinx dared. "We know why Max killed Dimitri, but why did you kill Pamela?"

"The oldest reason in the book," Stephanie replied. "Revenge."

"That might be an old reason, but in this case it doesn't make sense," Alberta said. "Pamela didn't kill your father, Max did. If you wanted revenge, why didn't you kill Max instead?"

"You really are so American, so blunt, so obvious, no sense of poetry or karma," Stephanie ruminated. "You people in this country love to throw that word around, but you have no idea what it means."

"You're wrong, Stephanie, I do know what it means," Alberta admitted, "I just didn't know karma could be so cruel. You killed Pamela to deny Max the object of his affection, the love of his life. You killed an innocent woman to get revenge for Max taking away the love of your life, your father."

Eyes widening, Stephanie's smile grew so she looked like a delighted young woman instead of a cold-hearted killer. "And now, Alberta Ferrara Scaglione, I think you're an honorary Russian."

"But still a very proud Italian," Alberta said. "Because as an added bonus you got rid of the boss who you had grown to hate."

"And once again I'm lost," Freddy opined.

"This one I know," Sloan assured. "Alberta told Stephanie that she killed two birds with one stone."

"You know something, Sloan," Freddy confided. "The more I see Mrs. Scaglione in action the more I like her."

Trying to hide his growing grin, Sloan nodded. "So do I."

"It seems that you embrace your heritage as warmly as I do mine," Stephanie observed. "Your Italian roots cling to you like a vine."

"Or in your case a noose," Jinx added.

"You think I'm going to pay for what I've done?" Stephanie questioned.

"With your life!" Jinx shouted.

"Hold on!" Joyce shouted. "We've figured out the motive, but before we move on to the prosecution phase, I need to know about the execution of the crime itself. How in the world did you pull this murder off, Stephanie?"

Grinning, Stephanie looked like she was just asked to the prom and not questioned to explain how she committed murder. Still, when she spoke she was beaming with pride.

"With planning, determination, and a little bit of luck," she said. "I knew all along I was going to use a skate blade to slice Pamela's wrists. I mean, it was beautifully symbolic. Skating is what linked Pamela to Dimitri and Max, it was her life for better or worse. Originally I was going to sneak in her room and kill her in her sleep, but really, that's so boring, isn't it? No sense of danger, no thrill. I mean, if you're going to take a life you might as well take yourself for a ride. Am I right? It wasn't until I saw Pamela practicing on the rink in the sunshine and with Lake Ariel and the mountains as the most gorgeous backdrop that I knew Pamela Gregory needed to die on the ice because it was on the ice where she was born."

Alberta winced, not because Stephanie's words and

tone were so callous and unfeeling, but because Vinny said the same thing. Where the hell was he? Before she could contemplate Vinny's disappearance further, Stephanie continued.

"But how to kill someone in daylight when they could fight back?" Stephanie posed. "When they're not capable of fighting back."

"You drugged her!" Jinx cried.

"Maybe you're not so stupid after all, Jinxie," Stephanie admitted. "The night before she was going to skate her routine, I added special ingredients to her protein shake. It was her habit, each night she'd make a shake, put it in the fridge, and drink it in the morning. She didn't disappoint."

"That's when we saw you sneak out of your room," Joyce said. "We thought it was to go on a rendezvous."

"It was," Stephanie said. "With fate. By the time I got on the ice, without my skates of course so I wouldn't leave a trace that someone else was on the ice with her, she was already groggy and was having trouble standing up."

"Poor thing must've been terrified," Joyce said.

"Let's hope so, Joyce!" Stephanie shrieked. "Seriously, that was the whole point. How do you think my father felt in the final moments of his life? When he realized the man he regarded as a son betrayed him?"

"Excuse me, why didn't Pamela scream?" Jinx asked. "We were all just a few feet away."

"Oh, Pamela did try to scream, but the poison I used makes it really hard to breathe and does some kind of damage to the vocal cords," Stephanie explained. "So as she was wobbling on her skates trying to stop the blood from gushing out of her wrists, all she could muster was a tiny, strangled, 'Help, help me.' "

Abruptly Stephanie stopped talking and was overtaken by laughter. "So pathetic. I wish she lasted a little longer before she collapsed, it was really entertaining. I also lucked out that Patrick was working in the shed so he didn't hear anything. And that Charlie sucks at his job and showed up late."

"I got a note from Pamela telling me not to arrive until the routine started and not a second before or else she'd—"

"Rip out your heart and take a photograph of it?" Stephanie said, finishing his sentence.

"How'd you know that?" Charlie cried.

"Who do you think wrote the note, you imbecile?" Stephanie replied.

"But Pamela was innocent," Cathy said.

"Pamela was guilty as hell!" Stephanie screamed. "She is the reason my father is dead."

"Your father set this in motion all by himself," Cathy shouted. "I should know better than anyone."

Once again Stephanie smiled broadly. "I know that you hated my father. I'm so glad it was your skate I used to kill that narcissistic, evil witch. Seriously, other than Max does anyone here really care that Pamela Gregory is dead?"

Alberta couldn't believe what she was hearing. "To think that I held you in my arms to comfort you after Pamela's body was found."

"I'm not a bad actress," Stephanie quipped. "I might have stumbled upon my true calling after all."

"Starring in the prison follies maybe," Jinx said.

Showing no signs of nervousness or anxiety now that she had confessed to premeditated murder, Stephanie surveyed the room and declared, "You underestimated me before, don't underestimate me now. I promise you I'll get away with this."

"Remember, *tale padre tale figlia*," Alberta said. "Like father like daughter."

"What do you mean, Gram?"

"Two things actually," Alberta stated. "Dimitri destroyed Max's life by using Pamela as a pawn, and Stephanie did the very same thing."

"And the other thing?"

"Dimitri paid for his deceitful actions with his life and so will Stephanie."

Any type of prosecution, retribution, or persecution would have to wait thanks to Helen's interruption.

"Max did it!" Helen shouted, running into the main room from Patrick's bedroom. "Patrick is awake and he said Max is the one who knocked him out and put him on the Zamboni all because they're both in love with dead Pamela!"

When no one reacted in shock, disbelief, or any emotion whatsoever, Helen wasn't entirely sure if anyone had heard her.

"Are you all *stunods*?" Helen cried. "I just explained what happened to Patrick, in his own words. Because he's awake!"

Finally she got a response, but still not the kind she was expecting.

"He's awake?" Cathy cried, running out of the room and to her brother.

"That's it?" Helen whined. "Nobody else cares that I solved the mystery?"

"Sorry, Helen, we already figured that out," Alberta confessed. "But thanks so much for letting us all know that I was right."

"What else happened while I was sitting vigil?" Helen asked.

"Stephanie confessed to killing Pamela," Jinx announced.

"That I did not expect," Helen declared. "Good work, ladies. I guess the only thing left to do is to call the police."

And yet again Helen said the wrong thing.

CHAPTER 25

È una tempest diversa.

When the police were introduced into the conversation, both Max and Stephanie realized that while they were sequestered in a hard-to-reach mountain lodge, there was a world waiting for them right outside, waiting for the snow to stop falling and the roads to clear so it could march right up to them, snap handcuffs onto their wrists, and haul them off to prison for the rest of their lives. The possibility of such action had been lurking in the backs of their minds since they had done their respective deeds, but thanks to Helen's statement it was thrust front and center. Unless they acted quickly, they would soon be at the mercy of the courts, begging for the leniency and salvation that they didn't show their victims. They came to the same conclusion at the same time.

Max ran into the kitchen and Stephanie ran for the front door.

Immediately the entire group sprang into action. Freddy and Sloan chased after Max into the kitchen followed by Alberta and Helen, while Jinx, Joyce, and Charlie ran after Stephanie toward the front entrance.

Max grabbed whatever he could from the kitchen counters and hurled them to the floor and into the air behind him to thwart his chasers from reaching him. Freddy deflected a large aluminum salad bowl with his forearm and Sloan jumped on top of the counter just in time to miss being hit in the head with a food processor.

"Sloan, be careful!" Alberta screamed from the kitchen doorway, clutching her sister's arm.

Just as Max opened the door at the back of the kitchen, Freddy leaped forward and tackled Max, pushing him against the door and slamming it shut. The two men tussled for a few moments until Max broke free and slammed his fist into Freddy's jaw.

Alberta and Helen cringed and cowered when they heard the impact. By the time they opened their eyes, Freddy was lying on the floor on top of Sloan, who he'd careened into on his descent to the floor.

The women waited for Sloan and Freddy to get up, but neither one of them moved. The only one on his feet was Max, and he was about to leave the room.

"C'mon, Berta, that one's getting away!" Helen cried.

She threw her pocketbook at Max and while the impact hardly hurt him, it did throw him off balance so he stumbled to the left, which was enough time for Helen to make it to the door and slam it shut once again. Alberta in the meantime ran to the other side of the kitchen so whichever way Max wanted to exit he was going to have to knock down an old woman to do so. Alberta and Helen were betting that he wouldn't be so violent, but they had forgotten that he was also desperate.

It took Alberta a few seconds to realize what Max was doing, but when she did she was terrified. He grabbed an aerosol can and shook it wildly. At the same time he turned on the stove so flames were licking the air where they should've been heating up the bottom of a pot or pan. Max positioned the can behind the flame and pressed down hard on the cap.

Like a cougar—or simply a devoted older sister—Helen sprinted toward Alberta and pushed her out of the way just as a blast of fire spread in a thin, angry line from the stove directly to where Alberta had been standing. Unfortunately, it was where Helen was now positioned so instead of the blast striking Alberta in the face, it struck Helen in her arm.

"Helen!"

Crawling on her knees, Alberta scurried to her sister grabbing the edge of the counter to stand up. She grabbed a towel to pat down the flames that had ignited on Helen's shirtsleeve. Pulling her sister to the sink, Alberta turned on cold water and placed Helen's arm underneath the faucet. The water quickly doused the flames and Alberta was able to peel away Helen's sleeve, which was both wet and charred, to reveal her burned flesh underneath.

"*Oh Dio mio!*" Alberta cried.

"It's nothing, Berta, I'll be fine," Helen protested.

"It's nothing?" Alberta scoffed. "You saved my life and look at you."

"Better a little burn on my arm then your face burned to a crisp," Helen remarked.

As Freddy and Sloan began to wake and get up off the floor, Alberta rummaged through the refrigerator and brought back a tub of butter. She handed it to Helen and said, "Rub this all over the burn, it'll soothe it and help it heal until we can get you to the doctor."

"Thank you," Helen said.

"What happened?" Sloan asked.

"Your girlfriend will fill you in later. For now will you three do me a favor?" Helen asked.

"What?"

"Go get that bastard who did this and make him pay."

They all looked around the kitchen, and their eyes fell on the open door that led to the hallway behind Cathy's office. Max had gotten away.

Meanwhile, a similar violent scenario had been taking place near the front entrance of the lodge. Just as Stephanie got to the top of the entranceway with Jinx, Joyce, and Charlie running up the stairs behind her, she was struck in the head by a shoe.

"Father Sal!" Jinx cried.

"I was trying to take a nap and you people kept waking me up with your shouting," he explained. "You were talking so loudly I'm surprised you didn't wake up Pamela."

"Did you hear what we were saying?" Jinx asked.

"Of course I did!" Sal protested. "I'm a priest, it's my job to listen. I overheard Stephanie confess and then saw her trying to flee the scene of the crime."

"Is it also your job to throw a shoe at the guilty?" Joyce questioned, standing over Stephanie's unmoving body.

"Well, I may not be without sin, but a shoe is not a stone so technically I'm not contradicting the Lord's word," Sal said.

"Guess my grandmother was right, Steph. You are going to pay for what you did."

Sal bent down to retrieve his shoe just as Jinx saw Stephanie's eyes open and wink at her. The personal assistant-cum-murderer wasn't yet ready to call it a day. For her, the fight had only just begun.

Stephanie grabbed Sal's hand as it was inches away from his shoe and yanked it down hard causing Sal to follow the motion and somersault on the floor. The motion caused his feet to bash into Joyce's legs and have her topple on top of him.

Next, Stephanie rolled to the left, grabbed the shoe, and swatted Charlie in the face as he lunged toward her, sending him sprawling down the flight of stairs that led up to the front entrance.

Without waiting to tackle Jinx, Stephanie got up and ran into the vestibule, the area between the exterior and the inside of Icicle Lodge. Jinx grabbed a chunk of Stephanie's hair just as she pushed open the front door, preventing her from getting outside.

"Let go of me!" Stephanie cried.

"Not on your life!"

Twirling around, Stephanie faced Jinx and stared at her with such venom Jinx thought poison darts were going to shoot out of every pore of her flesh.

"Not mine!" Stephanie howled. "Yours!"

With fury, both pent up and newfound, Stephanie pushed Jinx backward, and she landed with a thud on her back. Stephanie looked down at Jinx who was starting to pull herself together, and she smiled devilishly. She pressed a foot onto Jinx's hip and all it took was one little push for Jinx to roll down the flight of steps and lie motionless at the bottom. Stephanie allowed herself one moment of glory to soak in her victory before heading out into the snowstorm.

The landscape surrounding Icicle Lodge was seriously out of control. Snow was everywhere, on the ground, in the air, falling slantways, accumulating in mounds, clinging to branches, and turning the land into a world both beautiful and dangerous.

As Stephanie ran toward the parking lot, she saw Max running in the same direction about a hundred yards away. Hot on his tail was Freddy, Sloan, and Alberta. Grateful for the diversion, Stephanie smiled and turned to continue running in the opposite direction. When she saw what came between her and the parking lot, her smile faded.

"Did you really think one tumble down a flight of stairs was going to stop me?"

Jinx was standing directly in front of the entrance to the parking lot where a snow-covered Jeep was Stephanie's only hope of escape. But there were other obstacles. Joyce was positioned to Jinx's left and Charlie to her right, so whichever way Stephanie moved she would have to fight off an opponent. Unless she turned around and ran toward Lake Ariel and the mountains. It was not what she wanted to do, but it was her only chance.

Screaming something in Russian that no one understood, but which they all knew was not something that could be repeated around a dinner table as part of friendly conversation, Stephanie ran as fast as she could through the snow aiming for the same destination as Max—the ice rink.

When she was a few yards behind Max, he looked over at her. While he was disgusted by her and what she had done to him, they were both fugitives so he figured it was better to band together with the enemy who was in the same predicament than with the enemy who wanted to make sure you never tasted freedom again.

The wind made it difficult to see very far, but the

group was able to witness both Max and Stephanie jump over the side of the ice rink and slide across its length as a shortcut instead of running all the way around. They saw them pass the Zamboni still stranded in the middle of the ice since Patrick was rescued, but lost them after that. While visibility was compromised, their hearing was not.

"What was that?" Alberta asked.

"It sounds like thunder," Freddy said. "How can this storm possibly get any worse?"

"*È una tempest diversa,*" Alberta said.

"That's right, it's a different kind of storm entirely," Sloan corrected. "It sounds like a car."

Careening around the side of the lodge was some sort of sport utility vehicle. It slid a bit as it rounded the curve, but as it bounced over the uneven terrain and got closer to them they saw the writing on the side of the truck—Tranquility Police Department.

"Vinny!" Alberta cried.

The truck barreled past them and around the ice rink at the same time that Max and Stephanie ran through the opening in the barrier that the Zamboni previously crashed through. The truck swerved in front of them causing Max to sprint around the Zamboni shed and Stephanie to run in the opposite direction.

"I knew the chief wouldn't let us down," Freddy announced.

But when the door of the truck opened and the driver stepped out, it was obvious that Vinny hadn't attempted to save the day, but someone else did.

"Tambra?" Alberta cried as she, Sloan, and Freddy ran toward her.

"Why'd you lie to me, Alberta?" Tambra cried.

Alberta wracked her brain to figure out what Tambra was talking about. She was hardly innocent, but she couldn't remember the specific lie Tambra was referencing. "Which lie?"

"The one about Pamela being among the living."

"Oh that one! I didn't want to alarm you . . . wait, you know she's dead?"

"Of course I do, Vinny told me."

"He told us not to say anything."

"To the public, not the police," Tambra said. "He instructed me to keep quiet until the roads cleared. He was hoping to solve the crime on his own by then."

"Have you talked to Vinny?" Alberta asked. "Where is he?"

"That's what I came to find out," Tambra replied. "After your phone call, I got nervous when Vinny didn't show up. I called the Pennsylvania state troopers, but they're dealing with so many weather-related accidents they couldn't focus. I tried to call and text Vinny, but he never responded."

"We've been doing the same thing," Sloan said. "We have no idea where he is."

"I do," Tambra replied.

"You do?" Alberta said. "Where?"

"He's here."

"What are you talking about?" Alberta cried. "We've looked everywhere and we can't find him. We've been worried sick."

"I tracked his phone's GPS signal and it's coming from the lodge," Tambra explained. "He's on this property somewhere. He has to be."

"Oh my God."

They all turned around as Jinx, Joyce, and Charlie caught up with them.

"Jinx, what's wrong?"

"I think someone is sending us another signal."

Jinx pointed at the Zamboni shed and specifically to huge puffs of smoke rising out of the roof.

"It's on fire!" Jinx cried.

Acting on professional instinct, Tambra pulled her gun out of her holster and ran into the shed. The group as one freezing, huddled mass followed behind, but they all stopped when they saw a wall of fire separating them from getting to the man tied up in the back of the room. Vinny, however, was thoroughly relieved to see that he finally had company.

CHAPTER 26

Una storia finisce, un'altra parte.

Alberta could not believe her eyes.
For a moment she thought she was hallucinating—the circumstances and the snow and her own adrenalin pumping furiously through her veins had finally gotten the better of her. She couldn't possibly be looking at her friend, sitting on the floor with his hands tied behind his back and his ankles stretched out in front of him bound together by thick, black electrical wire. There couldn't possibly be a white piece of cloth shoved into his mouth and tied around his head. And she couldn't possibly see a barrier of flames separating the two of them. It couldn't be and yet it was.

"Vinny!"

At the sound of Alberta's voice, Vinny shook his body wildly and bounced up and down on the concrete floor. His eyes stared at his friend with a combination of fear and relief. He was grateful that he had been found but knew it would be difficult for him to be rescued.

"He must've been kept behind that door," Tambra

said, over the crackling of the fire and the howling of the wind.

"What door?" Jinx asked, not seeing anything but the back wall to the shed.

"The one over there lying on the floor," Tambra clarified.

They all looked in the direction Tambra was pointing and saw a door lying on its side up against the side wall.

"Vinny must have kicked it open and ripped it right off its hinges," Joyce surmised.

"I can't believe he's been in there this entire time," Jinx said.

"If we don't figure out a way to get him out, he's going to stay in there," Charlie said.

Alberta understood how Vinny could have gone unnoticed since the Zamboni had been housed in the shed and blocked the door from view. What she couldn't understand was how the fire had started. It couldn't have spontaneously combusted on its own so there had to be a rational explanation. Luckily, Tambra had one.

"It looks like Vinny knocked over that gasoline can when he kicked the door open and some gas leaked out," Tambra informed. "And that wire must've gotten loose during the storm and fell into the spillage, starting the fire."

Thanks to his own determination to free himself, Vinny may have secured his own death. Or proven that he had friends who would risk their own lives to save his.

"Freddy, are you afraid of heights?" Tambra asked.

"No sir, I mean, no ma'am," he replied. "But shouldn't you be asking if I'm afraid of fire?"

Shaking her head, Tambra replied, "No, that's a given, everyone's afraid of fire, it'll kill you."

"That's certainly reassuring," Jinx deadpanned.

Tambra grabbed a ladder leaning against the wall and shoved it into Freddy's hands. "Take this ladder outside and use it to climb up to that window."

This time she was pointing at a small window on the wall above where Vinny was sitting.

"And just in case the window won't open, take this hammer," Tambra added.

"Will do," Freddy replied. "Charlie, make yourself useful for once and come with me."

"Don't you give me orders!" Charlie protested.

"Dude! Shut up and come with me to make sure the ladder doesn't fall!"

"Be careful!" Jinx shouted as Freddy and Charlie ran out of the shed, each carrying an end of the ladder.

"Always, dude!" Freddy shouted.

"Stop calling me dude!" Jinx shouted back.

Alberta looked at the window and how high it was off the ground and wondered how Vinny was going to be able to climb up to it. Tambra had that covered too.

"I have industrial length cord that we use sometimes instead of handcuffs," Tambra confided. "I'll throw that up to Freddy and he can tie it against the pole that runs down the side of the building."

"How do you know there's a pole running down the side of the building?" Alberta asked incredulously.

"I'm a cop," Tambra said. "It's my job to notice things."

And take calculated risks.

"What are you doing now?" Jinx asked as Tambra took a large gray blanket that was tucked between several boxes and wrapped it around her shoulders.

"Somebody's got to get the rope to my boss."

Before Alberta and Jinx could stop her, Tambra ran straight into the flames, almost her entire body covered by the blanket, and dove into a side roll so she landed on the other side of the flames, falling on the ground on her shoulder and rolling several times before stopping right in front of the back wall. Grandmother and granddaughter shrieked as they watched Tambra fling the blanket off her body and stomp out the few flames that had ignited on the cloth. They were amazed at the woman's bravery, and while they understood that she was doing her job, Alberta and Jinx both knew that she had risked her life because of her admiration and love for her boss. Vinny truly was a lucky man.

Immediately, Tambra ripped the cloth out of Vinny's mouth.

"It's about time!" he shouted. "I didn't think you'd ever show up."

"Ye of little faith," Tambra joked. "You know how I like to make a dramatic entrance."

"You better untie me quick so we can still make an exit," Vinny said. "Otherwise your heroism won't be worth anything."

Tambra quickly untied Vinny's hands and then they both untied his ankles. She helped him to his feet and although Vinny was wobbly after being held captive, he was so elated at being rescued that his body was overcompensating and his desire to survive was far outweighing his need for rest.

"Alfie!" Vinny shouted. "Are you alright?"

"Ah, *Madon*!" Alberta cried, raising her hands up to the heavens. "Don't worry about me! Worry about how you're going to get out of there."

"And p.s., I'm fine, too, Vinny!" Jinx screamed.

"Of course you are," Vinny shouted back. "You're with your grandmother."

"Don't waste time trying to flatter me," Alberta said. "Focus on staying alive!"

"I'm sure Tambra's got a plan. She always does," Vinny said and then turned to his detective. "You do have a plan, don't you?"

"Of course I do, chief," Tambra assured. "But first, duck."

"Duck? Why?"

"Just do it!"

Tambra wrapped her arms around Vinny's shoulders and made him squat down on the floor as shards of glass sprayed over them. When the downpour stopped, they stood up and saw Freddy looking through the window waving a hammer.

"Dude! You were so right. The window was slammed shut!" Freddy cried.

Vinny looked up and down the length of the wall that led from the floor to the window and turned to face Tambra. When he smiled devilishly at her, Alberta could see him through the flickering flames and was reminded of how he looked when he was a teenager. She was once again amazed that as much as time changed, it stood still.

"You want us to climb up to the window, don't you?" Vinny asked.

"That's my plan," Tambra replied. She looked up at Freddy and shouted, "Dude! Catch!"

She unfurled the electrical cord and threw it up to Freddy, who caught it with one try.

"Tie it securely to the pole outside," Tambra instructed. "And I mean securely! Vinny and I are going to climb up and if it isn't tight enough we'll fall to our deaths. Okay?"

"Sure, no sweat!" Freddy cried.

"That's easy for him to say," Vinny murmured. "Don't you think it would be easier if we just ran through the flames?"

"I'm not sure if you've noticed, chief, but your legs are doused in gasoline," Tambra reminded him. "I don't think it's a wise idea to jump through a wall of fire."

"You were always such a smarty-pants."

"Just trying to keep you alive, sir," Tambra replied. "Plus, that fire's starting to get out of control." Looking up at Freddy, Tambra cried, "Is it all tied up and secure?"

"Roger that!" Freddy cried.

"So, chief, be honest with me," Tambra said. "Are you up for this?"

Vinny looked up at the window and then at the flames and took a deep breath. "Not really, but it doesn't look like I have a choice."

"Glad to hear it."

"After you, detective."

"Don't even think about it," Tambra replied, a conviction in her voice that Vinny knew could not be challenged. "You first and I'll follow in case you fall on your ass and I have to drag you up myself."

Respect and admiration poured out of Vinny's eyes. He smiled and grabbed Tambra's shoulder before taking hold of the rope and starting to shimmy himself up the side of the wall. Halfway up he stopped to catch his breath and the flames exploded and doubled in intensity.

"I know you're tired, chief, but this is no time to rest!"

Vinny looked over at the flames and he didn't need Tambra to repeat her command. With renewed energy and determination, he reached up, pressed one foot into the side of the wall, and hoisted himself up. Above him Freddy was pulling the rope to help quicken the pace, and below him Tambra had grabbed on the rope and started climbing as well. The flames were growing and there was no time to waste to get out of there.

Alberta and Jinx watched them and prayed for the fire to lessen or at least remain the same until they were safely outside. But their prayers were interrupted when they heard the sound of a motor.

"What's that?" Jinx asked, turning around to inspect the parking lot.

"I don't know," Alberta replied. "It sounds like another car."

"Maybe they hijacked Tambra's truck!" Jinx shouted, running outside.

When they saw the vehicle speed away toward Lake Ariel, they knew the truck wasn't stolen, but something much more conducive to traveling in the mountains. Max and Stephanie were on a snowmobile and driving full speed away from the lodge.

"They can't get away!" Jinx cried. "Not after everything they've done."

"And they're not going to," Alberta assured. "C'mon."

Before Jinx could contemplate what was happening, she saw Alberta running over to another snowmobile slightly hidden underneath the snowfall and some bushes. Alberta brushed off as much snow as she could, hopped on, and started the engine. Jinx was amazed at her grandmother's moxie, but decided she was going to go along for the ride. She and Alberta were a team after all.

Jumping on the snowmobile, Jinx wrapped her arms around Alberta's waist and shouted, "Go get 'em, Gram!"

"That's exactly what I intend to do, lovey!"

Prior to this encounter with this kind of vehicle, Alberta had never ridden, let alone driven a snowmobile. But that wasn't going to prevent her from pursuing two murderers.

Alberta raced through the snow-covered terrain in pursuit of Max and Stephanie, who were about five hundred feet in front of them. All she thought about was bringing the two murderers to justice and, to a lesser degree, how wonderfully free she felt cavorting into the wilderness on a snowmobile with her granddaughter hugging her tightly. What more could a sixty-five-year-old broad ask for?

For the first two hundred feet or so, the road was easy to manage primarily because Max had kept to one of the main trails on the lodge's property. Even though there was heavy snowfall, the ground was still rather level so the ride was even and not terribly bumpy. But once he made a right turn around Lake Ariel and into the nearby woods, the road disappeared and the landscape was no longer snowmobile friendly.

"Hold on, lovey!" Alberta screamed as they plunged down about a foot from the trail onto a more natural path.

Swerving from one side to the other, Alberta had to keep one eye on the trees in front of her that seemed to sprout up out of nowhere and the other eye on Max and Stephanie's snowmobile so she could follow in their snow path. Luckily their vehicle was bright orange so it stood out among the white and brown all around them and was easy to see. If only the snowmobile was as easy to control.

Every once in a while the snowmobile lurched in the opposite direction Alberta was trying to steer it to, either because she didn't have the strength to maneuver the handlebars as quickly as she'd like or because it had a mind of its own. Alberta was betting on the latter.

"Gram, you have to go faster, they're getting away!"

"I'm trying, but if I go too fast I'm going to lose control."

Max didn't seem to be following Alberta's logic, and just as Alberta was thinking she didn't have the skills to maintain a chase in such a densely wooded area, she saw Max's snowmobile take a hard left. The right side of the snowmobile lifted up and Max and Stephanie were almost horizontal as they made the turn at full speed. A huge spray of snow cascaded like a fan after they sped off, and only when the snow fell to the ground did Alberta see why Max had made such a daring turn. He wasn't trying to outwit Alberta, he was trying to avoid a huge boulder.

Thankfully, Alberta had more time to prepare for making the turn than Max did, otherwise she would've crashed right into the huge rock.

"Don't let go of me, Jinx!" Alberta cried as she turned the handlebars to the left and held on as tight as possible.

Once she leveled out she gunned the gas to take advantage of the fact that Max had to slow down after nearly crashing. From her vantage point, Alberta could see that Max was still having trouble keeping the snowmobile moving in somewhat of a straight line, and she figured he'd damaged the vehicle in some way when he made such a hairpin turn. As much as she heard him gun his engine, he didn't seem to move any faster.

Leaning forward into the windshield, Alberta hunched over and felt a sense of irrational calm take over her body. It was as if she allowed the snowmobile to react to the ground, the bumps, the curves, the icy patches all on its own, and Alberta was simply a passenger, like Jinx, with no control over their destination. It wasn't true, of course, but it's how it felt to Alberta, and she loved every freewheeling, dangerous second of it mainly because it was so unlike her and so unlike most everything she had ever done in her entire life. It wasn't cautious, it wasn't planned, it wasn't expected. It was, however, filled with purpose and necessity, and it made Alberta feel alive.

Sitting behind her, Jinx felt the same way. Although her life had hardly been as regimented, narrow, and confined as Alberta's had been, Jinx, too, was not known to take extraordinary risks other than defying her mother and moving back to New Jersey after college. But as she held on to her grandmother, she realized that all the other aspects of her life were rather traditional—she had a good job, a wonderful boyfriend, and a nice apartment. The radical element of her life consisted of her relationship with her grandmother and her two aunts. She howled into the oncoming wind thinking that she had to join forces with three women, all over the age of sixty, to understand how it felt to be alive.

As Alberta leaned to the right and navigated the snowmobile onto a smoother path barely missing the side of a huge tree trunk, Jinx said a quick prayer asking God not to let her die just yet. She was hoping to make it past sixty as well.

Max had to take another quick turn to the right and spun out in a complete 360-degree turn that gave Alberta enough time to make a wide left and wind up side by side with the criminals on the lam. But she was almost out of time. She looked down at the controls and saw that a capital letter E was blinking red indicating that the snowmobile would soon be out of gas. If Alberta was going to stop Max and Stephanie from escaping into the woods, she was going to have to act soon.

"There's nowhere for you to go, Max!" Alberta yelled loudly so she could be heard over the engines and the roaring wind. "It's time to give yourself up!"

Max turned to face Alberta, but her snowmobile started to slow down due to its empty gas tank. The negative was quickly turned into a positive when Max turned to look over his shoulder to find out where Alberta was going and why she was slowing down.

"Max, watch!" Stephanie cried.

By the time he turned back to look straight ahead and see what Stephanie was warning him about it was too late and the snowmobile drove up the side of a tree stump, rose about seven feet in the air, and landed on its side.

Max was pinned underneath the snowmobile and Stephanie was thrown into a snowbank several yards away. Neither of them was moving.

Alberta drove her snowmobile next to Max's and she and Jinx jumped off and immediately began trying to tilt his snowmobile back on its skis to free Max. They weren't worried that he would run away, they were only worried that he would suffer permanent damage if they didn't get him out from underneath all that metal.

"Gram, this is heavy!" Jinx cried as she tried to push against the seat to lift up the snowmobile.

"Keep pushing, Jinx, I feel it starting to move," Alberta commanded.

Alberta pushed as hard as she could against the side of the windshield as Jinx pushed against the seat, letting the snowmobile fall back into the palms of their hands, before they pushed back even harder. On the fourth try the vehicle tilted all the way to the right and wound up standing upright long enough for them to each grab one of Max's hands and pull him far enough away and onto flatter ground.

"Are you alright, Max?" Alberta asked, kneeling down by his side.

The only response was a groan and some slight movement of his head, but at least they knew that he was alive. They looked over at Stephanie to make sure she was okay and not only was she alive, but she was running off into the woods.

"Sorry, Jinx, you're on your own," Alberta said. "I feel about as bad as Max looks."

"Don't worry, Gram, I got this."

Jinx sprinted after Stephanie and after a few strides she wasn't as confident as she had proclaimed. Now that she had stood still for a few minutes, her adrenalin wasn't flying on all cylinders and she felt the chill all around her. Her legs felt like cement logs and her lungs felt like they were filled with blocks of ice. Every time she took a breath she felt cold air strangle her throat. She figured the only reason Stephanie was still moving with any speed whatsoever was because she was desperate to escape.

Not wanting to disappoint her grandmother or let Stephanie get away, she slammed her fists into her thighs and with a roar ran up the hill after Pamela's killer. At the same time she heard another roar, but this one was coming from Tambra's truck.

She and Vinny must've driven around the other side since they were coming in the opposite direction that she was running. It didn't matter, the sudden arrival of the truck shocked Stephanie so much that she tripped and had to scramble to her feet just in time for the truck to swerve in front of her and make her twist her body to the right to get out of its way. When she did, she fell into a snow-covered bush and Jinx was able to leap over a fallen tree and right onto Stephanie's back.

"I told you, you weren't going to get away with murder!" Jinx cried victoriously.

A half hour later they were back in the main room of Icicle Lodge thawing out in front of a blazing fireplace. Stephanie and Max were sitting back-to-back, handcuffs holding them together making it difficult for either of them to move. Spread throughout the room were the rest of the guests, all of whom were ready to get back to their lives and away from the past week's adventure.

"I can't believe you and your grandma literally saved the day single-handedly," Freddy exclaimed.

"Technically if we did it together it couldn't be a single-handed victory," Jinx corrected.

"Dude! Don't contradict me!" Freddy yelled in mock outrage. "I'm giving my girl a compliment so just take it."

"Okay, okay, I'll take it," Jinx said, hugging Freddy tight against her still-cold body.

"Thank you, Alberta," Cathy said. "I don't think I can ever repay you for what you've done."

Patrick smiled up at Alberta from the couch. He was conscious, but definitely needed medical attention. For the moment, all he wanted to do was express his gratitude.

"Same goes for me," Patrick added. "I heard every word you said when you were by my bedside."

Smiling and blushing at the same time, Alberta took both Cathy's and Patrick's hands and replied, "Just promise me that you'll work hard and make this place a success. You deserve it."

"We're definitely going to try," Patrick said.

"So Vinny, was Max the one who tied you up?" Charlie asked.

"Sure was, he came up behind me and just as I could tell it was him, I saw the crowbar come down on my head," Vinny explained.

"Ouch!" Joyce yelled. "Berta, I thought you said Max wasn't a violent man?"

"I can't be right about everything, can I?" Alberta asked.

"What about the note I found in our room, Vinny?" Father Sal asked. "Did Max write that?"

"He must have. I didn't," Vinny explained.

"Which makes sense because Alfie was spelled wrong," Alberta said. "That was the first clue that you were in danger. The second was your text that said 'Help, br.'"

"Would you finally solve that mystery, Vinny?" Sloan asked. "What does the 'br' stand for?"

"Bronze."

"What?"

"Once I realized that Cathy and Patrick were the O'Dells, the figure-skating pairs team, I realized that the bronze medal we found was theirs because they won bronze at the U.S. National Championships right before the Olympics," Vinny explained.

It took Alberta a few seconds to pick her jaw up from the floor.

"For crise sake, Vin, that was your clue?" she shrieked. "You're the chief of police! If we only had that to go on, you'd still be locked up in the Zamboni house."

"I thought it was clever," Vinny said. "Not too obvious so the wrong people could figure it out, but enough for you to deduce it."

"Let me tell ya something, Vinny," Alberta said. "From now on leave the detective work to us, we get much better results."

"Speaking of results, chief, two more squad cars are on their way," Tambra announced.

"Thank you," Vinny said. "We'll get you all home in just a little bit."

"Not all of us, I assume," Cathy said.

"You're not going to put them in jail, are you, Vinny?" Alberta asked.

"We did protect a murderer, after all," Cathy said.

"This is technically out of my jurisdiction, but I have friends here and can put in a good word," Vinny admitted. "For now, the Pennsylvania authorities need to question you both and get your statements."

"Before any of that happens, Alberta, I really do need to speak with you," Cathy confided. "It's important."

"I know you've been trying to talk to me privately ever since I got here," Alberta admitted. "I guess this is as good a time as any."

"It's like something my husband Mike always said, *Una storia finisce, un'altra parte*," Cathy said. "One story ends, another begins. And since you helped solve the mystery of who killed Pamela, it's only fitting that I help solve another mystery, this one involving you."

"A mystery involving me?" Alberta asked.

"It isn't about you necessarily," Cathy corrected. "But you do play a major role in it."

"Sorry, Cathy, I'm very confused," Alberta confessed. "What mystery are you talking about?"

"The one involving your Aunt Carmela."

CHAPTER 27

La mia famiglia è la tua famiglia.

"How do you know my Aunt Carmela?" Alberta asked.

Jinx, Helen, and Joyce wanted to know the same thing but remained silent and waited for Cathy to respond. They didn't expect Vinny to talk for her.

"Just hear her out, Alfie," Vinny said.

Alberta looked at her friend inquisitively, but he merely smiled reassuringly and sat down on a chair near the fire. He was exhausted, but it was obvious that he knew about the secret Cathy had been desperate to share with Alberta since the moment she arrived at Icicle Lodge. Only now had she found both the time and the courage to speak.

"What's this all about, Cathy?" Alberta said. "And what's this got to do with my Aunt Carmela?"

"I don't mean to be cryptic," Cathy said.

"Well, you have been," Alberta corrected. "You've been dying to get me alone and tell me something since I first got here. Well, you have my undivided attention."

"Let's sit down," Cathy said. "And you all might as well join us, Carmela was your family after all."

Cathy led them to the love seat and chairs in front of the fire and Alberta, Helen, Joyce, and Jinx joined Vinny to sit around anxiously waiting for Cathy to disclose whatever information she had about Alberta and Helen's spinster aunt. Their minds were racing with the possibilities, but as so often happens when too many thoughts invade a mind at one time the result was chaotic silence. All the thoughts and ideas canceled each other out so what was left was a blank slate of nothingness.

That's how Alberta's mind felt as she stared at Cathy. She couldn't imagine what Cathy was going to tell her about her aunt, nor could she fathom why she would be the one to tell her. She had just met Cathy; how could she know anything about her aunt? How could she know anything about Alberta?

"As I said, you should all hear this because Carmela was your family," Cathy repeated. "But *La mia famiglia è la tua famiglia.*"

"What do you mean?" Alberta asked. "How is your family my family?"

"Carmela was your aunt," Cathy said. "But she was also mine."

"That isn't true," Helen barked. "We never met you before we got here. There's no way Aunt Carmela was part of your family tree."

"She was related to my husband, Mike," Cathy said.

"That's impossible," Alberta replied.

Even though she was convinced she was right, there was a tingling sensation in her gut that made her realize that she should listen to Cathy, and that whatever the woman was going to tell her would change her life. She wasn't wrong.

"I think you should spell out exactly what you're trying to tell us, Cathy," Joyce advised. "We all loved Aunt Carmela very much."

"So did my husband and I," Cathy replied. "And so did Mike's mother, Annette."

Alberta wracked her brain, but couldn't remember her aunt or anyone mentioning an Annette Lombardo before. Who was this person and how was she connected to her aunt?

"Who's Annette?" Alberta asked. "I've never heard of her."

"Annette or Nettie, as everyone called her, was, well, she was Carmela's girlfriend."

The women were stunned into silence not because they didn't understand what Cathy just told them nor because they had a problem with a woman having a girlfriend, but because they couldn't comprehend their spinster aunt having any sort of love interest in her life that they wouldn't have known about.

Alberta and Helen looked at each other as if they were asking, "Did you know?" They then stared at Joyce hoping she would confess that she had always known.

"Don't look at me," Joyce replied. "I'm as stunned as you are."

"Aunt Carmela was a lesbian?" Jinx asked, finally saying out loud the *L* word, which had hung in the room since Cathy's announcement.

"I honestly don't know if that's the label they would have used," Cathy informed. "But she was in love with Nettie and Nettie was in love with Carmela."

"I'm sorry, I don't mean to be a *stunod*, but how did

she have time to have a girlfriend?" Alberta asked. "I don't remember ever seeing her with another woman."

"I do," Helen said.

"Really?"

"A few times at some gatherings, in church, once at the market," Helen admitted. "I never thought anything about it and just assumed she was a lady friend."

"And not a *lady* friend," Jinx added.

"Lovey, this isn't funny," Alberta scolded.

"Oh, Gram, don't tell me that you're upset that Aunt Carmela was in love with a woman?"

"Of course not! Don't be silly," Alberta said. "I'm . . . I'm upset that she felt she had to keep it a secret from us. Cathy's family obviously knew."

"It wasn't talked about openly, it was more like the pink elephant in the room," Cathy explained. "The truth of the matter is that Mike never approved of their relationship, not entirely, but it wasn't because it was two women, it was never that. It was hard on Mike because Nettie was his mother and his father's widow and he wanted her to remain that way. When she became something else, it was an adjustment that he was never quite able to make."

Alberta felt her heart race and the blood start to pulse at her temples. She didn't want to ask her next questions, but she had to.

"Was he nice to Carmela?" Alberta asked. "Did he make her feel welcome in his home? I'd hate to think that he made her feel uncomfortable."

"They got along," Cathy said. "After a few years they even got to like each other, but Mike could never shake the feeling that his mother had betrayed his father. It was petty and unrealistic and he acknowledged it, but it's how he felt. And I swear to you it had nothing to do with the money."

"Money?" Helen said.

"What money?" Alberta asked.

"The money that Nettie left Carmela when she died," Cathy said. "Carmela was well off and had saved quite a bit of money on her own, I think she even had some investments, but when Nettie died she left Carmela everything, all her worldly possessions including her house on Memory Lake."

"My house used to belong to your mother-in-law?" Alberta asked.

"Many years ago," Cathy said. "Trust me, Mike and I never wanted it. We didn't care that she left it to Carmela. We had our own house and the bottom line was that Nettie wanted Carmela to have it because they loved spending time there."

For a few moments the women were speechless. They tried to wrap their heads around Carmela's secret life and clandestine romance and weren't sure whether to laugh or cry.

"Joyce, did you ever see them together at the house?" Helen asked.

"Once or twice I saw Carmela sitting with another woman outside on the banks of the lake, but it wasn't like they were cuddling or holding hands," Joyce said. "I thought they were just friends."

"They were friends," Cathy said. "But so much more than that."

"They were committed to each other in every way."

The women turned to face Vinny, who up until that point had remained silent. At the same time they all realized that Vinny had known about Carmela's secret life all along since before Alberta moved to Tranquility and into her house.

"You knew about the two of them?" Alberta asked.

"I hope I find a love like they had some day," Vinny said, wistfully. "I still haven't given up hope."

"Why didn't you ever say anything?" Alberta asked. "You know I was shocked and couldn't figure out how she had so much money and property."

Shrugging his shoulders, Vinny replied, "It wasn't my story to tell."

But it was now part of Alberta's story. She felt the tears well up in her eyes and her instinct was to turn away from her family so they wouldn't see her cry, but she fought the urge. No more secrets, no more hiding. It was time to break the cycle.

With her family as witness, she cried for her aunt, who out of fear or shame was forced to hide her truth from her own family. Alberta also cried for herself because she finally understood why Carmela had chosen her as her sole beneficiary—she knew that Alberta was hiding her truth from her family just like she was. Maybe Carmela didn't know the specifics and didn't fully comprehend that Alberta wasn't truly in love with her husband, Sammy, and was pretending to be a good wife, but Carmela knew a compatriot when she saw one. Alberta was her kindred spirit.

Knowing the truth about how she had come into such wealth didn't immediately make Alberta happy. But she wiped away her tears and grabbed the hands of the three women she was closest to, three women who were family, but who were also her friends. At least Carmela had Nettie, and it was a great comfort for Alberta to know that Carmela had not lived her life alone or without love. It may have been a life lived partly in secret, but it was still a life well lived. And that was a sentiment Alberta would do her best to carry on.

A family, no matter what the shape or size, is still a family.

EPILOGUE

Senza famiglia sei perso.

One Month Later

The weather had improved considerably since the unexpected blizzard, but there was still a frosty chill that wafted in from Memory Lake. Winter clung to the earth and sky and wasn't about to let go, but the sun was shining defiant and bright as if to say have patience, spring will come and soon the land will be filled with flowers and lushness. Hope filled the air. And it was a perfect day to celebrate life. Two lives in fact.

Jinx bent down and secured the plaque in the earth next to a hydrangea bush that, defying nature, still sprouted some flowers as blue as the sky. She stood up and joined Helen, Joyce, and Alberta, who was holding Lola in her arms.

Jinx read the plaque aloud. "Carmela and Nettie. You gave love a name."

No one needed to say another word. They were all thinking the same thing, that it was wonderful that

Carmela and Nettie were together, openly and eternally. They were also thinking how wonderful it was that the four of them—Alberta, Jinx, Helen, and Joyce—were together as well as family and as friends.

As Alberta's mother, Elena, would always say, *Senza famiglia sei perso,* which means 'without family you are lost.' They knew how true that was and they also knew it would never pertain to them because they would always have each other. Just as Carmela would always have Nettie.

Alberta held Lola close to her heart and was thankful that her Aunt Carmela, who had once been lost to her, who for so long was a mystery, had been found. Her truth had been revealed and she no longer had to live in secrecy and silence and loneliness.

The clouds separated and the sun burst through, creating a golden halo over the lake, and suddenly Alberta realized with a full and grateful heart that because of her aunt's last act of kindness, leaving her money and her home to Alberta, that Carmela made sure her niece would never be lost. She made sure that Alberta would never have to live alone or in silence ever again. Carmela knew that she was giving Alberta more than wealth, she knew she was giving her life.

Alberta looked out at the majestic expanse of Memory Lake, the same lake her aunt had looked at with wonder and amazement, and she mouthed two words that she trusted in her heart that her Aunt Carmela would hear: Thank you.

Recipes from the
Ferrara Family Kitchen

ALBERTA'S ITALIAN WEDDING SOUP
(That she says she won't make again until Jinx gets married—but no pressure, lovey!)

½ pound extra-lean ground beef
1 egg
⅔ cup of Italian bread crumbs
2 tablespoons grated Parmesan cheese
½ teaspoon dried basil
½ teaspoon onion powder
5¾ cups of chicken broth (Joyce likes Rachael Ray's—
    Joyce isn't the greatest cook, but she's got great
    taste, so try it.)
2 cups thinly sliced escarole
1 cup uncooked orzo or baby elbow pasta
⅓ cup finely chopped carrots

1. In a medium bowl, combine the meat, egg, bread crumbs, cheese, basil, and onion powder and then shape into ¾-inch balls. This is one time where less is definitely more so keep them small.
2. In a large saucepan, pour in the broth and let it boil.
3. Stir in the escarole, pasta, carrots, and meatballs.
4. Once it gets back to a boil, reduce heat to medium.
5. Cook the soup at a slow boil for 10 minutes or until the pasta is al dente. If you don't know what al dente is, GET OUT OF THE KITCHEN!
6. Stir frequently to prevent sticking and serve.

JINX'S TOFU CACCIATORE
(Gram's never going to try it, but I promise you'll love it!)

2 pounds tofu, firm

1 onion, red bell pepper, green bell pepper—all
 sliced thin

3 cloves of garlic, minced

2 teaspoons dried basil

2 teaspoons dried oregano

3 14½-ounce cans of diced tomatoes

2 tablespoons tomato paste (Gram says to only use
 Cento tomatoes, and Gram knows best.)

¼ cup flour

Romano cheese for topping (Gram's fave is Locatelli,
 so go with that.)

1. To remove excess liquid from the tofu, it needs to
   be pressed. All this means is you need to place the
   tofu between two plates, weighted down by something heavy for about 30 minutes. You can dump
   the water at the halfway point. If you want the tofu
   to be really meaty, after it's pressed put it in the
   freezer until you're ready to start.
2. When the tofu is ready, preheat the oven to 350
   degrees.
3. Lightly coat a skillet with cooking spray and heat
   over medium-low heat.
4. Add onion and peppers and cook for about 5 or so
   minutes until they're soft.
5. Add garlic, oregano, and basil and stir.
6. Add the diced tomatoes and tomato paste, mix,
   and bring it all to a boil.

7. Reduce heat to low, cover the pan, and let it simmer for 15 minutes.
8. While this is happening, cut the block of pressed tofu into ½-inch thick slices.
9. Spray another pan with cooking spray and place over medium heat.
10. Cover the tofu slices with flour and place into the skillet, cooking for about 3 minutes on each side until brown. Respray the pan each time you add more slices.
11. Put the tofu slices in a baking dish, pour cacciatore sauce over the tofu, sprinkle on the Romano, and cover with aluminum foil.
12. Bake for about an hour.

HELEN'S SICILIAN ZABAGLIONE

4 egg yolks
¼ cup very fine sugar
4 tablespoons Marsala wine (You could use sweet sherry, but Helen will get upset if you don't use Sicilian Marsala. If you go rogue, you're on your own.)
Entenmann's Madeleines on the side

1. Put the egg yolks and sugar in a large, heatproof bowl and whisk with an electric beater. Don't ask how long, just keep doing it until the mixture looks pale and thick.
2. Fill a pan with water and heat it on the stove until it simmers. Do not let it boil.
3. Go back to the mixture and add the Marsala 1 tablespoon at a time, whisking after each addition.

4. When the water is simmering, place the bowl over the pan and whisk for about 5–7 minutes or however long it takes for the mixture to get really thick. Do not get impatient and stop beating or else the zabaglione will be too runny, like a raw egg, and nobody but Jinx will eat that.
5. Pour into four warmed mugs and serve immediately with as many Entenmann's Madeleines as you want.

MAMA ELENA'S RISOTTO BALLS

1½ cups water
1 cup uncooked rice
1 teaspoon salt
2 eggs
⅔ cup sundried tomato pesto
2 cups panko bread crumbs
Marinara sauce, warmed (As Mama always said, a real Italian makes her own sauce. If you buy it from a bottle, you'll have to live with yourself.)

1. Preheat the oven to 375 degrees.
2. Combine water, rice, and salt in a large saucepan and boil.
3. Reduce heat, cover, and let simmer for 20 minutes.
4. Leave it alone for 10 minutes, then transfer it into a large bowl.
5. Add in the eggs, pesto, and 1 cup of the bread crumbs.
6. Put the rest of the bread crumbs on a plate.

7. Shape the rice mixture into 1¼-inch balls and roll them in the bread crumbs.

8. Place them on a greased baking pan and bake for 25–30 minutes.

9. Serve with the marinara sauce, which will either be your pride or your shame.

Connect with Us

Visit us online at
KensingtonBooks.com
to read more from your favorite authors, see books
by series, view reading group guides, and more.

for sneak peeks, chances to win books and prize packs,
and to share your thoughts with other readers.

facebook.com/kensingtonpublishing
twitter.com/kensingtonbooks

Tell us what you think!

To share your thoughts, submit a review,
or sign up for our eNewsletters, please visit:
KensingtonBooks.com/TellUs.

Grab These Cozy Mysteries
from
Kensington Books